Hands Like Clouds

Hands Like Clouds

Mark Zuehlke

A Castle Street Mystery

THE DUNDURN GROUP
TORONTO · OXFORD

Editor: Marc Côté
Design: Jennifer Scott
Printer: Transcontinental

Canadian Cataloguing in Publication Data

Zuehlke, Mark
   Hands Like Clouds

"Castle Street mysteries".
ISBN 0-88882-228-6

I. Title.

PS8599.U33H36 2000   C813'.6   C00-931903-4
PR9199.3.Z83H36 2000

THE CANADA COUNCIL | LE CONSEIL DES ARTS
FOR THE ARTS | DU CANADA
SINCE 1957 | DEPUIS 1957

Canadä

ONTARIO ARTS
COUNCIL

CONSEIL DES ARTS
DE L'ONTARIO

We acknowledge the support of the **Canada Council for the Arts** and the **Ontario Arts Council** for our publishing program. We also acknowledge the financial support of the **Government of Canada** through the **Book Publishing Industry Development Program, The Association for the Export of Canadian Books,** and the **Government of Ontario** through the **Ontario Book Publishers Tax Credit** program.

Dundurn Press	Dundurn Press	Dundurn Press
8 Market Street	73 Lime Walk	2250 Military Road
Suite 200	Headington, Oxford,	Tonawanda NY
Toronto, Ontario, Canada	England	U.S.A. 14150
M5E 1M6	OX3 7AD	

Readers familiar with Tofino, Ucluelet, and Pacific Rim National Park may find some discrepancies between their world and that of Elias McCann. This is as it should be for Elias's world is as fictional as the people who populate it while such readers live in a world that is presumably more closely linked to reality.

Chapter One

Dawn came warily, reluctant to brighten the day. The furtive light remained grey and colourless, subdued by the threatening blackness. Rain spiraled down, while a biting wind plucked at the foam-specked waters of Tofino's sheltered inlets. By mid-morning a heavy veil of fog had crept in from the sea to further the day's gloominess. The rain and fog enshrouded the ancient forests of Clayoquot Sound's surrounding slopes, as morning gave way to afternoon. Even the old growth on Meares Island, directly across the water from my cabin, became veiled in the fog's eerie cloak. Thumb-sized raindrops, turgid and lazy as mercury, splatted flaccidly upon the cedar roof shakes. Water languished in the shrink lines of the plank deck jutting from the cabin's westerly side out over the dank inlet waters.

For the next twenty-five days the rain seldom relented. Throughout those dreary days I was haunted by a causeless sense of foreboding.

On the twenty-fifth day, when Nicki the dispatcher at the police station called, I felt oddly relieved — freed from some prescient insight that could do nothing but bode ill for someone dear.

Naked, shivering, and fresh from the bathroom, with the hair on one side of my head trimmed and half my beard clipped, I scrawled down her directions, inappropriately thanked her for the call, and hung up. Realizing it might be wise to finish the job at hand I returned to the bathtub. Picking up the magnified shaving mirror and the barber's scissors, I resumed my awkward barbering. My blondish-brown hair loves to grow into hanks and stray rooster-tails that leap out from above my forehead and the crown of my scalp. The anarchy of my hair growth has resulted in my abandoning barbers and hairdressers in favour of my own innate understanding of the rebellious nature of my hairstyle.

Trimming finished, I pulled on faded jeans and a denim shirt. As always, when Nicki called, there was no need for haste. So I took my time dragging rubber bib overalls over my jeans, yanking on heavy gumboots, buttoning the snaps of my weather-and-dirt-seasoned brown Filson hunting jacket.

When Fergus, the last of the pups from my father's long dead breeding pair of purebred Brittany spaniels, saw the Filson he sat on his haunches before me, rust and white ears twitching alertly. His disappointment was palpable when he learned I was to go alone. A quick compensatory effort of hard fingers scratching behind floppy ears failed to chase the disappointment from his eyes. At 12, Fergus has entered his twilight years and I wondered passingly how many more we would have together, wandering rain forest trails to flush grouse from the briar. My father always said the Brittany was a fine hunting dog, but high strung and consequently short-lived.

Shaking such morbid thoughts aside, I covered my head with an old bush hat, also a Filson, and dashed across the gravel drive from the house to the Land Rover. Inside, I paused to shake the rain from the hat to the floor.

It had been days since I had bothered going anywhere but the engine agreeably turned over. Built in 1967, the Rover is a paint-chipped green antique with a temperament Vhanna alleges is as independent and irascible as my own. She should talk. It was Vhanna after all who had hung up the phone on me the previous week. We hadn't spoken since. Compounding matters was the fact I had genuinely called with the sole purpose of apologizing for my latest wrong against her.

Today, perhaps sensing my impatience could turn cranky, the Rover cooperated, running like a finely tuned machine twenty years younger. All except the wipers, which gamely, but more or less in vain, tried to sweep the perpetual rain from the windscreen. One wiper slapped downward while the other struck upward, as each, powered by its own motor, sought its own rhythm.

I drove Highway 4 south into Pacific Rim National Park. At Florencia Bay, I veered left up a gravel road awash with sloppy run-off from the deluge. Winding inland, away from the wide spit upon whose northernmost tip Tofino sits, I drove up into the mountains, climbing in gentle S-curves through dense forests of western hemlock, amabilis fir, and monstrous cedars whose upper branches were cloistered in an impenetrable fog. Below me, the fog blocked all view of the waters of Tofino inlet. I drove through a world rendered surreal and lonely by the dour weather.

After several kilometres of this ghostly passage I saw a track, little more than a tunnel cut through trees, running on an angle to the approaching ridge-line. Swearing at my own lack of foresight I stopped and clambered out into the rain to throw the hubs in on the front wheels. Hat, jacket, rubber pants, and short-clipped beard were all running with water by the time I got back inside. I engaged the four-wheel drive on the transmission and probed slowly down the track, the Rover bucking and kicking like a recalcitrant mule over the rocks and muddy water-sluiced ruts.

I didn't have to drive far. A few hundred metres in I found Gary Danchuk's RCMP Blazer parked in a small clearing. The blue and red emergency lights wigwagged back and forth. An ambulance stood alongside the Blazer. No lights flashed on its roof. Not surprising. I don't get called to such godfor-saken places if there is any urgency. Indeed, the only reason the dispatcher issued her summons was my own obstinate insistence that, being the coro-ner, I should be involved at the very beginning of these investigations. Normally I would have been pleased that Danchuk had finally cooperated, but, given the conditions of the day and the location, it was all too apparent he operated more out of spite than professional courtesy.

Driving into the space between the two vehicles, I noticed for the first time a blue Chevy four-wheel drive pickup with monster tires and a garish rack of halogen spotlights crowning the roof. CB-radio whip antennas were mounted on either side of the cab. The truck was nearly hidden amid a clump of wild ferns. One heavy cleated tire crushed casually down on the new growth rooted in the rotting husk of a fallen cedar that had been a young sapling about the time Sir Francis Drake sailed past these mist-shrouded coastlines in 1579. The truck's rusted back bumper sported a sticker reading *Real Men Hug Women Not Trees*. On the opposite side of the bumper was a *Dauphin Logging Company Ltd.* sticker. I didn't recognize the vehicle, so doubted it hailed from Tofino.

A movement at the ambulance caught my eye. Scrambling out of the driver's seat, Joseph Samuels, hunched against the rain, trotted through the mud toward me. Jerking the Rover's passenger side door open he climbed aboard. In the small space, his arms and legs coiled awkwardly about his torso. Rain dribbled off his ambulance crewman's slicker, which began to steam from the little bit of warmth fitfully thrown out by the heater. Samuels is a full blooded Clayoquot, now called Tla-o-qui-aht; he is a large, hulking man who wears his hair in a razor-close crew cut and has a soft voice that eternally surprises even those of us who know him fairly well. "Up the road about a kilometre, Elias," he near whispered.

Despite the apologetic-sounding voice, his eyes were bright with a mocking challenge. "Danchuk didn't try?" I asked.

"Couple creeks with a wallow between."

I pushed down hard on the gear levers, shoved the drive into bull low. Samuels grinned like he might have when he was a kid breaking out of residential school — a kid who cared less about the punishment that would inevitably come when he was captured. Thinking this, I returned Samuels' look with one as wickedly delinquent.

Before my father's parents had comprehended his true nature and exiled him to Canada, he witnessed — with the natural respect of a person who admires fine machining in such things as vehicles and guns — how British farmers used the Rover's bull-low gear to drag their plows through the soft, rain-sodden, English loam. For these farmers the Rover performed a multi-purpose role — that of tractor and general-purpose family runabout. Over the years he often recounted this testimony to the little four-wheel drive's prowess. This was probably one of the few times he didn't lie. His other undeniable areas of truthfulness revolved around matters concerning sporting guns, outdoor clothes, and the breeding and nature of hunting dogs. Fitting that these are all subjects of little real consequence to the human condition. Still, his truths exerted an immense influence upon me, for I too have come to place inordinate value on excellence in these matters. And in the case of the Rover his anecdote about Old Country farming practices led to my owning a battered relic from the days when British engineering remained something to be admired. Now, keeping a light foot on the accelerator, I drove this squat box on tires up the track. The Rover lurched forward, wheels barely turning.

There are two ways of driving through mud — a right way and a wrong way. The wrong way, favoured by everyone who watches American television truck ads, is to hurl the vehicle at each obstruction with the abandon of someone driving an M-1 Abrams Main Battle Tank in the sands of Kuwait. The tactic works fine if the obstacles are few, quickly crossed, and you're driving a tracked vehicle. But on the back country roads of Vancouver Island's west coast the mud runs slick as grease, runnels of icy water slice away the road surface and spread to form bogs, rocks as hard-headed as Gibraltar rise up out of the road bed, and the slopes on the high side like to slough down to erect blockades you have to claw a pathway over. On these roads the Rover is king, turtling with slow, churning determination past one hurdle after another, its narrow wheel span providing a vehicle virtually impervious to imbalance.

In this way we made our way up the track to where a small knot of people stood near a cedar tree, the trunk of which was as widely girthed as the Rover. It wasn't until I was outside and walking with Samuels toward the others that I saw the figure hanging from one of the cedar's log-sized lower branches. "Damn," I muttered.

"Yeah," Samuels said.

Danchuk broke away from the group and approached us. Rain dribbled relentlessly off the bill of his police cap and down his full-length brilliantly orange slicker. The garish slicker gave him a sort of Halloween festiveness at odds with the setting. "Good to see you, McCann," Danchuk said in a voice that said the opposite. He gestured toward the still shadowed figure hanging from the branch. "Body's over this way."

If the Mounties were to select one of their own for a recruitment poster they would never point a Nikon lens toward Danchuk's apparition of officialdom. Small, squat bodied, Danchuk has a heavy gut and sluggish jowls that seem to pull down the skin beneath his watery blue eyes so the pupils appear in constant danger of toppling out. It's an illusion rendered all the more realistic by the way his forehead recedes away from his eyes to meet the level playing field of a perfectly bald skull. The man made it to sergeant in Tofino through sheer longevity and is, I fear, doomed to remain until retirement. Danchuk, having this same apprehension, is consequently a bitter and spiteful man.

"You could have cut him down."

Danchuk wheezed a grim laugh. "Didn't want you to miss anything." Resisting a scathing reply, I walked up to the rest of the men. Samuels' ambulance driver, Lou Santucci, whose dad owns the local lumber store, stood with apparent deliberateness apart from the other two men. He raised a weary hand in acknowledgement. The duo bumping shoulders beneath the branches of the tree near the body's feet, which swayed back and forth gently as the wind caused the slightest of vibrations in the tree, offered no greeting. Both wore muddy rubber ponchos with hoods that hung down to obscure their faces. I gave them an unreturned nod and turned my attention to the body.

There was a time when death affected me greatly and I feared to look upon its face. This was when I was young; doing the things of a young man, like serving in the army in defiance of my father's insistence that I was failing my class by entering into a military career as anything less than an officer. But I, wanting no burden of responsibility, became a private. In that role I spent a tour as part of the Canadian Forces' United Nations peacekeeping detachment in Cyprus. It was easy duty in a land where women's eyes were dark and dancing, their hair thick and wiry, and their laughter low and husky as they shared bottles of acrid retsina with us soldiers. I could have lingered there forever. Then one sun-drenched morning a terrorist bomb tore open the chest of a four-year-old Greek girl. Her gorgeous large black eyes foretold how she would have some day rivalled beauties, like the one whose bed I had left in the first dawning moments of that new day. Left via a window as her husband, returning early and unexpected from his job at the shipyard, made a more conventional entrance through the front door.

From the dirt of a street broiling with flame, smoke and screams I scooped the ragged doll-like body of the little girl into my arms and raced toward the platoon armoured car. Her blood soaked my fatigues as I bundled her into the vehicle's iron-sided safety. Through narrow, snaking streets we rocked and tilted in a desperate race against death. No sooner did I apply a pressure bandage to the bloody wound in her chest than it soaked through, forcing me to exchange one dressing for another. As I begged her to keep living in a language she couldn't understand, the light slowly faded from those dark eyes. Years later I still wake in the night from dreams in which those eyes again gaze up at me — confused, terrified, questioning. But I still know no words of comfort and can offer no explanation.

Since finding my wife Merriam's body and witnessing my father's death I have no more squeamish fear. Death no longer shocks or sickens me. It merely is. Something as immutable and beyond understanding as life's own peculiar incomprehensibility.

Which doesn't mean I experienced no feelings as I looked up at Ira Connaught's body hanging from the branch by a corded nylon rope tied around his neck. He wore a green plaid jacket, heavy grey wool pants and work boots. His mottled red and gray beard was thick and as unkempt as the shoulder-length hair streaming out from under a blue tuque that somehow still clung wildly to the right side of his skull. Ira's face and neck were dark red and swollen. This indicated he had died slowly and terribly as the rope choked him to death. With his bloated protruding tongue, bulging eyes, and the rakishly angled tuque there was something almost playfully obscene about Ira in death, as if he were taunting those who still lived and who now gazed up at the soles of his well-worn boots.

The heavy rains offered a blessing of sorts in that the odour of death failed to blanket the scene. Indeed, it was held somewhat at bay by the richly spicy bouquet emanating from the sodden cedar boughs. Perhaps this had served to keep the scavengers from finding Ira's corpse, for he was remarkably free of the mutilation that normally attends a body exposed to nature's recycling. Black flies swirled about and crawled upon his face and clothes, but beyond that he had not yet been subjected to the indignities of carrion.

Ira had obviously fought for his life. The leather of his workboots was torn clear through to each steel-capped toe. The cedar tree's bark was scoured and ripped away in strips where the boots had clawed desperately in search of a purchase. Both hands were shredded to bloody fly-matted pulp. With a shudder I imagined how he must have clung and scrabbled at the rope around his neck in a futile effort to climb up to the heavy knot on the branch about six feet beyond his reach. It was easy to imagine Ira's struggle; the vain efforts to go up the rope hand over hand, trying to overcome the inevitable pull of gravity, the impossibility of dragging a body larger than my own six-foot 195 pounds up by arms that could never reach the right muscular angle to start upward, feet clawing at the rain-slicked bark.

"I took pictures," Danchuk declared proudly.

"Fine. Let's get him down."

Which proved a problem and it was then I realized Danchuk hadn't just left Ira hanging there for my benefit. Truth to tell, he was stumped over how to get up and undo that rope. We all stood for a while looking up and wondering. During this time I found out the two men in the ponchos had happened on Ira while hunting deer. Their names were Rick and Chuck Greer, brothers who had driven up from Ucluelet (pronounced YOO-CLOO-LET, emphasis on the CLOO) to hunt deer. God knew why they'd come out hunting on a day like this, but the days had been this way for twenty-five, and I suspected their licences must have been close to expiring and the freezers still barren of venison. Some people will do anything to avoid supermarket meat prices.

Maybe it was the damp and cold creeping into my body that made figuring out what to do so difficult. Or maybe it was the bluff blabbing of Rick and Chuck with their tale of stumbling on Ira's corpse and bustling back to the truck to use their radio to call the authorities. Whatever the reason, I found myself unable to sort options. Finally I turned from their hearty depiction that had now backtracked to when they first sought shelter from the rain under the cedar's outstretched canopy of branches and stumbled into Ira's boots. Letting the rain splash my face, and no longer having to see Ira's swaying corpse, I was able to realize the obvious answer.

I walked to the Rover. After turning it around, I backed through the heavy undergrowth of ferns, vines and chuckholes until the Rover's boxy back-end was next to Ira's body. Samuels, realizing my intent, used the little ladder next to the back door to climb onto the vehicle's roof. Easing one arm about

Ira and lifting his body upward to relieve the rope's tension, he carefully untied the knot with his free hand. Then, with reverent gentleness, he lowered Ira by the rope into Rick and Chuck's waiting arms.

One of them told the other with a short hard laugh to watch out for maggots as they abruptly bundled Ira into the back of the Rover. By the time I got back to them they had already roughly folded his body to make it fit, so there was no point in telling them or Samuels I had intended to strap the body to the rack on the Rover's roof. When I got home I would just have to deal with the smell that was going to be all through the vehicle. Luckily, there is a cure. I often bum bottles of the odour eliminator the provincial ambulance service uses to remove death's stench from the body bags and interiors of their ambulances. A wonderful chemical, it also works more effectively than commercially available products to eliminate the unpleasant scent of soot, dirty canines, and anything else that tends to linger in the household. It's even bio-degradable.

Ira was well past the stage of rigor mortis that makes the body stiff and unbending, so I guessed it hadn't been difficult for Rick and Chuck to cram him inside so quickly. This told me Ira had been hanging there for at least twenty-four hours and possibly as long as forty-eight, for this is how long it takes for rigor mortis to pass out of the body and return it to suppleness. The limbs seemed looser than the torso. This, too, made sense. Ira had struggled hard with his arms and legs. Muscles engaged in demanding physical activity before death enter rigor mortis more quickly than those that are less active. Consequently, the first muscles to loosen are those that first enter rigor.

Ignoring the strong fetid odour that made the bile

rise in my throat, I clambered into the back of the Rover. Then I gently moved Ira so the slate grey daylight dusted his face. The lips were laced with clots of blood that had ruptured in razor thin lines. I opened his mouth and saw the same purple traces of dry blood there. The lids of his eyes were similarly veined and here and there small pricks of blood had surfaced and dried to form black crusty specks. These bleeding sites are called *petechiae* and are caused by strangulation. In this case, as the rope compressed Ira's veins, the arterial flow continued to pour blood into the head causing an immense iron pressure to build that could not escape toward the heart via the closed veins. Seeking an outlet, the blood burst out of the thinnest veins available, those of the mouth, lips, eyes, and probably the inner veins of the nostrils.

Circling Ira's neck was a vivid, bloody laceration surrounded by dark bruising. Typical of a hanging death, this circle pulled up in a symmetrical V-shape on the right side where the noose had come together at the knot. According to the medical books on such subjects, this is indicative of a suicide rather than murder. In the case of violent strangulation by another person the wound is level all the way round the neck as the killer cinches the rope in tight at the back of the victim's throat.

Even as I made these observations about hanging wounds, burst blood vessels and limbs freed from rigor, I was surprised by how much I had learned after less than a year as Tofino's coroner. But the surprise was unaccompanied by pleasure, for I knew now that I faced the job of determining the why of Ira Connaught's ghastly demise.

Chapter Two

It is an idiosyncrasy of British Columbia's provincial law that community coroners don't have to be medical doctors. Drawn from all walks of life, they are only required to be upstanding members of the local community. I'm sure Danchuk is still trying to comprehend how I could possibly have been deemed as qualified for the position. But Tofino is fiercely loyal to its eccentrics. Besides, in this case, no one else wanted the job. Even I had to be coerced by Mayor Reginald Tully. His argument was that I should not persist in a life of unbroken idleness. Then, because Reginald isn't just a politician but also my doctor, he advised from behind his bottle-thick wire frame glasses that perhaps the work would enable me come to terms with my grieving process.

As if confessing to a great invasion of privacy, Reginald said he had noted my behaviour seemed a little erratic of late. I knew that by this he referred to my tendency to take Fergus for long, late night rambles around the community in such a way that I would pass within eyeshot of Vhanna's sprawling ocean-side home which stood at the opposite end of the community from my own modest cabin.

"Reginald," I said carefully in the manner one uses when taking great care to say the politically correct thing, "Merriam has been gone for two years."

He shrugged, embarrassed by his ill-thought intrusion. "Well, I just think you could do with something to concentrate on. Something...." His voice trailed off weakly.

I glowered at him, guilt crescendoing through my soul. "Fine, I'll do it," I finally grumbled without being able myself to comprehend why was agreeing to this lunacy.

It didn't matter that I could fault Reginald's argument about idleness. That was utter nonsense. There was a cornucopia of things to be done. There were pheasants, grouse, and ducks to flush with Fergus's aid. Untamed stacks of books looted from my father's magnificent library awaited reading. At least a dozen CDs ranging from Mahler's Symphony No. 9 with Leonard Bernstein conducting the Berlin Philharmonic Orchestra to Roseanne Cash's latest album of lament cried out for the careful listening they properly deserved. There was even a bearing on the right front wheel of the Rover I was certain required changing. Yet none of these things provided the distraction Reginald correctly recognized I needed. Yet he misdiagnosed the cause of the pining sense of loss that sent me forth into the misty dark nights on long fruitless sojourns.

For how could I tell this old friend I grieved not so much over the loss of Merriam but over Vhanna's absence and the words that stood between us like a black impenetrable storm front. Yes, I still grieved for Merriam, was in fact torn by a guilt I believed would never know release over how she had died and what I believed was my culpability in her passing. But, more than that, what seemed far and again of greater triviality but was not, I needed distraction because Vhanna had been gone two months, would be gone another, and, for what was then the first time, harsh words stood between us. I could not even post a letter to her or call to admit I was wrong and should never have fought her determination to lead the tour. But it was impossible to reach a woman supervising a walking trek of thirty-five other women across the Himalayan saddlebacks from Katmandu to within a whisker of Everest in Nepal and on across the Tibetan wildernesses to follow the frigid waters of the Huanghe River to Lanchou, a village where the mountains finally tapered off into the rugged heart of northern China. By heading the first such trek by any Westerners, let alone a group of North American women escaping careers, husbands, and children, Vhanna ensured Artemis Adventures Inc. a place within the pages of *National Geographic* and herself status as the virtuosa of women-only adventure company owners.

Meanwhile, feeling abandoned and desolate with worry about her safety in this latest and most dangerous expedition launched by her then-neophyte company, I saw a certain logic and the potential of escape from my own melancholy thoughts to be found in assuming the position of coroner. So I told Mayor Tully, my doctor and friend, I would take the job. Within hours he called to say the provincial attorney general had agreed to my appointment and I should come in to the council office to swear the required allegiance to the Queen and government and all other such authorities.

With fingers crossed behind my back I did so swear and the deed was done.

I blame my becoming coroner on a temporary lapse of sanity brought on by the inexplicable feelings of loneliness I had at Vhanna's absence. Possibly, too, since Merriam's death I've had a bizarre fascination with the mechanics and reasons for violent passings from this life. It's not something I allow myself to brood upon much — or so I tell myself. I am the local coroner. Enough said.

Extracting myself from the back of the Rover, I found the rest of the party had apparently already departed the scene and were on their way back to where the ambulance and RCMP Blazer waited. It seemed they preferred to stay out in the rain than take cover from the weather inside the Rover with Ira and myself. There was no hurry to overtake them so I took another walk around the scene of the death. There wasn't much to see. The rain had turned the soil into a muddy quagmire riddled with our six sets of boot prints. Somewhere in among all the prints no doubt were also those of Ira's, but all the boots were cleated and I couldn't sort one from another.

Propped against the tree was a worn green camouflaged rucksack with an aluminum pack frame. As I started to open the pack, Danchuk came up. "It's Connaught's. Not much inside. Guess he didn't need much." I jumped at the sound of his voice at my back because I had assumed he had left with the others. When I turned to face him, I saw the vindictive gleam in his eye that told me this surprise was deliberate.

Studiously I ignored the policeman and turned my attention back to Ira's pack. Danchuk was right. The rucksack contained little of value. Some mixed nuts, chocolate chips, and dried fruit sifted together in a plastic bag to make a form of trail mix, a half empty water bottle, and a grey woollen sweater riddled with moth holes. Nothing else. No note. No answers. There were, of course, also the tools of Ira's trade, or what might have been called his self-appointed mission in life. These consisted of a short-handled five-pound sledge hammer carefully wedged into the bag so as to be invisible to anyone who might meet Ira on the trail. Lying heavy on the bottom of the bag were several pounds of twelve-inch railroad spikes as thick as a finger.

"This make sense to you?" I asked Danchuk, while pointing out the gear inside.

Danchuk shrugged his disinterest. "Maybe he left a few parting presents for some logger." He reached around me and closed the flap on the rucksack, hefted it with difficulty and slung it over one shoulder. "Time to get out of this goddamned rain, McCann. By the time we put him on ice and get the report written up it'll be way past dinner. Told Donna I'd be home early, too." He slouched off down the hill without looking back. Obviously he also wasn't going to accompany Ira back in the Rover.

Not yet ready to quit the scene of Ira's death, I lingered and took one more look at the branch high up in the tree. Again I checked the trunk of the ancient cedar, but found on its mud-caked surface only the scouring marks made by Ira's scrabbling boots. Then I walked up through the small stand of timber and out into the opening beyond. As rain streamed off my hat and puddled around my boots I stared at the great empty expanse that stretched off into the shrouds of fog hanging low on the distant heights. Not a single tree blocked the line of sight and only a thin covering of new growth salmon berries, salal, and other low

lying vines and bushes, had taken root in the tortured
soil. I could have been looking at a landscape stripped
bare by the blast of bombs, the carnage of war. But it
wasn't that at all. This was the devastation of a massive clear-cut logging operation. It had been more
than five years since the loggers had come with chainsaws and skidders. For weeks all that was heard here
was the scream of machinery and the shudder of
ancient timber crashing down to the earth in a final
death throw. The stink of diesel and mixed chainsaw
fuel carried on the wind. Neither the sound of a
thrush singing or a deer stepping lightly through dense
brush was heard. Finally the tree cutting was finished
and the loggers had moved on to another forest to
continue their work. Behind they left a giant scar, a
wound the earth could not heal in the next few cen-
turies. And never again would the giant western hemlocks and cedars cast protective shade over this land.
It would stand naked and bare to erosion by rain and
wind and still be a wasteland long after the loggers,
myself, and even Vhanna were dust or ash.

I wondered why Ira would come to this place,
a place already destroyed. Why come here with the
spikes he and the other ecological saboteurs, who
called themselves The Sunshine Warriors, used to
sabotage logging operations? Why come here carrying the spikes he drove into the guts of trees to
render them deathtraps for timbermen? A chainsaw
blade striking a spike could shatter into dozens of
bits of deadly shrapnel. Shrapnel that could maim
and even kill. The hammer and spike — the misguided ecological warrior's weapon. A weapon Ira
had carried and used in a personal war against
those who sought to log the bastions of the
Clayoquot forest surrounding Tofino's inlets.

But instead of going to the fringes of Clayoquot, where he normally operated, Ira came here, to a land already devastated. He chose to come here to die. To hang himself from an ancient conifer amid the wasteland. Was it some last act of protest or despair? And why, if that were the motive, haul along twenty pounds or better of spikes and hammer? As a legacy, as some twisted message? Try as I might, I couldn't fit the presence of the spikes together with Ira's suicide. And I also couldn't find an explanation for the site chosen.

When I die I want to be on my deck looking out on the inlet and lush green wooded mountains that bridle Clayoquot Sound and which have been a soft place for my eyes to rest upon for years. Would not Ira, who loved the woods so much he went to war for them, have sought something similar? But, then, I was no suicide. How could I begin to divine Ira's mind? I could no more understand Ira's thoughts at the moment of his death than I could comprehend his becoming an ecological warrior. Perhaps I simply didn't have the passion of commitment or belief that would allow me to make ultimate sacrifices or to make a last stand for any kind of belief.

On occasion, Vhanna has said I believe in nothing of worth. Perhaps she is right. As I grow older, I fear I am all too much like my father. Just another remittance man, living without effort, standing on the outside of life, looking in at the struggle and strife of others without understanding. Who was I to try and make sense of Ira's reasoning?

Despite these all-too-common thoughts, however, I still could not explain away the contradictions surrounding Ira's death. There were too many things that didn't link together, that begged consideration. Before leaving the police station I tried raising them with Danchuk but he expressed no interest. Instead he grumbled and mumbled about the burdens of his duty; of how this investigation was hindering his preparation for the imminent Tofino visit of an American senator named Jack Sloan who came to investigate whether the attempts by loggers to get renewed access to the verdant Clayoquot Sound forests would destroy a natural wonder of the world. With an American senator in the wind, Danchuk had no time for wondering why an ecotager like Ira Connaught would hang himself before a clear-cut site. Long after Ira's body was shipped off to the hospital morgue and Danchuk and I completed an initial investigation report attributing Ira's death to suicide, the questions still remained.

Upon getting home, I brushed aside Fergus's eager efforts to investigate the smell on my skin and clothes. With abandon I soaked the interior of the Rover with the odour eliminator and sprayed it liberally onto the canvas of my Filson jacket and hat, for there is no way to wash either of these wonderful items without destroying the oil treatment that renders them fully waterproof. The beauty of Filson is it ages like something real and natural without need of cleaning. This is why those of us who wear these rugged clothes love them. I've carried many pheasants, grouse, and ducks back from the hunt in the coat's game pouches, but there is something about the stench of dead humankind that lingers unlike any other death smell and so the odour eliminator came to the rescue of my old coat and hat.

Inside the cabin, I locked Fergus out of the bathroom and took a long, steaming hot shower. Since having made this insane decision to be Tofino's monitor on death I keep lemon-scented shampoo and bath soap on hand for just these kinds of occasions. The lemon seems to penetrate deep into the hollow centres of the hair shafts and remove the lingering stench.

When I emerged from the bathroom wearing a thick green terry robe, Fergus took a few inquiring sniffs and snorted his disappointment. There was still one other matter that needed attention — the reek of death lingers in your sinuses. I've developed an excellent cure stumbled on by experimentation after we found Margaret James sitting bolt upright in her bed watching game shows. The poor old soul had been gone for at least a week by the time a neighbour decided to complain about the twenty-four-hour-a-day electronic racket and glimpsed her through the living room window.

As always when having to deal with a somewhat ripened death, I diced up strips of tenderloin beef, green pepper, tomato, onion, garlic, celery, and carrot and stir fried it all vigorously in very hot olive oil over high heat. Into this mixture I blended generous helpings of chili powder, cayenne pepper, oregano, the juice of a whole fresh lemon, and a cup of white wine. Throughout the last moments of cooking Fergus looked up from his bowl of crunchy dry food and sneezed profusely with such vengeance that his ears flopped wildly about his head. My chuckle of amusement offended his dignity, so he returned to his bowl and ignored me throughout dinner. But then he isn't fond of spicy food and seldom bothers assuming a position of intense-eyed supplication when I cook something that offends the mild training of his tastebuds. When the mixture had thickened I served it like a fajita, rolling the ingredients inside a couple of warmed tortillas.

Several ice-cold Vancouver Island Premium Lagers, straight from the bottle, washed it down nicely.

Throughout supper, I managed to avoid thoughts of Ira and to concentrate simply on the pleasure of food and drink. But soon after, as I finished washing up the dishes, the questions crept again into my mind. Far into the night I sat in one of my faded antique green wingback chairs staring into the glowing embers of a dying fire on the grate of the stone fireplace, a glass of Glenlivet forgotten in my right hand. Fergus looked up worriedly from where he lay on the braided rug at my feet. The questions still haunted me, lurked in my consciousness, offered new angles that needed consideration — but always kept understanding far beyond my grasp.

Near midnight I tried calling Vhanna, but her answering machine came on with a curt message instructing the caller to leave a message she would later return. I hung up without speaking and tried her office line, where the scenario repeated itself. For a moment I considered driving over to her home but decided the timing was all wrong and to let it go until morning. Again, as I had throughout the days since before the twenty-five day storm struck Tofino, I cursed myself for a fool who could not hold his tongue. I remembered with chilling clarity the cutting words I had thrown at Vhanna, the accusation that she was incapable of allowing herself to care about others, namely myself. How I chided her that perhaps it was something she learned as a child during the flight out of Cambodia across the sandstone escarpment of Chuor Phnum Dangrek into Thailand. No sooner had I blurted out this inanity then she said simply into the receiver, "I don't understand you. I don't think I want to know you at all." A light click was all that followed as she cradled the phone and cut off the words I wished to say, the words that were spilling forth as I desperately tried to make her understand that I wasn't thinking, wasn't saying my true feelings — which was a problem that plagued us both.

Now, in the midnight-shrouded darkness of my cabin, with the fire dying in the grate, regret for my ill-thought words again washed over me so intensely I could no longer put my mind to the questions of Ira's death. My desire to have Vhanna here by me and to explain to her why I sometimes lashed out at her cool reserved way was so strong I could think of nothing else. But I could not go to Vhanna tonight, could not offer explanations. She was either not home or sought no company.

Despondently, I climbed the stairs to the mezzanine and crawled under the heavy-blue loghouse-pattern quilt Merriam had sewn the year before she died — the quilt she had worked on incessantly as if possessed. And there, lying in the darkness, Fergus stretching and sighing contentedly in his oversized wicker basket that stood beside the bed, my sleep muddled brain swirled with images of Vhanna and of Ira. I saw Vhanna, wrapped tightly in the white linen and lace Portuguese tablecloth I had on a whim bought her and which she preferred as a shawl instead of as a table covering. Her black hair, plaited into a long rope hung to the base of her spine, dark mysterious Oriental eyes watched me without expression, the rest of her face remained shadowed and unreadable. Ira was beside her, hair red and wild as a Viking's. Clots of purple blood dappled his closed eyelids, spattered his lips. I forced aside the images and found no peace, for the questions surrounding Ira's death swirled to the surface of my consciousness. Sleep proved as elusive as the answers I was seeking.

In the early morning hours I became aware of a pale light falling through the pane glass window and dusting my room. Rising, I stood at the window and looked out at a full moon gleaming down through huge gaping holes in the black clouds that raced past like ghost riders borne on a darkening wind. After twenty-five days the nearly endless track of storms had broken.

Chapter Three

With the dawn, I abandoned the quest for sleep in favour of a morning walk with Fergus. A wind, raging high in the stratosphere, ripped the storm's few leftover clouds into cotton candy-like strings. At ground level, however, the air was calm. A light misty fog rose off the inlet. We walked the inlet trail, moving beneath a canopy of still-dripping trees, our feet squishing on the sodden carpet of needles and leaves. Fergus raced far ahead, stopping here and there to sniff or dig, pausing often to mark his territory. Hands plunged deep into my Filson's pockets, I followed at a brisk pace.

In the calm bays of the inlet, flocks of bufflehead ducks pausing in their migration northward here for a protracted rest bobbed serenely on the shimmering surface. Their bodies were such an intense black that the dash of white on the backs of their heads and breasts gleamed in the dappled sunlight filtering down through the tree canopy onto the water and the trail. Circling above the buffleheads, seagulls, like street punks, lurked, waiting to plunge down and rough up any duck that might happen upon something edible. The gulls' shrill cries were the only sound breaking the morning stillness. Dwarfed scrubby shore pine lined the water — branches and trunk as twisted and distorted as its Latin name *Pinus contorta* implies. Perched amid the intertwined storm-shattered branches of two lone hemlocks a blue heron peered down with studied disdain upon the passing of dog and man.

After twenty-five days of continuous rain, the trail teemed with the Pacific Northwest's most famous creatures — banana slugs. They were swollen with water and stretched as long as my hand, antennas arcing up from black, grey, or mud-coloured bodies as they crawled along on their bedding of slime, heading, it seemed, nowhere in particular. I stepped carefully to avoid squashing them. Fergus, however, shunned such delicacy and his big cat-like paws left many a mushed slug in their wake.

Here and there I paused to dig with the toe of my boot, in the same manner as Fergus, through the covering of needles and leaves to the soil below, which was black and rich with peat from the rotting blanket of leaves and needles that sheltered it from any drying by the sun. The dirt was laced with fat earthworms. Everywhere I looked this morning there was life and it was hard to think on death and dying, so I allowed myself this reprieve.

Fergus kept up a constant bounding entertainment. Suddenly he would be at my side, the next moment crashing far ahead through briar to send grouse fleeing skyward in an explosion of flashing wings. Each time, he stared at me in growing dismay when I failed to snap the twelve-gauge to the padded shoulder of my Filson to pull down a pair in perfect syncrhonization with Fergus's efforts. Try as

I might, I could not make Fergus understand the reality of legal hunting seasons or that I did not always want to play the predator. Nor did he seem capable of comprehending that the antique 1942 Parker Brothers side-by-side gun remained in the security locker back in the cabin.

After walking a mile or so, I called Fergus and we started homeward. Fergus's coat was sodden from dew and the dripping trees. Mud covered his paws and legs, caked his chest and belly. His floppy ears were bedraggled and his hair a filthy tangle. He grinned with delight and sheer joy, jumping up at my side, while being extremely careful not to brush his filthy body or paws against me. I gave him lots of praise for this consideration, which it had taken years of patient scolding to drill into his nature. Back at the house, I put him into the covered kennel run standing against the south wall and left him there to dry out. After changing out of gumboots into a weathered pair of Chukka Boots, I tossed the gummers into the Rover, just in case my day's journey took me where they would be needed. Then, I drove into town.

Hardly more than one thousand souls call Tofino a permanent home and of those there are a good many only passing through. In the summer and the whale watching season of March and April the town core throngs with tourists come to wander the wild, windswept beaches of Pacific Rim National Park or, dressed in garish orange floater suits, to cluster in boats offshore in hopes of seeing a school of thirty-ton grey whales. We locals tolerate their presence grudgingly, take their money, give them poor directions, and grumble to ourselves about their many, many failings. We are like people of tourist towns everywhere in this respect. And at times, in our more honest moments, we might acknowledge that were it not for their presence, and more importantly their dollars, we would not enjoy the few good restaurants we have or the scatter of other businesses that make life easier. And for some, like a remittance man, embarrassingly profitable.

It is a fact that all you need to make money is to begin with money. I'm living proof of this reality. Through absolutely no fault or talent of my own I am not only financially well off but becoming ever more so. Yet, to achieve this happy state of affairs, I do nothing at all.

I have had the simple luck — or curse, depending on your viewpoint — to be born a remittance man's only son. Angus McCann was the second son of Hedric McCann, whose family owned and operated one of the largest ceramic pot foundries in Scotland. As a young man, Angus showed no aptitude for business, was rejected as an officer candidate by Sandhurst, flunked out of public school, and created a scandal in Glasgow by having affairs with one married society woman after another when their husbands were fighting for King and Country in Flanders Fields and such places. In 1919, Hedric McCann finally threw up his gnarled hands in despair and shipped Angus off to Canada, which I gather the old scion still referred to as the Colonies. As long as Angus remained on the opposite side of the sea he would receive a healthy monthly remittance from the family business. A business that Alex, the eldest son and undeniable heir, ran with typical Scottish miserliness and wily business smarts — to such an extent that between the end of the War to End All Wars and the one that followed McCann Industries grew to have factories throughout Scotland producing an array of household essentials ranging from steel cooking pots to ironing boards. With World War II, the company branched off into the lucrative sidelines of cannon barrels and shell casings.

When Angus passed on at about the same time I turned 30 I inherited his share in the rewards of Alex's thrift and zeal, now being ably run by his eldest son. So the monthly remittances come to me and, despite the recessions that have plagued Britain for decades, the sums continue to grow exponentially.

It's hard sometimes to know what to do with all this lucre. I put it in banks, term deposits, bonds, all the stuff my financial adviser suggests but this causes it only to grow some more and require further investing. Mostly I leave the management of it to my financial adviser as she is more interested in these matters. Sometimes, however, I make independent investments. These are usually strongly opposed by my adviser because she finds my investment rationales illogical. She's right, of course, because I don't marry logic with financial matters. Simply put, I follow my heart and dump money into enterprises of friends who need a grub-stake to get going. In this manner, I have come to be known as a financial wizard in Tofino business circles. Oddly, every business I invest in thrives. Perhaps I am lucky in the friends I have.

I am now in the position of owning a 30 percent interest in Tofino's most successful restaurant, The Crab Pot Café, Tofino's fastest growing home building company, Do It Right Construction, and, among others, probably the world's most successful women-only adventure touring company, Artemis Adventures Inc. This last was the only investment my financial planner endorsed and encouraged. On my behalf, James Scarborough cooks up crabs, David Larson pounds nails into boards, and Vhanna Chan takes women on adventure tours that pit their courage against challenges that would daunt any sane person.

All this entrepreneurial success, however, leaves me with the leisure to do whatever I like, explore any passing fancy. To live, in short, as remittance men historically always lived. Only in the 1800s and the early 1900s, when remittance men were thick upon the land of the British colonies and the western United States, they referred to this as living in the manner befitting an English gentleman. I've not often considered myself as being able to lay claim to such august status. My father still exhibited some of these attributes, but I have tended to shun the lifestyle in favour of simpler things.

This is not from any noble desire to share the lot of those less fortunate. Rather, it's more a response to my own innate liking of simplicity. For this reason my home since Merriam's death is a pleasant, rustic Steiner Arch cottage surrounded by a small plot of land I leave as unlandscaped as I found it; my vehicle is a battered Rover; I tend toward clothes that are rugged and functional; and I like my single malt scotch straight with no mix or ice. Oh, I certainly enjoy my pleasures and don't stint on expense when I feel it worthwhile or likely to give me some reward. I just don't go out of my way to flaunt my economic independence or the freedom of spirit money allows.

In this sense I doubt the remittance men of old would approve of me. They were, by and large, pompous, self-important souls; or, even worse, insecure about their position in life, so given to boasting and excessive behaviour. They wandered the Colonies in absurdly heavy and old-fashioned English tweeds, dragging along their gun cases and fishing rods, seeking adventure and recognition. Having, as my father did in a later time, failed to succeed in the pursuits allowed a gentleman in the Old Country and now pensioned off to the Colonies, they sought to prove themselves worthy by remaining stoically dedicated to playing the role of the Britisher of good breeding.

Perhaps this is one of the reasons I have parted company with the tradition. I'm well aware of the failures of my breeding. My father remained childless until he was well into his fifties and I was his only progeny. Angus, like myself, had little reason to strive to succeed in the usual paths recognized by the middle class society that came to dominate North America and the world following World War II. Angus differed from me, however, in that only late in life did he set down roots. Instead, as a younger man he wandered in true remittance man tradition from the foothills of the Himalayas, to the open veldt of South Africa, to the Cassiar Mountains of British Columbia, seeking something elusive — meaning, perhaps or simply, love. Who can know? In the end he washed up on Vancouver Island and, apparently having tired of a drifter's existence, bought a small land holding and set about being a gentleman farmer.

And, as we all know, a farmer takes a wife. Except Angus didn't bother with such formalities. He was a handsome man and well to do. It was easy for him to attract women. Even as a child I always respected his fine wit and perfect charm. He could beguile the most dubious skeptic. Often enough he worked his magic on me and from virtually my first word I was an all-too-eager critic.

A few years after Angus settled in the rich farmlands of the Comox Valley, just across the mountains on the east side of the Island from Tofino, he brought a scandalously young woman with eyes blue as the sky and hair red as a Viking's to live with him. Her name was Lila and after a year she became pregnant with me. Two weeks after I emerged kicking and squalling into the world, Lila, so the folk tale goes, took one battered suitcase full of Angus's cash and caught a passing bus out of town.

I didn't know this until I was a boy in school and some of my fellows started taunting me about being a bastard. I beat the whole sordid story out of them even as I forced them to recant the name they called me. When I arrived home with bloody knuckles and questions my father denied it all with great vigour and sincerity. He told me Lila died in childbirth and there had been a secret marriage. For a long time after I believed nothing Angus ever told me and assumed the opposite to be true. Of Lila I knew little at all but bits and pieces I overheard from others through the years. My father would not talk of her except in the finest of terms and always assured me she had passed on to a happier place but still loved us both.

Years later, when I was settling my father's affairs following his death, I found a small packet that contained perhaps a dozen or more letters with Angus's awkward handwriting. I read the first few paragraphs of the one topping the packet. It was a letter to Lila. A love letter, really, that told of how we both were and how she was missed. Angus, of course, had no idea where to send the letter so never posted it. I wondered, then, why he had bothered writing it. I have since come to understand. To understand the heart of a man entwined in an inescapable web of love I think you must have stepped into the same gauzy web yourself. I neither finished reading the first letter, nor looked at the rest. After burning his words in his den's fireplace, I carefully sifted the embers with a poker so no trace remained. Throughout the minutes it took to carry out this simple task I remember my eyes being wet and a pressure filling my chest.

I am careful never to think of Lila; never to wonder if she ever has thoughts of Angus or myself. If she wonders how I turned out. Does she know that my father no longer lives? Probably. He would be a very old man by now and so statistics favour the probability of his death. Does she care though?

Vhanna says I brood too much. She's right. This day, however, brooding on my family tree and the circumstances that brought me to this place in time and the unusual position of being Tofino's coroner served a purpose. It allowed me to avoid dwelling on the unusual death of Ira Connaught, or on my role as death's messenger to the woman with whom I seemed destined to be eternally, hopelessly, and infuriatingly in love.

Chapter Four

After ringing the doorbell and eliciting no answer I opted for the direct approach by climbing over the rugged stone wall enclosing the grounds of Vhanna's home. Dropping to the rain-soaked grass below the eight-foot wall I couldn't help smiling at the realization that an unknown number of pressure sensors and motion detectors must be sending hysterical ringing signals through Vhanna's alarm system.

Here was a woman who never thought twice about the wisdom of guiding a pack of Women-Who-Run-With-Wolves-hearted females through the chilling terror of a white-water canyon run, yet who surrounded her home and office with the kind of security equipment guaranteed to set even a ninja's teeth on edge. I used to attribute this contradiction to the ordinary feminine fear of the streets seemingly inevitable in the violence typifying our troubled times. Recently, however, it seemed to me to symbolize some darker, barely disguised pathos.

Not that I spent a great deal of time wondering about this contradiction, merely that I noted it as yet another possible source of the troubles plaguing our relationship. It was something I wished explained, but I knew better than to raise the subject with Vhanna.

The woman I love was on the sweeping deck, that fronted her expansive grey cedar-sided home. From the deck, or anywhere inside the house's interior, the view is singularly stunning. It was especially so on a day like this when the sun was out and the sky clearing rapidly to a blue so sharp it made your eyes ache. The ocean was calm all the way to infinity. Several fishing boats were barely visible on the sea's far horizon. The house clings to a cliff and a long cedar stairwell switchbacks down to the rocks and brilliant white sand of a wide, stretching beach.

Vhanna's back was turned toward me as I stepped off the path circling from the housefront to the deck. She wore black denims, a white cotton bush shirt and black, thick-soled Doc Marten shoes, which look like something old hoboes might wear but which Vhanna swears are comfortable. Her hair was tied back and plaited, just as she had worn it in my half-waking dream of the night before. Seeing this, an unexpected shiver slipped up my spine. Not for the first time today my instincts warned me to tread carefully.

As I approached, Vhanna pushed a couple of buttons on a cellular phone and turned to me with a look of mock surprise. "I just told Jabronski to put away his guns and go back to Elma's for breakfast. Remember doorbells?" She tossed the phone on a cushioned chaise lounge and gave me a little smile that rendered her words friendlier than they might appear.

I thrust my hands into my Filson's deep pockets and shrugged, deriving a wicked sense of pleasure in having disrupted Jabronski's security-man routine. I thought of reminding Vhanna that his was yet another of my investments she had stridently protested and now she was probably Jabronski's biggest customer. Instead I said, "You've had a way of ignoring such things as doorbells and phones lately."

Vhanna turned away to some wooden pots scattered along the length of the deck railing. Her lean hands and fingers were delicately plucking withering lavender and plum polyanthus blossoms. Below the deck, surf rolled against the shore; slowly, eternally, breaking on the white sandy stretch of beach in lazy lines that flowed in and out as gently as a breath. In the deck's sheltered corners stood several varieties of ancient bonsai trees in their shallow tubs. Precisely plucked and trimmed by Vhanna, the leaves remained small and the trunks were dwarfed and gnarled, as if they were tormented souls forever twisting in upon their own suffering. I don't like these little trees. I cannot understand why Vhanna derives such satisfaction from providing them with constant grooming. To me they seem artificial and perverse. But Vhanna gives them hours of her labour and apparently finds something in their imposed sufferings that gentles her own spirit. I have long given up understanding what it is about bonsai gardening that soothes Vhanna. Given her past and her love of what is natural, it seems yet another contradiction.

"How's shorty?" I asked, pointing at the closest bonsai plant, which looked somewhat like a dwarfed beech tree.

Pursing her lips thoughtfully Vhanna decided to treat my question as a serious inquiry. "It's desiccated. The winds during the storm were full of salt. See." She pointed at the small green leaves and I noticed that the edges were yellowed and curling.

When I took one of the petals between my fingers it broke away from the branch.

Perplexed I said, "This isn't the first storm they've been through."

Vhanna brushed a finger lightly down one of the leaves. It, too, snapped loose from the stem. Her voice seemed far away when she finally spoke. "So many days of continuous rain, the unending wind. It's a miracle they live at all." Vhanna stared off at the ocean. "Sometimes I wonder how any of us survive such storms."

She turned from the distraught bonsai and brushed fingers lightly down my cheek. I almost put my arms around her and pulled her close, but held back — uncertain if we were again in the process of declaring a truce or not. It was the troubled, haunted expression on Vhanna's face that gave me pause. Her eyes seemed to look inside me and beyond. "I dreamed of you last night." Her fingers traced across my lips. "It was very bad. You were alone and running from something. I could see, but couldn't reach you." She shuddered.

I took her thin hand in mine and squeezed it gently, brushing the fingertips with my lips. "It was only a dream."

Vhanna pressed against me and snuggled her small head into the hollow between my neck and left shoulder. I circled my arms behind her back and squeezed her lightly against me. As always, I felt huge and awkward. Vhanna is so lean and thin her bones seem small and delicate despite the hard, thin covering of muscle built by the life she lives. Her bones seem terribly vulnerable to the pressure of my arms. It is a fear of causing damage that I think leads me to touch her with something akin to reverence. That and the fact my feelings for this woman are often over-whelming. My instinct is to compress her into my own body so tightly that we are forever, inseparably, bonded together. Is it my own intense need of Vhanna that forever sets us apart?

I started to apologize for the hard words that had driven her away on the eve of the twenty-five-day storm, but she stopped me by pressing her fingers against my lips. Vhanna is not one for expla-nations, neither is she one for apologies or declara-tions. I could see in her eyes she wanted only to put the past yet again behind us and start afresh. This is her way. Consequently, we have had many a new beginning; and we shall, I suspect, have many more as the years flow by. I put my lips to hers and for a long time was free of thoughts and concerns, feeling only the spicy taste of her mouth and inhaling the soft musky scent of her hair and body. From the back of her throat came a slight moan, a hint she would like this to go further. Which, even as my body began to respond, reminded me I was here on a very different kind of mission. I had news and it would not wait.

Reluctantly, I broke off the kiss and stepped back from her. Seeing my expression, Vhanna's smile faded and her face became guarded, closed. I waited for her to ask me what was the matter, but she didn't speak — just remained warily watchful.

I cleared my throat and in a flat, straight for-ward voice told her of Ira's death. I knew better than to leave any of the more gruesome details out. Vhanna is less a stranger to death and suffering than myself and would tolerate no false consideration for supposed delicate sensibilities. When I finished, we moved to the deck rail and stood side by side staring out at the surf. I wanted to put a comforting arm around her, but the rigid set of her body rendered her aloof and solitary.

So I remained beside her, watching her face out of the corner of my eye. I was half reading her expression, half enjoying her beauty. Vhanna's mother was half-French colonial and half-Cambodian Chinese; her father was pure Cambodian Chinese. The European genes have given Vhanna a lithe tallness and angular facial features. Her cheekbones are high, her nose thin in memory of the French tobacco planter who bedded and married her mother's mother. Her hair is thick and shines with a high gloss of health from a life spent in the outdoors. I could look at Vhanna all day without becoming bored.

When Vhanna at last turned toward me her jaw was set with determination. "Ira didn't kill himself," she said. "They murdered him."

Since becoming Tofino's coroner a year earlier I had handled several accidental death inquiries, three suicides, if you count Ira's, and a handful of natural passings in unusual settings such as Bert Frederick's dying of a heart attack while driving down Main Street and Guenther Brecht's stroke-sparked drowning while windsurfing off Vargas Island. Not once had I been faced with an inquiry into a murder or other violent killing of one person by another. On this day, after a twenty-five day storm and the coinciding strife between Vhanna and myself, I was wary of such a complexity entering my life, so I didn't want to entertain Vhanna's wild speculation. No matter that I felt an instinctual distrust of the obvious explanation of Ira's death, had myself darkly worried the matter throughout the previous night. "There's no indication that it was anything else but suicide. All the signs are there and there are no signs of physical violence. I know you were friends, but...."

She cut me off. "Ira wouldn't take his own life. Never. It's just not a possibility."

"Why?"

She bit her bottom lip for a moment, considering. I could almost sense her mind conjuring up one explanation and discarding it, processing another. This is the way Vhanna looks when she's examining my financial records and countering my intention to invest in another friend's seemingly shaky business scheme. Vhanna knows the importance of logic in an argument and that she can also best me in this field with ease.

But today her logical mind was perhaps short-circuiting. "He was a devout Catholic, so it would be a sin to have done so," she said finally.

I gaped at her and then snorted. "Good God, Vhanna, he was a criminal who spiked trees and endangered the lives of countless loggers without a whim of conscience. Sin seemed to come easily enough to him."

"That was a mission, not an unjustifiable sin," she snapped back. "He confessed and made atonement. Ira was at peace with himself over what he did."

"Would he have been if one of his spikes had caused a logger injury?"

Vhanna glared at me. "We have to do something to stop them from destroying the forests. And now they've murdered him."

"You're not one of Ira's mob, so don't use 'we.'

And who exactly is the 'they' that are supposed to have murdered him?"

"Maybe I don't approve of Ira's methods but at least his heart was in the right place. And we shared the same beliefs." She paused, her eyes riveting me like two gun barrels. "You should try having some beliefs sometime. Ira did what he thought he had to do. He didn't think there was any other way."

Her rebuking my lack of beliefs stung, despite my being slightly proud of this fact. Perhaps it was that stinging wound that caused me to lash back at her. Perhaps, too, it was an irrational jealousy sparked by her obvious admiration of the dead Ira. Whatever the reason I shoved my hands into the Filson's pockets and retorted, "Pol Pot did what he thought he had to as well. That didn't make him right, did it?"

Vhanna's eyes met mine steadily but the colour drained from her face leaving her pale and gaunt. "Go to hell, Elias," she said very softly. With that, she walked to the patio door, pausing only a moment to turn back toward me. "You have a job to do. Like it or not you have to find out who killed Ira and why."

"I'm a coroner, Vhanna, not a policeman. My job is only to determine how Ira died. Nothing more."

"Fine, then prove he was murdered and Danchuk will have to find out who and why." She hesitated, obviously considering. "And when you're done I don't think you should come back here. I can't take this back and forth stuff anymore." She passed through the French patio door and closed it behind her with a definitive thump I realized drowned out my calling of her name.

For a moment I thought to go after her, to start yet another apology, but the futility of it all was apparent even to me. "Pol Pot," I muttered under my breath as I walked off the deck and across Vhanna's open grounds. "What the hell is the matter with you? Jesus." I couldn't help wondering, too, why I hadn't told Vhanna of my own uneasiness over the circumstances of Ira's death, of the incongruities I saw in the location and manner of his demise, of how troubled my thoughts had been the night before — of the vague uncertainty I felt over the matter. If I had been open with her, instead of dismissing her contention it was murder, perhaps the conversation would have gone another way entirely and we could have finalized the truce negotiations so favourably begun.

Getting over the wall was more difficult this time as the ground inside the compound slopes away, but I managed to scramble up without any serious scrapes. As I opened the Rover's door I took one last look toward Vhanna's house. Perhaps a shadow moved in the upper window of Vhanna's bedroom but I couldn't be sure. Feeling weary, defeated, and lost, I started up the Rover and headed into town. I pulled into the Shell service station on the edge of town and rang Mayor Tully with instructions for Ira's body. Then I spent several minutes filling in the necessary forms to begin a formal coroner's inquiry. For some reason I had carried these forms with me this morning when I left to tell Vhanna of Ira's death.

As I did so, I realized I never pressed Vhanna about who she thought it was that had killed Ira. She had spoken of a "they" with authority, but I wondered if there was really a distinct group she had in mind. If so, the other question was why she thought this party responsible.

Vhanna, like many people in Tofino, is deeply involved in the environmental movement, especially the battle to stop the Island's rain forests being destroyed by the strip-mining technique industrial loggers call clear-cutting. As a result of her involvement in the politics of environmentalism, I knew she had more familiarity with Ira and the other direct action environmentalists of The Sunshine Warriors than I did. It was reasonable to assume she had some knowledge of who their enemies might be. I realized it had been foolish not to ask her more about her suspicions and how she came by them. But only in the days to come would I realize the extent of this deadly oversight. I should have swallowed my pride, gone back to the house, and asked her for an explanation; indeed, demanded one. Failure to do so set into action a chain of tragic events.

Chapter Five

Ira Connaught's home was a twenty-foot wooden scow grandly named *Sojourner*. The boat was moored at a dock a few hundred metres from my cabin. Once the craft might have been seaworthy, but the wooden hull was in a state of advanced rot. She wallowed low in the water. Latherings of caulking and ragged sheet metal patches kept the salt water sufficiently at bay to enable the craft to remain tenuously afloat. The balance between sinking and floating was further maintained in favour of seaworthiness by a snake's nest of thin black hoses leading from the bilge to drain out of the scuppers.

"This is a waste of time, McCann." Danchuk's voice grated against my shoulder. Ignoring him, I continued down the length of the dock to Ira's home. The sun's warmth sucked a mist of steam up off the dock's sodden timbers and swirled it about my legs. With each gentle swell, water slopped lazily back and forth across the deck of Ira's boat.

"Bloody shithole." Again I chose to ignore Danchuk's bitching, which had been more or less constant from the moment I tossed the papers necessary to launch a formal coroner's inquiry on top of his meticulously organized desk.

"Suicide," he had immediately sneered. "Tully's autopsy will confirm it. One less crazy."

I ignored his grousing then, I ignored it now. I was perversely pleased that Danchuk could do little more than grumble. Once I started an inquiry he answered to me, not the other way around. Just how much this role change infuriated him was apparent in his every word and his anger-tautened shoulders.

"Should be preparing for the Senator's arrival. Not buggering around with you," he muttered.

Danchuk was openly fretting the arrival of Senator Sloan. I wondered if he were really that insecure about his own abilities. What serious duties could shepherding a senator around Clayoquot Sound possibly pose? All Danchuk need do was be polite, avoid scratching private parts in public, and keep his red serge formal dress uniform buttoned and clean. On reflection, perhaps the sum of these tasks did constitute a tall order for him.

Unlike Danchuk I was in no hurry, so I took a slow look around the small dock. The majority of the fleet using this dock were usually crabbers. Only a couple boats were in harbour today; the rest would be out working their lines. The vessel immediately in front of Ira's was one of Vlassis Mavrikos's small fleet. It was a paint-weathered fishing boat, but Vlassis had long ago removed the net drum from its stern and here round chicken wire crab pots were now piled in a rough kind of order. The door leading down to its tiny cabin was partially open. I wondered who was using Vlassis's boat.

"Come on, McCann, let's get moving."

An antique wooden soft-drink crate, reading Coca-Cola in faded reddish scroll, served as a step down from the dock to Ira's deck. Gingerly I boarded the vessel. Water sluiced about my rubber gumboots, making me glad of the foresight I had shown in donning these boots before coming here from the RCMP station in Danchuk's Blazer. The rains had covered the deck to a depth of about three inches. It slopped back and forth over the toes of the boots. I sloshed across to the cabin's low doorway.

"If it's locked, I ain't forcing it. We'll have to get a warrant." Danchuk was balancing on the Coke crate. He looked down distastefully at the filthy water flooding the deck. His shoes were police-issue heavy patent black leather. Suppressing a grin, I wondered if he had any dry socks in the Blazer.

Such thoughts kept me from worrying about the problems getting a warrant might pose. The courthouse was in Ucluelet. The area judge and magistrate both lived there, too. I wanted this investigation done. Wanted answers. Some sixth sense nagged me, warned that time was of the essence. It was the same sense of impending doom that had haunted me since the rains stopped, since Ira Connaught's body was found.

Fearing the resistance of a lock, I turned the little rusted brass knob. My breath of relief was audible as the door swung freely inward, squeaking on it hinges.

"Fuck a duck," Danchuk muttered. He was still on the box, piggy blue eyes skewering me meanly. Not for the first time, I wondered what I had done to so earn this man's undying rancour. Having earned it, however, I had long ceased trying to curry his favour and acceptance. We both had jobs to do. Right now our jobs included learning all we could about Ira's last hours to uncover what might have prompted him to take his life. If, indeed, he had. Vhanna's words plagued me. My own unease fueled her accusations, powered my suspicions.

Stepping over the sill, which was high enough to keep the water on the deck from running below, I descended three small steps into the blackness. Fumbling along the wooden paneling I found the windows were covered with crude wooden shutters fitted into slides. I tugged the first open and sunlight cast a small pool of light around me. By the time I had forced the last of the main room's shutters open Danchuk was coming down the stairs. He glared about at the rubbled interior. "Good housekeeper." I noticed he was able to stand upright, the peak of his cap just barely scuffing the paneling on the ceiling, whereas I was forced to stoop uncomfortably. Ira was a good few inches taller than me. I wondered how he had tolerated hunkering around inside his home. "So, Coroner, what do we look for?" Danchuk's head was cocked to one side with mocking attentiveness.

Baffled myself, I offered only a shrug. Now that I was here, I really had no more idea what to look for than Danchuk did. "A note, something that might explain his death," I muttered unconvincingly. I glanced about, tried to find order amid chaos. The place looked like it had been tossed over by reckless thieves, but it was all too apparent this was the normal state of affairs aboard *Sojourner*.

Ira Connaught gave new meaning to the word slovenly. The small U-shaped galley just off the entry stairs swarmed with grease-stained aluminum pots and pans. Steel plates and stainless flatwear overflowed the sink. Grimy glasses and chipped mugs were wedged into the little counter space that was free of dirty pots. The gas four-burner stove had once been white, but now it was a graffiti work created by various coloured sauces that had spattered and overflowed. Most of the stains ran toward the residue left by boiled-over tomato-based sauces. A stack of cans in a plastic garbage bin confirmed Ira's taste for canned spaghetti, chilli, and lots of ravioli.

I gingerly opened a few cupboard doors, expecting an avalanche of debris to pour out. But they were mostly empty, awaiting Ira to clean his kitchen and restore the inventory to its rightful resting place. When did he do this? Once a year? Bi-annually? Before major holidays? Or would he just clean a pot, plate and cutlery as the need arose?

Danchuk's voice pulled me back from this pointless musing. Ira's housekeeping practices no longer mattered. "Just a bunch of old newspapers on the table. There's nothing here, McCann. Waste of time."

I stepped past the sergeant, having to turn sideways to crowd past his stomach girth. The rest of the room was taken up with a small pedestal table that was bolted to the floor. On the opposite wall was a low bench, upholstered in a tattered, greying yellow-flowered material. Bookshelves ran above the grimy windows. They were jumbled with popular paperbacks. I recognized among the authors and titles Tom Wolfe, Ed Abbey's *The Monkeywrench Gang*, Heller's *Catch-22*, Keysey's *Sometimes A Great Notion*, Jim Harrison's *A Good Day To Die*. I saw nothing current.

The papers on the table were equally eclectic and aged. A couple of copies of *The New York Times*, a *Globe and Mail*, several *Vancouver Sun's*, the odd *Vancouver Province*. One headline leapt out at me: "Loggers Want Into Clayoquot" pronounced the bold black letters just below the *Vancouver Sun* masthead. Another from the same paper proclaimed "Government Approves Clayoquot Logging Plan." I riffled through the rest of the stack. Most carried a story in the first two or three pages about Clayoquot. Many were dated back to the summer of 1993 when the provincial government had given the forestry companies permission to log a large percentage of the sound and hundreds of people from around the world flocked to Tofino to form blockades across the logging access roads. More than eight hundred, too, ended up being arrested in the largest mass arrest in Canadian history. A good many of the protesters were sent to jail or faced stiff fines for violating a court injunction that ordered them to stop blockading the roads. But they also disrupted the loggers' operations and forced the government to broker a deal that would supposedly preserve Clayoquot from further clear-cut logging. This year, that deal was in jeopardy as the government was bending to increased pressure from forestry-dependent communities and the forestry companies themselves to open up parts of Clayoquot's pristine ancient rainforests to smaller than usual clear-cut logging operations. I suspected the government's proposed compromise would lead to this forthcoming summer repeating that of 1993. I also tended to rather cynically believe that the struggle between environmentalists and loggers would continue for summer after summer, with the loggers slowly gaining ground bit by bit until the last of the giant trees of Clayoquot fell to their chainsaws.

Besides the historical record of the 1993 Clayoquot summer frolics, only one other headline seemed of relevance to Ira's Sunshine Warrior mission. In a little box printed at the bottom of a

Victoria Times-Colonist front-page a small headline read "U.S. Senator to Tour Ancient Forest."

A concise story set out how Senator Jack Sloan was to tour Clayoquot Sound's old-growth forests in an attempt to examine the truth behind the provincial government's decision to allow limited logging in the area. He would then take his findings back to what the senator assured British Columbians was a very concerned American public. This concern, the story seemed to believe, derived from a series of advertisements taken out in *The New York Times* by a coalition of American environmental groups opposed to any logging of this last remaining vestige of Vancouver Island's once-mighty rain forests. The forest industry and its supporters naturally took umbrage at what they termed interference by a foreign power. The province's premier had gone so far as to recently label anyone opposing logging in Clayoquot as an enemy of the people of British Columbia. The senator, however, argued that the environment was owned by all humankind and that his inquiry was a responsible action and not meant to be an attempt to further inflame a controversial issue. I noticed his arrival was but two days off.

I wasn't here, however, to catch up on old news. I knew all about the impending visit of the senator. In a curious twist, Vhanna had been requested to act as his guide during his visit to Clayoquot. It appeared her renown as a world-class adventure guide had spread even to the hallowed corridors of Washington D.C. When I heard of this plan I pondered why she would bother to sully herself chaperoning about some politician on a self-promotion junket. She'd just given me her tolerance smile. That's the one she reserves for when it's clear to her I'm utterly naïve about the ways of the world. "You sly dog," I said, after a moment's reflection. Where junketing senators go, of course, follow a covey of media. Vhanna was cashing in on a chance to reap copious amounts of free publicity and promotion. The woman is nothing if not resourceful.

Leafing through the rest of the papers, I could see only the normal doom and gloom of world events. There was little there of interest to me. I find world events depressing, irrelevant, or beyond comprehension, so make an effort to remain uninformed. I've done this since returning from Cyprus.

Danchuk was meanwhile pulling the upholstered pads off the bench and rooting about noisily inside the bench's storage lockers. With a gleeful snigger, he triumphantly raised a small plastic bag containing something greenish. Carefully he tossed it up and down in the palm of his hand as if to test its weight. "A junkie," he said, as if this constituted an explanation to all the world's sorrows.

"It's only a little grass, Danchuk."

"Still illegal. We're dealing with a pot-head. Would make him unstable."

I decided not to probe this line of reasoning. Something else had captured my attention. I ran my fingers along a row of small Polaroids tucked into the seam of a ledge above the benches. They were all more or less alike. Snapshots of laughing young and middle-aged people with wild hair, heavy wool sweaters, outdoor weathered faces. All except one. One that was very different. It set my heart tripping and made my skin flush and tingle. I slipped this photo free and, after checking to ensure Danchuk was still absorbed in his search for more proof of a drug-crazed Ira Connaught, tucked it away in my inner jacket pocket.

Methodically I finished my search, but saw little of what the various drawers I opened contained. Instead, my mind replayed the scene from the picture I had palmed. Finally I moved into the small bedroom in *Sojourner's* stern. This contained nothing but a ragged pile of blankets and dirty sheets laying in an untidy mess on a bare mattress. I returned to the main cabin to find Danchuk finally finished his search of the storage lockers. He had discovered no further drug stashes.

As we left the boat I realized the search had yielded nothing but a baggie of pot and a mystery I was unsure I wanted to unravel. It was a mystery that gnawed, however, at my guts. How could I know nothing of this?

"Waste of time, right?"

I nodded grimly. Danchuk was wrong, of course, but I wasn't about to tell him so. With his suspicious mind and vindictive nature, showing him the photograph would be all the provocation needed to set him off stirring up trouble. And right now I had enough troubles of my own.

As I climbed back onto the dock a figure stepped through the cabin door of Vlassis's boat. I squinted against the sunlight and made out the shape of a woman in a heavy wool sweater, who had a thick mop of golden hair that glittered with sunshine tracing through it. The hazy figure waved. I walked over to where she stood in the boat's stern next to the crab pots. "Hello, Tassina. When did you come in?"

"Been here a week. Papa's letting me use the boat until I get set up."

"Be more comfortable up at his house wouldn't it?"

She smiled thinly at that. "You know how it is, Elias."

I nodded. I knew the enmity between father and daughter. Had other families been pulled apart by the battle over the fate of Clayoquot? In 1993, Tassina had joined a line of about fifteen protesters, mostly women from Tofino, to form a human chain across the logging road. They had all been arrested and fined. When Tassina refused to pay the modest fine she was jailed for two weeks by an indignant judge. Tassina's father, Vlassis, believing logging Clayoquot was the only way to save the jobs of the loggers, had refused to accept his daughter's differing opinion. Since her imprisonment the two had barely exchanged a word. Were it not for some compelling reason I knew Tassina would not be here on her father's boat.

Tassina shrugged. "Papa and I both do what we must."

I waited. Behind me I could hear Danchuk's feet impatiently scraping the dock.

"I'm not going back this time." She grazed fingers around her eye and over the brow. Perhaps it was the gesture, perhaps it was a shift in the sunlight, but I now saw the purple and red swelling around her right eye, the discolouring that trailed down from her forehead past her ear to her neck. The bruises confirmed what I had been thinking.

"Anything I can do?"

Her smile was rueful, tinged with regret. She shook her head. "Thanks anyway."

"No problem."

"McCann, we gotta be going."

I started to introduce Danchuk to Tassina Mavrikos but she said, "Oh, Sergeant Danchuk and I know each other well. He arrested me that day, you know. Very brave he was." She hitched her fingers into the belt loops of her faded denims and gave him a mocking smile. I grinned at her for that and saw a little glimmer of light dance in her eyes as a reply.

From inside the boat cabin came rustling sounds and a moment later a small head covered in thick, wavy dark hair peered out sleepily at me and Danchuk. "Hello, Eleni, you won't remember me," I said. I introduced myself and Danchuk. The little girl's eyes widened at the sight of Danchuk's uniform. She looked scared and nervous. I wondered how many times police had been called to Tassina's home in Port Alberni by the neighbours. How many times had she and Tassina left under their protection, or watched William Gatos be taken away to spend the night in the drunk tank? Tassina's child was a beauty, with the dark Greek complexion of her mother's father and also his hazel eyes and thick hair. Her body was thin like Tassina's. I smiled at Tassina. "Vlassis must consider himself a lucky grandfather."

She nodded, smiled widely, but then the joy that had touched her face faded. "Vlassi is Vlassi," she said, using the contraction by which Vlassis was normally called. I nodded to show I understood. Eleni listened intently to every word that passed between us. I sensed she was trying to break through the allusions. Perhaps she realized more than we thought her five- or six-year-old mind could comprehend. It was all too probable given the experiences that had already troubled her short life.

Tassina and I passed a few more pleasantries but Danchuk's impatience was increasingly obvious from the scuffing and squelching of his sodden shoes. I also noticed there was something akin to rage emanating off him like strong body odour. The man was a puzzle. Before I said good-bye to Tassina I learned she had no car. I told her to call me at the cabin if she needed anything and either I'd pick it up or give her a lift downtown.

Danchuk slammed the Blazer into gear the moment I closed the door and roared off in a spray of mud toward the police station. We both ignored the other for a while, but finally just before reaching the station I decided this was ridiculous. "What's eating you, Gary?" I thought perhaps using his first name would ease the tension between us.

The policeman didn't answer me. Instead he braked hard and swung the four-wheel drive off the road onto the gravel shoulder. After levering the gear shift into neutral and yanking on the emergency brake he scowled across at me, eyes narrowing like he was peering down a sniper scope. "You're a real work of art, McCann. A fucking knight in white armour for every little bitch down on her luck. That's you. But we both know better, don't we?"

I waited.

Danchuk grinned like a tiger might before sinking its teeth into helpless prey. "Some day you'll make a mistake. Some day."

"What's this about, Danchuk?" I had my suspicions and they made it hard to keep from slamming my fist into his face. It also filled my voice with more malice than I intended, a fact which just made Danchuk grin all the more.

He wagged an accusatory finger at me. "You know, McCann. You know." He nodded at the answer he saw in my eyes. "Yeah, I ain't forgotten. And one day I'll find the evidence. And when I do I'll come shit all over you, Mr. Coroner."

"There's nothing to find, Danchuk. You're wrong." But I could see my denials were nothing to him; just as they had gone unbelieved three years earlier when then-Corporal Danchuk and Sergeant Bellows, who had since been transferred off Vancouver Island, came to the house and found me standing over Merriam's body with the Remington sixteen-gauge over-and-under shotgun in my hands. In that moment Danchuk had made up his mind. I had been tried and convicted on evidence so scanty and absurd that it was inconceivable this man could still believe in his obviously flawed interpretation of events.

Merriam had died by her own hand. She had used the shotgun while I was away from the house. This was a fact easily proven. A fact later confirmed when Vhanna testified on my behalf and informed Bellows I was with her at the time. She had further testified, when pressed, that we were lovers. And when she opened up our lives and secrets to Danchuk and the always courtly Bellows the latter believed the truth and pressed no charges. But I realized now that Danchuk never believed; that he still thought me guilty. "Let's go," I told him.

Danchuk continued to glare at me and it took every ounce of willpower I possessed to not drop them in the admission of guilt he sought. For I was guilty. Not in the way Danchuk suspected but in a way that, in my eyes, damned me every bit as much as if I had pulled the trigger of that shotgun. Many times mayor Tully has told me I wasn't responsible for Merriam's death, that the demons writhing inside her mind that ultimately led her to suicide were sown in another time and place. If Merriam had known about my affair with Vhanna, the doctor assures me, that was not the reason for her suicide. Tully, Vhanna, innumerable others, have all painstakingly assured me of this fact. But who could know? And even if that were so, how could I have failed to recognize how far Merriam's depression had settled? How could I have failed to see the decision she was reaching? I had failed her. And at the time she took her life, I had been at Vhanna's, lying warm and close in her arms, tasting her love, soaking up the joy I found in this woman's bed. Oh yes, I was guilty all right.

The truck pulled into the police station parking lot. I climbed out and banged the door behind me without looking back. As I opened the door on the Rover I heard Danchuk's mocking laughter carrying across the yard but chose to ignore it. Inside the Rover, I brushed aside the wetness from my eyes and fired up the engine. As I drove away from the police station, I saw Danchuk standing just inside the doorway. His face was shrouded and unreadable beneath the bill of his policeman's cap, but I sensed he was still grinning, still enjoying his revenge over me.

Chapter Six

Can anyone explain love? Why the exchange of a glance can lead to a heart being irrevocably lost to another?

I pondered these questions on the way to the hospital. Questions that eluded answers. The kind of questions that often trouble the romantic, melancholy mind of a remittance man.

When we think of moments spent with someone we love, the memory is not inevitably overtly sexual in nature. Instead, we may recall a moment of sweet gentleness. I often fondly recall a time shared on Vhanna's elegant black leather couch. She was propped up by a thick cushion and I leaned against her, my head rested lightly between her small breasts. For several days I had been plagued with a case of insomnia brought on by an unhappy marriage and the inability to break it off and openly declare my love for Vhanna. In Vhanna's embrace, I drifted on the edge of sleep, lulled all the more by her fingers gently tracing the lines of my forehead and cheeks. "I love you so much," I whispered.

"I know," she replied as softly.

"Do you mind?" Vhanna never declared her feelings for me, or for anyone else, as far as I knew. She seemed to believe such pronouncements tempted fate.

Her lips brushed the top of my head. "No. But for you it may be bad."

"I don't think so."

"No, not now. But later."

"Not if we stay like this."

A soft laugh. "Yes, perhaps not then."

"Well?" My heart was beating faster. I was ready to make the stand, to offer any commitment she would accept.

Her fingers pressed down on my eyelids, brushed them closed. My hands squeezed her arms below the elbows, tucked them in close under my chin. I wanted to dissolve inside her, attach myself physically to her heart so as to be ever melded with her spirit.

In that same moment, I later wondered, did Merriam lock Fergus in the outside kennel, return to the living room and press the barrel of my second shotgun — a Remington sixteen-gauge over-and-under — into the cleft between her breasts? Did she hesitate? Reconsider? Or simply bring the gun into place and then squeeze the nearest trigger with the big toe of her right foot?

That is how the police determined my wife ended her troubled life. The gun was too long barreled for her to have reached the triggers with her hands. So she sat down in a living room chair, braced the gun against her chest, then extended her bare foot until the big toe slipped inside the trigger guard. A light push and the gun fired. In an instant Merriam attained the peace in death that had so eluded her in life.

Did she really do this while I was lying in Vhanna's arms? Or was it later? About the time I was driving home? Wondering, over the short distance between my home and Vhanna's, how much longer Merriam and I would have continued to live together in a life where we were so emotionally estranged and our home was consequently gloomy and cold. Had Merriam fired the gun while I was being haunted by these thoughts?

More likely, her suicide took place barely minutes before I drove up to the house. That timing coincided with the time logged by Nicki, the local police dispatcher, for a call reporting that a shot had been heard at my house. As I arrived home, the RCMP were already on the way. I had no sooner found Merriam's body and picked up the gun lying before her than Sergeant Bellows and Danchuk entered the house. Bellows, tall and lank; Danchuk, short and brutal looking.

Seeing me with the shotgun, Danchuk's hand drop to his holstered gun. But Bellows touched the back of the junior officer's hand restrainingly and the gun remained undrawn. Bellows then turned his attention to me. Our eyes met and I saw his were sad and possessed of a weary wisdom. "What happened here, Elias?" he asked quietly.

"Merriam," I murmured. Then I spoke her name even more softly. It was all I seemed capable of saying, so I continued to repeat it in a dull, fading rhythm. When Bellows put both hands on the gun I let him take it from me without resisting. He passed it behind him to Danchuk who turned stiffly, as if made from wood, and, holding the gun at port arms, walked out of the house. As he left, Bellows knelt beside Merriam's body. She lay on her back, the chair flipped over and beneath her, so her legs draped over the seat and between the chair legs. I saw him reach out and softly close each eyelid and press her open jaw shut. I remember thinking it was kind of him to do that for her.

My memory of what happened after this becomes clouded and confused. I recall Bellows leading me by one arm out of the living room and into my study. He spoke quietly but none of the words penetrated. At some point Danchuk and he had a short, sharp discussion in the living room, while I waited in the study. Danchuk's voice rose angrily at various times during this conversation, but again his words made no impression on me. Nor did I take in the snap of Bellows's obvious rebuke. Of what concern to me was this discussion between policemen? I believe I thought of nothing at all. Perhaps for the first and only moment in my life my mind was completely inactive, inert, as lifeless as Merriam's own tormented mind would now forever be.

Merriam left no note, offered no explanation. When I counted the pills of her medication I determined she had dutifully taken the prescribed amounts. No medical oversight explained the irrational act. What was it that led her to suicide on this particular day? How was it different from any of the others that had preceded it or promised to follow? Perhaps that was the problem. Did she finally reach a point where the unending sameness of the days became unendurable? Was there anything I could have done? Had I not been with Vhanna might I have been able to prevent her death? Or would I have been off with Fergus flushing game? Would she have simply waited for another moment? Was it something she had decided upon over weeks of brooding and resolved to do? Or did she act impetuously?

This is the suicide's revenge. The suicide leaves no explanation and offers no absolution. If I had not failed Merriam, this terrible thing would not have come to pass. It is an indictment against which no defence can be offered. What had I done to push her toward suicide? Did I play a leading role? Or only a bit part? Perhaps I did nothing. Maybe it was the demons of her childhood about which she never talked, perhaps not even with her therapist. In the aftermath of Merriam's death I was left to dole out ladles full of personal responsibility, culpability, and guilt.

Would those who knew Ira Connaught haunt themselves with such questions and measures? Would they try to figure out how they could have prevented his self-inflicted death? If he in fact had committed suicide.

As these morbid thoughts on suicide and Ira ghosted and swirled through my mind I came to the southern edge of Tofino's tiny downtown core. Passing the Crab Pot Café I spotted Father Welch's Volvo sedan parked out front and pulled in alongside it. Business in the café was brisk and the smell of cooking crabmeat filled the air. Father Welch sat on a stool at the bar sucking thin slivers of meat out of the legs of a platter-sized Dungeoness. The hard-shelled body lay flipped on its back, every last scrap of meat meticulously eaten clean away. Allan Welch's fingers glistened with butter. At his elbow was a half-emptied pint of dark draft. His shoulder-length grey hair was tied back in a ponytail and the muscles in his shoulders bulged out visibly within the tight black T-shirt he wore along with black jogging pants and ankle-top canvas Converse runners. Father Welch's biceps were bigger around than fence posts and his shoulders rose at a precisely geometric angle to an apex point that started just below his ears.

I leaned into the empty space at the bar beside him and fished a crab leg off his plate. Snapping it in the middle, I put one half up to my mouth and pulled the meat out with my teeth. Down where the bar joined the open kitchen James Scarborough, Crab Pot's owner and my active partner in this venture, was giving live crabs a quick killing blow with a small mallet he held below counter level so the customers, especially potentially squeamish outlanders, couldn't see the final seconds of execution. The dead crabs were then tossed into a boiling vat of water. His motions were quick, deft, and as merciful as the whole process of killing and cooking fresh crab can ever be. Scarborough flashed his boyish grin at me and arched a thick black eyebrow in silent query as to whether I needed him for anything. I shook my head in his direction and ate the other half of Father Welch's crab leg.

"Good?" Father Welch asked as I chewed down the last of the meat.

"Wonderful. Food's always excellent here."

"Especially when you don't have to pay for it because you're eating off another man's plate. Want some of my beer next, no doubt."

I examined his mug thoughtfully and he put a huge fist around the glass, pulling it protectively toward him. Small beads of oil from the crab had pearled in the hair of his thick, drooping moustache. He looked more Mexican bandit or professional wrestler than priest. "Too dark," I said. "I'd prefer a blonder ale." Using the brass footrail that ran the length of the bar as a step I reached up and hooked a mug from the ceiling rack. Bending across the counter I drew a pint full from the blonde ale tap.

"Do you put money in the till when you do that?"

"Sometimes."

"Eat one man's crab, steal another man's beer. You are a reprobate, Elias McCann. A scoundrel."

I nodded to all of this and took a long pull on the beer "Every time I see you it's harder to see a neck," I replied. "One day all this weight training is going to transform you into something akin to the Goodyear Blimp."

Father Welch slapped the palm of one hand against a stomach that was as flat and hard as granite. "Ever see a blimp looked like this?"

I laughed and leaned my back against the bar. "So how you keeping, Father?"

He swallowed some beer, looked with pleasure upon the carcass on his plate and released a delicate burp. "Saving souls. Doing God's work. The usual. It's demanding work, as you well know." His demeanour turned suddenly serious. "I heard about Ira, Elias. Hell of a thing."

I nodded. "I understand he was Catholic."

"Yes, there weren't many Sundays when Ira Connaught failed to attend Mass. He may have been misguided in some things, but never in the matter of his faith. I liked him very much. So did most who knew him."

I worried this for a few seconds, hesitated, then said, "It looks like Ira committed suicide, Allan."

Father Welch's normally ruggedly cheerful demeanour washed instantly off his face as his mouth turned into a hard line that matched the flintiness that had entered his eyes. "No," he said with a hard shake of his head. One powerful hand settled over the back of mine and pressed it gently against the wood of the bar. "Ira would not have done so."

Shrugging I said, "Even Catholics sometimes take their lives, Allan."

Removing his hand from where it covered mine Father Welch carefully drained the last of his beer and signaled Scarborough for another. I gestured for him to make it two as I was finding investigating death thirsty work. Scarborough plunked brimming mugs before us and gathered away the plate containing the crab carcass. When he was out of earshot and we had drunk the heads off our pints, Father Welch said, "Ira was a very literal Catholic. Under no circumstance would he take his own life. That simply is not possible. Ira's faith was far too strong."

"What about the ecotage? Did that not contradict his faith?"

Father Welch considered this over a long swallow of beer, the fingers of one hand tugging at his moustache. "I believe Ira saw that as a matter of the world, Elias, not a challenge to his eternal soul. Have you ever known anyone to actually be injured because of tree spiking?"

I thought about that. Vague stories of injuries suffered in the Olympic forests of Washington State. No definite accounts I had ever actually read about or known of directly. Still — it seemed a dangerous thing, an impersonal form of potential violence. Not like strewing bombs or mines across a landscape, but still an act of indiscriminate malice. I told Father Welch this and he did not disagree. "In his mind I believe he saw himself as a warrior on one side of a war and the loggers as fighters for the other side. In that context the small risk the spikes posed to the loggers who chose to fall an old growth tree were acceptable."

I realized that Father Welch was saying that in Ira's mind the forests were both symbolically and literally the country for which he waged battle. It was a soldier's rationale for the use of force, also a rationale to which any terrorist could adhere. But we were off topic, probing Ira's motivations for spiking trees rather than whether he could also have been motivated to take his own life. I had Father Welch's certainty that this was not possible, I had Vhanna's equally strident rejection of this theory. I had a man hanging by his neck from a tree and no sign or evidence that it was anything other than suicide. I drained my glass, put it on the bar, and said good-bye.

"Go with God, my son," Father Welch said with an irreverent grin that robbed the phrase of its usual piety.

"Always, Father."

"Reprobate." He was chuckling as I walked out the door.

From the café I drove to the hospital. As I had expected Mayor Tully's rusted blue Cadillac angled crookedly into his assigned parking stall. Perhaps the good mayor-cum-pathologist-cum-family-doctor-cum-friend would be able to provide some answers about Ira's death. I found Tully in a cubicle, deep in the bowels of the small hospital. A metal and Formica desk was wedged awkwardly into the doorway so I had to shuffle in sideways to reach the wobbly visiting-room-style chair facing Tully. Next to me was a four-drawer black file cabinet bulging with papers so that it appeared none of the drawers could be firmly shut. Across the desk, the doctor was squeezed into the remaining sliver of cubicle space. The walls of the office were of that paint-chipped institutional pastel green favoured by hospitals. There appeared to be no ventilation; the air was thick and rancid smelling. The room was appallingly over-heated. I draped the Filson over the back of the chair and put my hat on the desktop. Sweat broke out in small beads on my chest. There were no windows, no means of getting fresh air. Tully's office was the sum of everything I hate about hospitals. Hospitals are intensely dangerous places, cloistered prisons into which loved ones go for treatment and seldom emerge again into the light. Had it not been so for my father? Are hospitals not where most of us will inevitably spend our last days? Does anyone manage to die in quiet peace at home anymore? Either death comes violently or we wither away in places where the air is stale and the temperature unnatural.

"How can you dress like that? You must be melting." Tully wore an open doctor's white lab coat over a grey woollen sweater and blue striped oxford shirt. His brow was dry. He looked cool and collected. Perhaps Tully had acclimatized to the unnatural environment. Sweat dripped down my sides. Small patches darkened my shirt front.

Tully ignored my question. "Danchuk is very upset with you. He called. Said he hasn't time to waste on Ira Connaught."

I shrugged. "What did the autopsy reveal?"

Tully glanced down at an open file balanced pre-cariously on a stack of other files. "He died by stran-gulation. Some time in the past forty-eight hours.

With the weather conditions an exact time of death isn't easy to calculate. I would guess he had been dead for more than a day before he was found. But it's really only a guess. If we sent him to Victoria for a forensic pathology examination we might narrow the time of death down somewhat, but probably not much. Determining time of death is more difficult than you'd think." He took off his glasses and rubbed the red spot on the bridge of his nose, like weary men who wear glasses are often prone to do. "Humidity, changes in temperature, all these things influence the way the body cools, passes through rigor, and begins to decay. It's not an exact science."

Putting his glasses back on, Tully stared across at me. His eyes were less tired, I realized, than clouded by trouble. "What else?" I asked, feeling my heartbeat quicken.

Tully took his glasses off and again rubbed his eyes until they were red and watery. He sighed. "I don't know. Could be nothing at all. It's strange."

"Godsakes, Reginald!"

"I'll have to show you. I haven't completely sewn him back up yet." He must have seen me pale, as Tully smiled ruefully. "It won't be that bad."

It was worse than bad, it was a descent into horror. The Ira I knew was no longer. Gone was the thick tangle of red hair and the beard. Stitch marks circled his shaved head, closing the surgical opening Tully had made in the cranium to allow his examination of the brain. Another line of stitch marks extended from his pubis to the top of his chest and then slashed over to each shoulder. This, I assumed, was the classic "Y" incision that allows a pathologist to examine the internal organs. Permeating the room was the cloying stench of death and I was grateful Tully had insisted we both change into surgical clothing for the inspection. I didn't want to have to spend another evening trying to banish death's stench from my clothes.

The body lay on a metal autopsy table positioned squarely in the centre of a sterile room sparsely fitted with gleaming stainless steel equipment, a powerful spotlight above the metal table, pastel green walls and a battleship-grey linoleum floor. Ira, so large in life, was dwarfed into insignificance by this clinical facility. I thought of my father. I remembered Angus lying under the hospital bed covers, the machines ticking and wheezing, sustaining the life that had long fled in spirit from the withered body those bed covers concealed. It had been such a simple act of kindness to use my Swiss Army knife to sever the air hose trailing from one wheezing machine to the mask covering my father's face. Alarms rang as the knife severed the hose and nurses came quickly to repair the damage, but by the time the machine was again working Angus had gone peacefully. I only wished I could have taken him out of that place of death and let him drift off in his bed in the Comox Valley farmhouse that overlooked lush, green pastures and a tree-lined trout brook.

"I left his neck open," Tully said. I returned from my reverie to the stark room and grim task at hand.

Ira's neck was what I had studiously been trying to ignore. Now Tully was forcing me to focus on it. I turned away for a moment, took a few deep breaths, in a futile effort to steady myself. Turning back to Ira, I found that my nausea had passed but that my hands still trembled lightly. During the autopsy, Tully had meticulously flayed the flesh of

Ira's neck back layer by layer in what seemed a hideous form of post-death mutilation.

Now he had several layers rolled back so I was looking down at a skin filament that must have been half-way between the veins, arteries, and windpipe and the surface skin. This layer of skin, normally so deep beneath the surface, bore a livid bruising wound that was shaped like a rope. "You see?" Tully asked.

I nodded, unsure I could successfully talk and keep my stomach contents in place.

Like he was peeling back a layer of onionskin, Tully slipped the filament of skin away to expose the layer immediately underneath. The rope wound was still there, dark and raw looking. But there was something else. I forced myself to look more closely. Around the rope wound was a larger, more blockish looking bruising; bruising every bit as brutal looking as the rope wound. I looked up questioningly at Tully.

"Look at the outer edges. What's it look like to you?"

Where the skin began to disappear around the back of the neck on either side I noticed four distinct areas where the bruising was broken by undamaged skin, forming a definite recognizable imprint on Ira's throat. When I looked right where the jugular was, two precise bruises far darker and blunter looking than the rest of the damage were evident. "Hands," I whispered. Huge bloody hands. As big a pair of hands as you could imagine. "The thumbs on the windpipe, the other fingers around the throat. Whoever it was used both hands." I paused. "But why weren't the same marks duplicated on the outer skin?"

Tully sighed, a troubled sound. "I'm not sure. It happens. I think probably it has to do with the size of hands. The pressure was so dispersed that it was only on the deeper layers of skin that the extra bite of the fingers and the overall crushing strength of the killer's hands left its mark. Again, a real forensic pathologist might know the answer."

"Doesn't matter a lot, though, does it? Ira's still dead. And somebody murdered him and tried to cover up the killing." I pondered this for a moment. "He would have struggled." I remembered Ira's ragged hands, the signs of his scrabbling feet on the tree, the scars on the boots. The memory sickened me. "He was still alive when the killer hanged him. The choking was only to render him unconscious."

Tully nodded. He pointed at the damaged hands. "Can't tell how much of the injury to his hands came from a struggle with the killer and how much from trying to climb the rope after he regained consciousness and," Tully's voice trailed off. I imagined Ira waking, finding himself hanging, strangling, the world spinning, a rope dangling him from the branch of a massive cedar. I clutched the side of the table to steady myself. It was hideous, brutal and sadistic. "There were lots of bruises and cuts on his body. They could have come from a struggle or from when he was hanging from the branch."

"You've taken samples?"

"Yes. I've scraped all the wounds and taken blood samples. It'll take a couple weeks for the labs in Victoria to come up with any blood type identifications or anything else."

"How long would Ira have been rendered unconscious by the choking?"

Tully shrugged. "Impossible to tell. A few minutes, an hour. It would depend a lot on his physical constitution and how close the killer took him to the point of death before releasing his hands. Perhaps he thought Ira was already dead. He might not have intended the hanging to be the thing that killed him."

"But where was Ira at the time the killer attacked him?"

It wasn't something Tully could answer. He shrugged again and pulled the sheet up to cover Ira's body. He gestured for me to follow him and I willingly fled the room, my head pounding with questions that could only be answered by Ira's killer.

"What does it mean?" I asked back in Tully's office. He had returned to digging at his eyes with tense fingers. I was sweating again and wishing we were on a beach breathing in fresh salt air.

"I could be wrong about the injury to the lower layers of the skin. But if I'm right, and those injuries were caused by hands and not the rope, then Ira was strangled first."

"And whoever did the strangling hung Ira up by the rope to make it look like a suicide."

Tully nodded. His expression was grim. "I should tell Danchuk," he said.

"No." The word escaped my mouth before I realized what I was thinking.

"Elias."

"No, listen, Reginald. If you tell Danchuk he'll start a murder investigation. Which means he will call in detectives from Nanaimo or even the mainland. It will be days before they get started. Give me forty-eight hours and then call him."

"Why?"

I looked down at my hands, suddenly uncertain. How could I explain? After taking a deep breath, I said, "Ever since this thing started I've had a sense that Ira's death is part of something bigger. And that whatever it's a larger part of is going to come to a head very soon. We need answers now, Reginald, or something worse is going to happen."

Tully's patience was obviously being tried and he did little to conceal the fact. "You think you can solve Ira's murder and save the day."

I shook my head. "No, but I know that if we tell Danchuk he'll throw a lid on this thing until after his damn senator has come and gone. And it might be too late then."

"Too late for what?"

All I could do was shake my head. How could I explain that my reasoning was based primarily on the premonition that I had had since the first day of the twenty-five day storm; the haunting sense that disaster was imminent, that lives were in danger? Intuition was a poor justification for concealing the immediate evidence of a murder.

"No, Elias. I'll tell Danchuk. And I'll pretend we never had this conversation. Dammit, there are procedures to follow."

I got up, slung the Filson over my shoulder and donned my hat. "Do what you have to do, Reginald." I was suddenly drained. I wanted only to find some fresh air, to feel a breeze upon my face, to escape this house of death. "I'll be on my way."

As I squeezed past his desk and out the door Reginald said, "I think you best leave this to the police. They'll probably want the regional coroner to take over the inquiry as well."

From under the brim of my hat, I looked back

over my shoulder at him. I started to speak, to assure him I would do the correct thing. Conversely, I was tempted to tell him that I was the coroner and, there-fore, technically seized of this inquiry. From the moment I drafted the inquiry papers, nobody — nei-ther the police nor the regional coroner nor even the provincial attorney general — had the right to tell me what I could or could not do in carrying out that inquiry. Such was the law. These thoughts roared like a runaway train through my head. But instead of saying any of this to Tully, I merely nodded a farewell and walked down the corridor toward the sunlight and air that irresistibly beckoned.

Chapter Seven

The decision to take a matter into your own hands in defiance of authority can, to use the current mumbo-jumbo words of pop psychology, uniquely empower an individual. This was as true now as it had been years before, when I severed the breathing hose attached to my father's slowly wasting-away body. I would continue my investigation into Ira's death despite the fact that I had no true legal authority to continue. My duty as a coroner was solely to determine cause of death. Ira had been strangled, either by a murderer's hands or by a murderer's hangman rope. Ira was a victim of a homicide. That was certain. With that certainty my coroner's inquiry was technically complete. I should stand aside, write my report and allow the police to carry out their murder investigation. Just as I should have allowed the doctors and nurses to continue pumping air and fluids into my father's dying body, while at the same time using other devices to extract and dispose of his bodily wastes. That would be the legally correct and personally safe course of action.

On the day I euthenized my father it seemed likely I was in a great deal of trouble. I had realized the gravity of potential consequences even as I drew the knife from my pocket and started cutting. That knowledge had failed to slow my hand as the knife sliced cleanly through the hose. When a nurse, with short-clipped red hair and vivid china blue eyes, arrived in the doorway and let out an hysterical shriek, I wondered in an oddly detached way whether my actions would see me in prison.

But there was no such dire result. Instead, the whole affair was quietly hushed up. My father's death was explained as resulting from a mechanical failure. I was fortunate in having taken my action during a time when the right to die was a heated national issue, one that continues today. The courts of the day were routinely having to weigh the balance between a family's desire that a terminally ill relative be allowed to die when the spirit seemed to be seeking to depart the body and the medical community's insistence that its machines and medicines could sustain life and should be allowed to do so for as long as the body continued to survive. What constituted life and whether a family or health institution should have the power of life and death over the terminally ill was so hotly debated that the authorities feared prosecuting me would give the right-to-die movement an ideal *cause célèbre*. Other than for a short interview at the hospital, the police never placed me under arrest. During the interview, I claimed no knowledge of how the hose had come to be severed. The police obviously didn't believe me, but they also seemed to welcome the arrival of my father's lawyer who helped extract me from their interrogation. Over the ensuing days Angus's lawyer and the Crown prosecutor negotiated.

I waited at my father's home in Comox, spending the daylight hours jigging for trout in the little brook that faced the old farmhouse. By night, I browsed through his extensive library of aged books penned by writers from the Victorian and Edwardian eras.

Finally the lawyer called to say the Crown would not press charges. "You knew of his will," he said as a statement rather than a question. I told him I had yet to see it. "You are, then, a lucky man, Elias, because it's his will that is providing the Crown an excuse to not prosecute you for murder." It transpired that Angus had the foresight to write into his will that, in the event he became ill and disabled, no life support systems should be utilized. Unfortunately Angus, who seldom even remembered to file his tax reports, had failed to validate the will by having it witnessed. He had then compounded that oversight by locking the will away in his safety deposit box where it lay undisturbed until the lawyer, acting as Angus's Estate Executor, discovered it and realized the opportunity it presented for exonerating me. "I wouldn't tell them you were ignorant of his will," he warned.

Knowing Angus as I had and sharing enough of his beliefs about what constituted a meaningful life, I was not surprised by the contents of his will. It was that knowledge that had given me the strength to commit the merciful act of ending his life. I knew that doing so had been a great risk and that when charges were not preferred I had been very lucky. For weeks after, I worried that the hospital staff would raise a cry for their concept of justice being done. I remembered the red-haired nurse with pretty eyes and her horror at my actions. She had even pounded her fists against my chest while her eyes streamed with tears. I watched the newspapers for headlines blaring her or

Angus's doctor's accusations. But all remained silent. Beyond the obituary, which I authored, no further mention was made of my remittance man father's passing. In due course, he was properly buried and I set about administering his estate, trying to give little further thought to how he died.

I seldom think of it now. Certainly I feel no guilt. There are, I know, many who would say what I did was wrong, that I had no right to decide whether my father should live or die. They would argue that such a decision should have been left to a higher power or to nature. But there is no nature in machines that sustain a body alive while rendering the mind and spirit its helpless prisoner. I know this for certain. A man who loved to hunt the briar, to feel dawn mist on his face, who wrote love letters to a woman long lost, could think of no greater indignity than being trapped in a sterile hospital room while machines replaced his lungs, fed him, and emptied his intestinal tract.

Ever since my father's death I have hated and feared hospitals. My skin crawls and becomes clammy whenever I must enter one.

By the time I reached the Rover, I had managed to shake off the effects of my visit to Mayor Tully's morgue. It was almost noon and my stomach growled hungrily. I needed to think about where to begin the inquiry into Ira's murder.

I drove home. Before attending to my hunger, I had to see to Fergus's. In the kennel that sided the cabin, he had dried out from our morning's meander and was now pacing restlessly. I spent a few minutes with the slicker brush, freeing his coat of dried dirt and loose hair so he once again looked fairly well groomed. Inside the cabin, he headed straight to the kitchen and stamped an expectant paw on the linoleum before his bowl. When I dumped some dry food into it, he greeted this offering with a snort of annoyance. "Okay," I conceded, feeling no urge to wage a protracted battle I would certainly lose. I cut and cubed a couple of large slices of cheddar cheese and sprinkled these into Fergus's bowl. Without so much as a thank-you he happily dug into his gourmet lunch.

I washed down a ham and cheese sandwich with a bottle of Vancouver Island Piper's Pale Ale. As I ate, I flicked through the telephone book until I found the address I wanted. There was no listing for Rick and Chuck Greer, but Dauphin Logging had a Ucluelet listing and address.

Grabbing up my hat and coat I headed out the door, Fergus so close on my heels he was wriggled outside before I could shut the door on him. I paused. Fergus did a perfect down-sit and looked wishful. I relented. "Want to go for a ride?"

His eyes met mine quite literally as he managed to jump skyward while standing in place. For a second we met each other's gaze before gravity inevitably dragged his body down to earth. Then in a flurry of legs Fergus headed for the Rover, back-legs slithering in a drift through the driveway's gravel as he came to a halt before the passenger door.

I climbed into the driver's side and opened Fergus's door from the inside. He leapt up on the passenger's seat and leaned against its back with his front legs stretched out between those of his rear. A lopsided, floppy grin was his thanks or just as possibly an order to get the Rover into gear and moving. Next to flushing birds from the briar, Fergus's greatest joy is going for a drive.

We set off down the highway toward Pacific Rim National Park, leaving Tofino in our wake. I pushed hard, forcing the speedometer up to somewhere between 80 and 90 kilometres, virtually the Rover's top speed. It's hard to tell the vehicle's true speed because the needle bounces erratically between 0 and 100 kilometres, pausing for only the briefest second in the speed range that the Rover is actually traveling. The 2.25-litre engine screamed, the transmission whined, and the drive chain howled; peering out through the small windshield, we watched the road-side scenery pass by in a seeming blur that defied our actual speed. Occasionally the road topped a rise and I could see over the small hillocks to where long rolling breakers crashed in upon the sweeping expanses of Long Beach. The sky was still brilliant blue, the sun starkly etching the white foam capping the waves.

Fergus's head twisted this way and that as he tried to take in all of his domain. With his scrawny hind legs thrust out before him and his long body sitting bolt upright, he looked like an old, wizened dour Scot. Or he might have, were it not for the tongue lolling smiles he kept casting my way and the gleam of contentment in his eyes.

After about twenty kilometres the manifold exhaust running directly beneath the driver's footwell on its route to the Rover's tail started heating up the interior. My foot on the accelerator became uncomfortably warm. This heating of the steel floorboards by the heat thrown off by the manifold used to be much worse before I installed a sheet of asbestos under the carpeting. Once it was almost intolerable and I would have to stop and let the engine cool, now it was merely uncomfortable.

The sun blazed through the windows and the heat kept rising. I reached over to Fergus's side and cranked open the plate door below the windshield that served as an air vent. Fergus leaned down and let the streaming air play over his face and flip his ears about. I opened the identical vent before me and mimicked him. The air felt wonderful, clean, and cool. It tasted sharply of salt and smelled of rotting kelp beds.

We hurtled along until just before the exit from the south end of Pacific Rim National Park when, responding to Fergus's imperative, serious stare, I pulled over and let him out. He raced into the bushes with all the urgency of a politician rushing toward a bribe. Although our mission was the same, I set a more leisurely pace into the screen of brush. A few minutes later, we emerged feeling more able to concentrate on the serious business before us.

Tofino and Ucluelet stand forty-two kilometres apart at opposing ends of the thirty-three-kilometre-long stretch of Pacific Rim National Park's Long Beach. This opposition of locations is both physical and psychological. Ucluelet is a town of loggers and fishermen. It's proud of its resource-based past and determined to preserve this heritage despite the fact that there remain few forests left to quarry, or salmon to harvest. Like many small towns on Vancouver Island, Ucluelet is glued to the old ways, to a time when forests stretched up mountains without limits and no man could envision the last great western red cedar being felled. In my mind, Tofino has claimed the promise of the future. The surrounding Clayoquot is the last bastion of ancient rainforest. There is opportunity here, the chance to build a future based on preservation of resources and living in mutual harmony with nature. Tofino and Ucluelet are the two opposing camps in this struggle between the past and the future. Clayoquot is their battleground. Perhaps Ira's death was a shot fired in this battle. It was to explore this possibility that I had traveled to Ucluelet.

After driving through the more ramshackle portion of the town past ill-painted clapboard houses where rusting trucks served as lawn ornaments, I came to a wide gravel lane fronted by a weathered yellow sign that bore in faded black hand-scrawled paint: *Dauphin Logging Company Ltd. No Trespassing. Private Road. Keep Out. Beware of Heavy Trucks. Machinery Working.* A gate constructed of heavy welded-together metal pipes that could probably bring a charging bulldozer to an abrupt halt yawed open. Ignoring the sign's litany of threatening messages, I drove into Dauphin Logging Company's work yard.

The road inside the compound was heavily oiled to keep dust down and help prevent muddying in the rains. After twenty-five days of constant rain, however, it was quite greasy. Mud, flicked up by the tires, drummed against the Rover's wheelwalls and roostered out behind us. On either side of the road, regimented by their type, stretched Dauphin Logging Company equipment.

First came a long line of yellow logging trucks painted with black trim. These were heavy trucks built to drag the long trailers confined to the forest licence roads and capable of hauling out entire fallen trees without the need for them to be first cut into sections. A trailer might manage to hold three, maybe even four, fallen cedar giants per load. I have seen these trailers groaning and bulging perilously under the weight and girth of just one huge raincoast tree.

After the trucks came yellow-painted log skidders

and bulldozers with blades that stood higher than the engine cowlings. The driver's seat on all this equipment was fully encased by protective steel cages to protect the worker from tree and branch falls or in the event the machine overturned while working on the steep mountain slopes. Graders and dump trucks formed the tail end of this neat, awe-inspiring line of mechanical behemoths. The road terminated abruptly, too, right before a large grey-metal Quonset workshed. In front of the shed several men in flannel shirts and green work pants held up by wide red suspenders tinkered with chainsaws mounting blades taller than the largest of these husky loggers. Seeing me drive up, one of the men walked over. As he approached the window, the man tipped a shiny steel hard-hat back on his head. "Help ya?" he said like a challenge and spit a stream of tobacco juice from the corner of his mouth. In one big paw he held a chainsaw sharpener with a good foot-long file.

"I'm looking for Rick and Chuck Greer," I replied. "Need to talk to them."

"You being?" The man's face was grimed with grease from the chainsaws and his teeth were yellow. Grey eyes looked straight through me.

I told him who and what I was. He stuck the file in his back pocket and pointed down a narrower lane than the one running between the logging equipment toward the kind of portable office trailer often seen on construction sites. It was white with yellow trim bordered by thin black lines. On one side of the building, a high chain link pen held a large black pitbull-cross of some sort. The dog paced frantically from one end of the pen to the other, then retraced its steps.

Thanking the man, I drove up the slight rise toward the office building. In my rearview, I noticed the man still watching me. He was gripping the dagger of the sharpening file in one hand and sliding it back and forth through a hole he made by joining the thumb and forefinger of his other hand together. The movement was slow, thoughtful, vaguely threatening.

Two four-wheel-drive vehicles were parked in front of the office. Both were Jeep Wagoneers. One was red, the other gunmetal blue. Their paint was shiny and new. Each vehicle bore pinstripes that contrasted stylishly with the body paint and the door panels sported Dauphin Logging Company decals.

These were the kind of off-road vehicle you see in rush hour traffic trying to cross Vancouver's Lion's Gate Bridge or passing the Empress Hotel in downtown Victoria. Vehicles called SUVs or sometimes sport utes, both of which stand for Sport Utility Vehicles, as if that provides an explanation of their purpose. It's as if the military's penchant for acronyms of meaninglessness has crossed over into the realm of civilian transportation. SUV? As senseless sounding as MBT. What else could a tank be built for than to be a Main Battle Tank? Are there tanks built for Lesser Battles? LBTs? The same applies to four-wheel drive vehicles. Their purpose is obvious, it requires no further labeling.

As I stepped out of the Rover, the door of the office opened and a man came out. He had to bend his head slightly to avoid scouring the upper door jamb with it. He straightened up and gazed down upon me from the small, raised porch.

I looked up at him, feeling, because of his towering presence and the position of height afforded him by the porch, like some penitent come to see royalty. "You Mr. Dauphin?" At the sound of my voice, the dog in the enclosure suddenly started roaring and throwing itself against the wire with what seemed near-demonic rage. Fergus replied from the safety of the Rover with a short, sharp bark but then, as the other animal's barking reached a wild crescendo, obviously thought better of further heroics and quieted after giving one last show of defiance, a rather meek-sounding little woof. The man in the doorway bellowed, "Shut up!" The dog stopped barking as abruptly as if he had been pole-axed.

At least six-foot-six, with the kind of shoulders a linebacker would envy, the man's voice was as intimidating as his stature and looks. His head sat like a square block of concrete on a neck that rivaled the post used to close the gate at the bottom of the compound. He wore his blond hair long on the sides and combed up to cover the sun reddened skin of his balding crown. He had a florid face and hands as big as dinner plates. "Dauphin." He pronounced it Doffin. "Phil Dauphin. And you?"

I held out my hand, having to almost go up on my toes to make it extend to where he stood above me on the porch. Dauphin enfolded my hand inside one of his paws with such crushing force I winced. I didn't miss the little smile that twitched the corners of his mouth when he finally released his grip.

As I started explaining who I was, and my purpose for the visit, he ran meaty fingers through the wisps of hair topping his head. Then he donned the kind of cowboy hat Garth Brooks has made popular in the suburbs — a wide brimmed bluey-grey thing with a high top and the look of money about it. He wore jeans and a blue and white cowboy shirt. The jeans sported a wide black leather belt with a silver buckle that had an embossed gold bulldozer in the centre. Hand-tooled cowboy boots added another inch or two of totally unnecessary loft to Dauphin's height so that he appeared to be a not-so-friendly giant.

When I finished my spiel and passed him my coroner's business card, he tucked the card and his hands in the jean's back pockets and looked off at the hills. From this angle I could see his nose had once been crushed and bent to one side. It didn't look like he had done much to try and correct the injury. The deformed nose had the effect of distorting Dauphin's face so his pale blue eyes looked beady. "They ain't here," he rumbled and continued to study the hillsides.

"You know where I might find them?"

He shrugged. "Said they was going huntin'. Up around Woss. Or maybe Zeballos?" He had just described two of Vancouver Island's most isolated points. Woss has a population of about 400. Zeballos, maybe 220. Both are surrounded by country that could swallow entire military divisions without a trace. And the residents of Woss and Zeballos were likely to be about as helpful and talkative as Phil Dauphin.

"I need to talk with them."

"About the terrorist?"

For a moment I was confused. "Terrorist?"

Dauphin nodded. "That long hair with the spikes. Feller that hanged himself."

"Yes, I need to talk to them about Ira Connaught. The dead man they found."

Dauphin grinned. It wasn't a nice expression. "You welcome to do so when you find them. But I think they said they was goin' to be gone a week, maybe two."

Behind him the office door opened and a woman

with long blond hair that was dark at the roots and a bosom that paraded before her like bumper bullets on a 1950s car stepped by Dauphin and descended the steps. Her acid-wash jeans moved like skin on her hips and legs. She wore a sleeveless red sweater that was as tight as the jeans. Ten years ago she would have been a marvel to behold but there were bulges where there shouldn't have been and pockets of flesh under her eyes. As she passed by a waft of perfume redolent with jasmine nearly caused me to sneeze. She pegged her way across the lot on perilous white spikes to the fire-red Wagoneer. "You be home for dinner, honey?" she asked over her shoulder in a voice bordering on a whine.

Dauphin nodded curtly. She graced me with a smile that glittered of more than routine dental polishing and climbed into the vehicle. As she drove away Dauphin turned his attention back to me. "You need anything more, mister?"

I pushed my hands into my Filson's pockets and looked up at him in a futile attempt to see his eyes beneath the brim of the big hat. "Did you know Ira Connaught?"

"No. Ain't never laid eyes on the man. Least ways I don't believe I ever did."

"But you knew of him. Knew he carried spikes. Knew enough about him to think of him as a terrorist."

It might have been the sunlight playing with the shadows cast by the brim of his hat but Dauphin's skin seemed to pale slightly for a moment and then darken to a deeper shade of red. "We know all about those damn fools, Mr. McCann. Them and their spikes. Them and their tryin' to stop us loggin'. Stop us takin' the timber out. Stop us makin' a livin'. We know our enemies, mister. We know 'em, alright."

I turned to stare off at the hills beyond Ucluelet. It wasn't a pretty sight. In the saddles between the mountain peaks the scars of clear-cuts stretched. The slopes and even the peaks of several of the more rounded mountains were also totally denuded. I thought of the green Clayoquot mountains visible from the windows of my home and wondered if this was their future. "Somebody killed Ira Connaught, Mr. Dauphin. Somebody thought him enough of an enemy to want him dead."

The silence hung between us for a long time. I did nothing to ease its passage. I continued to look at the ravaged hillsides because I could not read Dauphin's face beneath the protection of his Stetson. Eventually he broke the quiet with a wicked little laugh. "Can't say I'm sorry. The little son of a bitch had it comin'."

Dauphin was probably one of only a few men who could describe Ira Connaught as a little man and not appear foolish. "Why would you say he had it coming?" I trained my eyes on him now, trying to read his face as best I could. But it was hopeless. The snort, however, spoke volumes about what his expression would have been like.

"You see those hills up there?" He thrust a huge fist toward the mountains and then extended one meaty finger like a cannon barrel sighting in on its target. "Timber's gone from them, eh? Ain't nothin' left here to log. No way for a man to make a living here from the forests. So we need into Clayoquot. We need those trees, mister. People's livelihoods are at stake here. And men like him and their Birkenstock-wearing bitches who drink herbal tea and eat that tofu shit chain themselves to barriers across the fuckin' roads, spike the trees, vandalize our equipment. Do all they can to stop us doin' what we gotta do to survive."

Dauphin came off the step and settled a paw on my shoulder. As a man might with a small child he swiveled me around so I was looking at the equipment in his compound. He bent down next to my ear, his big head next to mine, his arm, on the other side of my face, pointing out across my shoulder. "More than a million bucks' equipment out there. Jobs for eighty, a hundred men. Contract loggin'. Haulin' out the timber, cuttin' the roads to get in there. A livelihood. That's what matters. That's all that matters. And there ain't no tree spiker's goin' to stop us from makin a livin'. No fuckin' way." As he straightened up, Dauphin spun me around again with a surprisingly deft and yet gentle move so I faced him. Huge teeth grinned down at me. "But ain't none of us would kill him, mister. Type like that ain't worth killin'." Chuckling, he started toward the blue Wagoneer. "I gotta get home." He turned and waggled a finger at me. "You all want to talk to Rick and Chuck you best be drivin' up north. They like the back country, where the Roosevelt elk roam. You maybe find them up there by one of them lakes between Woss and Zeballos." He chortled deeply as he folded himself into the Jeep.

I walked over to the Rover and opened the door. Behind me the Jeep fired up. Gravel crunched beneath its wheels as Dauphin backed down alongside me. The power window whirred down. He stuck his right hand out at me. Reflexively I took it and my palm and fingers were crushed as if caught in the jaws of a steel vice. "Been a pleasure meetin' ya, Mr. McCann. You all drive safely on the way back to Tofino now." The big teeth flashed again and the window slipped closed. As Dauphin drove away I heard strains of Garth

Brooks singing about having friends in low places.
Dauphin's jeep went down the road fast, barely slow-
ing to pass the men working in front of the Quonset
shed, and roared out of the compound.

A few minutes later I followed, passing the men
working on the chainsaws. There wasn't a man there
who didn't have hands more than capable of matching the ones that strangled Ira Connaught. And
Dauphin? There might be motive there. But I had
learned nothing here. All I had were more questions.
Would Dauphin have enough reason to kill Ira? Had
Ira been that much of a thorn in the sides of the loggers? Why Ira? Why not any of the other Sunshine
Warriors or ecologists? And why had Chuck and Rick
Greer gone off? Had they gone to ground? Or had
they just gone hunting because their permits were
close to expiring and the chances of finding game
were better up north?

I drove out of town, passing between the bleak
and weathered buildings of Ucluelet. Here and there
people walked past the stores, grey children played
in the yards, men stood in the doorway of the local
bar and eyed the Rover as it passed. I found myself
looking at every man's hands, measuring their size,
pondering their motives. Most would qualify in size,
or had a buddy beside him who was bigger, more
than large enough to have hands that might match
those that strangled Ira. When I was finally out of
town I felt a palpable relief. Wherever the answer to
who murdered Ira Connaught was to be found I
knew Ucluelet was not the place. Not that Ira's killer
didn't live there, but to find his identity I needed to
look elsewhere. But I had no idea where that other
place might be.

Chapter Eight

The tree in which Ira Connaught had been hanged seemed even more immense beneath a sunny sky than it had the day before, when shrouded in fog and dripping rain. I wandered beneath its dense canopy and peered up at the branch from which Ira had been suspended. There was a deep scar in the cedar bark where the rope had bitten through to the yellowish meat. It was a huge branch, large enough for a man to crawl out upon easily.

Fergus wandered about, sniffing this and that bush, distractedly leaving signposts of his passing. From time to time he gave me a puzzled glance, as if wondering why we had paused here in this fragment of forest bordering the bleak devastation of a clear-cut.

Slowly, I circled the tree trunk. The trunk, other than for the side facing the branch, was covered only with large patches of moss. On the flank beneath the branch, however, thick crusted globs of mud splattered the tree's rough hide. I noticed that the mud covering the trunk only extended to a few feet below the height of the branch used for hanging Ira. Digging my

Swiss Army knife out I flicked the steel wedge attachment free and carefully scraped some of the mud away to expose the layer of bark it had concealed. Encouraged by what I found, I scraped away more of the dry mud.

In the bark that had been covered by the mud was a sharp slashing wound cut through to the hard wood. I had seen these kinds of scars on utility poles alongside the highway. These were the marks left by the climbing spurs a utility employee might use to scamper up a pole without the need for a ladder. Loggers sometimes used these spikes as well when taking down trees in sections rather than in one fell swoop. So that was how it had been done. The killer had climbed the tree to the branch, then strung Ira from it and fashioned the knot that had suspended him in the air. Had Ira gained consciousness while the man did this, or had he awakened later when the killer was back on the ground? Had the man witnessed his desperate struggle to live? Had he enjoyed watching Ira die?

I reconsidered for a moment and realized my mistake. I tried imagining a man, with dinner-plate sized hands, straddling the branch. He held a rope whose other end was knotted around Ira's neck. Hand over hand the man started pulling Ira up by the rope. When he had the body to the right height he started tying the knot around the branch. But each time he tried to tie the knot I imagined the rope slipping in his hands, unwinding, and Ira tumbling back to the ground.

Two of them, then. One up on the branch to tie the knot and one on the ground holding Ira's body up so the man's weight was off the rope. Only when the rope was unweighted would it be possible for the knot to be tied around the branch. Two killers. Not one. But who? And where did they first attack Ira? Why bring him here?

The obvious answer was that they found Ira here and for some reason set about assaulting him. So I walked carefully around the site in ever widening circles that turned up nothing. No crushed brush, no broken branches, no disrupted ground to indicate a struggle between three large, powerful men. When I finished this futile exploration, Fergus shook his head, causing his dog tags to jingle ferociously, and went to stand impatiently by the Rover's passenger door. Confused by my illogical-seeming actions he was ready to leave.

But I wasn't free to go yet. The killers had smeared mud on the tree trunk to conceal the scars left by the climbing spurs. Might they have taken other precautions to hide any evidence of their presence? I studied the ground leading up from the old track of road into the site. A thick carpet of needles and leaves blanketed it, disrupted here and there only by the tires of my Rover. These were the tracks left when I backed up to the tree the day before to enable Joseph Samuels to free Ira's body from the rope.

I went to the Rover and dug out the trenching shovel I kept stored in the back. Using the side of the metal spade, I skimmed away layerings of the needles and leaves to expose the soft earth. The Rover's utilitarian tire tracks were imprinted heavily into the soil. And a few inches over from this track was a thinner, less deeply treaded tire marking. I found its mate a little beyond the second line of the Rover's tire impressions. The tread markings seemed to be those left by a mid-size pick-up truck or, and I paused with

this thought, one of the showy new SUVs. Skimming
aside the covering of camouflage I followed the two
sets of tire tracks all the way up to a position directly below the branch. Then, skimming away leaves as
I went, I followed the tracks back all the way to
where they joined the abandoned logging road. Here,
the marks blended with other older impressions,
becoming indistinguishable.

Not only were there two killers, but they had
definitely brought Ira to this place in a pick-up or
SUV. They had backed the vehicle all the way up
beneath the branch selected for the hanging. And
after that? Had they put his body in the box of the
truck? Or, if it was an SUV, did they lift him up onto
the cab? That seemed too difficult, but it was also
what Samuels and I had done to get Ira's body down.
I remembered Samuels standing on top of the Rover's
cab, gently lifting Ira's body by one powerful arm
while he worked the knot free with his other hand. So
either vehicle type — pick-up or SUV — would have
served the purpose.

Danchuk and the RCMP could take castings of
the tire treads and determine the brand of tire that
had left this print. From that they could narrow
down the type of vehicle used. But all that forensic
work would take time. Days? Weeks? Would
Danchuk even bother? He had Senator Jack Sloan
coming. That responsibility alone stretched his capa-
bilities to the limit. He also would be less than
thrilled to have me advising him on the proper ways
of conducting a murder investigation.

The sense of urgency surrounding this matter
had not lessened as the day slipped past and
answers came so slowly. The presage of disaster still
hung on me, haunted my thoughts.

Fergus, having resigned himself to being stuck here for a while, had wandered off into the brush in search of some entertainment. I whistled sharply and seconds later he flushed from a thicket looking relieved and optimistic that I had called to take him away from this place. On the drive back to the highway, I passed the spot where Danchuk and the Greers had parked their vehicles the day before. Seeing the imprint of the Greers' swollen monster tires left on the rotting hulk of a fallen cedar, I got out and walked over to take a closer look. The tread was unmistakably at least twice as wide as that of the vehicle that had backed up to Ira's tree. But perhaps the other Greer owned a smaller-tired truck and they had wisely not returned to the murder site with this vehicle. Returned so as to fake finding Ira in a clumsy attempt to deflect suspicion away from themselves. But why come back at all? Why not leave him there for the ravens, the crows, the maggots, and the rot of death to further conceal the evidence of their crime? In a few days or weeks rain would have washed away the tire treads. In the same time the obvious signs of the climbing spurs on the tree's bark would also have become less easily identifiable. Why choose to draw attention to themselves by coming back here and pretending to have found Ira's body while on an improbable hunting expedition in the driving rain?

Were they sent by Dauphin? But, again, what possible purpose was served? If he had murdered Ira or ordered his murder, why would the logging company owner seek to establish a link between himself and his victim when none existed before?

I climbed back into the Rover and stared wearily out the window for a time at the green shrubbery bor-

dering the logging road. There was nothing more to
see or learn in these woods. My suspects for the murder of Ira Connaught began vaporizing before my
eyes. There was no logic in any of the evidence I had
gathered. But then perhaps that was the logic. Perhaps
Dauphin and the Greers realized the best way to
deflect suspicion was by confronting it head on. Or
perhaps the Greers, acting alone, had reasoned such a
strategy out. But I could not see bluff Rick and Chuck
thinking so cleverly. Dauphin, with his sneering chides
about my chances of finding the Greers, could perhaps be so devious. Indeed, the more I thought about
it, this seemed precisely the kind of stratagem of
which he would be capable.

But it was all so much futile speculation. There
was no motive. I still had no idea where Ira had been
when he was choked unconscious and then kid-
napped to the murder site. Why had he been wherever he was that motivated his murder? And who had
been with him? These were the questions that
required answering. But how could I find answers?

The Sunshine Warriors maintained a base of operations of sorts. It was an old shack on the shore of
Flores Island near the small village of Ahousaht.
More like a fraternity house than operational command centre, the base was, like all of Flores, accessi-
ble only by boat.

This fact brought me to Tassina Mavrikos. I could
have probably borrowed Vhanna's splendid forty-foot
yacht for the trip, but I'm not especially adept at piloting boats. The dual sixteen-cylinder diesel engines that
power her boat require a deft hand on the wheel when
docking. Besides, I had not yet decided what to say to

Vhanna the next time I saw her. There was much to discuss and I could see no happy conclusion to the conversation. Thinking of the prospect of seeing her again depressed and worried me.

When I explained to Tassina my need to go to the Sunshine Warrior clubhouse she happily offered to give me a lift. We cast the crab boat off from the dock and powered up the inlet, heading for the gap between Vargas and Meares islands. Once through the passage a short run would carry us up to Flores Island's southern tip, where the Sunshine Warriors gathered to plot their next offensive against the forestry company operations.

I sat on a bench in the cramped wheelhouse. Tassina stood behind the wheel. Eleni and Fergus were playing among the crab traps in the boat's stern. They were involved in a complicated game in which Eleni explained at great length the personality and habits of each of a menagerie of troll dolls who all possessed hair dyed similarly to many of the street children you see on inner city streets. Hair, dyed brilliant purple, yellow, pink, and green, extended in long spikes from the crowns of the little trolls' heads. Fergus's role in the game was to sniff each troll doll as it was presented and then stare in confusion at Eleni's face as she briefed him on the doll's characteristics and familial history. Like myself, Fergus is neither used to nor comfortable with children. He shrinks into a corner when they confront him and looks at them with a slightly wild-eyed stare. Children usually construe this expression as reflective of his being as fascinated with them as they are with him. In reality he is more likely on the verge of hyperventilating and desperately tries to catch my eye to gain permission to beat a hasty retreat behind my legs or, if possible, outside in the neighbouring brush where they can't follow him. Today, however, there were no nearby woods to provide Fergus sanctuary. About the time we reached the passage between Meares and Vargas islands Fergus realized his position was inescapable and resigned himself to enduring Eleni's attentions. Resignation rendered his expression somewhat less crazed and desperate.

We cruised along at a good clip, Tassina puffing down one Winston after another and flicking the ashes out the window beside her. Her honey hair was pulled back in a ponytail and her coppery skin looked fresh and soft except where the bruises still showed around her eyes and down her cheek. She wore a frayed grey wool pullover sweater, faded denims with holes in the knees, and a pair of canvas runners riddled with saltwater holes. On the ring finger of her left hand was a thin white line where a wedding band had kept the skin from tanning.

It turned out Tassina had known Ira quite well. They had even been chained side by side to a barrier across a logging road in 1993. "When the police came we all went limp so, after they cut the chains away, they had to carry us to the paddy wagon. It took four of them to carry Ira and he kept accusing them all of trying to tickle him, so he could squirm and wriggle around making it difficult for them to get him to the paddy wagon without dropping him on the ground. That drove Danchuk crazy, of course, which made it all the funnier. Ira could always make me laugh." This last she said wistfully. I wondered if there had been much laughter in her life these past years. Repeatedly, Tassina expressed dismay at the idea that anyone would have wanted Ira dead. I told her some of what I had discovered and in the telling realized how the sum of it all amounted to very little.

I asked if she had seen Ira since coming to live on the boat. Tassina replied that she had knocked on the door of his boat a few times but had never got an answer. In fact, in the time Tassina and Eleni had lived on the crabber, Ira's boat had never shown any signs of life. She looked a bit misty eyed for a moment, her mind probably drifting back to the beating Billy Gatos had given her that had finally driven her to flight.

To change the subject, I asked, "How long you staying on the boat?"

She glanced away from me and out to sea. We were coming up to the headland of Vargas Island, cutting between the island and an isthmus extending from the mainland. Both were heavily wooded, soft and green beneath the blue sun. The ocean was swelling in a light chop. Heading into late afternoon, it was still a lovely day. "I'll stay until I can find some work. Then we'll get a place of our own."

"You're going to stay in Tofino, then?"

Tassina dragged her cigarette down to the stub and flicked the butt out the window into the sea. "No where else to go," she said. "Besides I wouldn't miss this summer for anything. It's going to be long, hot and wonderful. We'll give them a time." In my mind I saw angry loggers, people forming human barricades to block the logging roads, Sunshine Warriors vandalizing logging equipment and spiking trees. Every summer the fighting worsened, the ante rising with every tree felled. Had the stakes become so high that, in the minds of some, murder became justified?

"And Vlassis?" I asked.

She shrugged. "He has his side. I have mine."

"Is it worth it, Tassina?"

Fishing a Bic lighter from the watch pocket of her jeans she fired up another Winston. Her hand gripped the boat wheel so tightly the skin whitened. "No one is going to tell me what to do anymore, Elias. No one." She smiled my way to take away the harshness of the words. And then she turned her smile on Eleni, who had stopped her play and was glancing nervously at her mom. Tassina's smile did the trick. The little girl grinned back and returned to telling her stories to Fergus.

When Tassina spoke next her voice was soft, barely audible above the regular drumming of the boat's engine. "When I was 17 papa wanted me to go back to the village in Greece where he grew up. It's up north near the Albanian border. Even today they do things the traditional way there. When a woman marries she is known by the feminine form of her husband's name. You marry some guy named Nikola and everyone, until the village finally forgets your existence generations after your death, will know you only as Nikolina. Nikola's woman, you see?" I nodded. The custom had been much the same in Cyprus.

"You know what Tassina means?" I shook my head. There was a light sheen on her eyes and I had an illogical urge to comfort her by holding her close in my arms. This seemed a poor idea for many reasons. "It means Tasso's woman. That was the name my father gave me. He wanted me to be known by the name of his grandmother but couldn't remember what her name had been before she married Tasso. She was killed by the communists. He sought to honour her, but could only give me the name that had described her as property.

"I didn't want to see his fucking village or the relatives there. I wanted to go to university, so I could study marine biology at the institute in Bamfield." She laughed, remembering. "We went to Bamfield on a school outing and it seemed exciting." She shrugged. "But papa said I got nothing if I didn't go to Greece as he wished. So I thumbed a ride down to Victoria and took a job working at a checkout counter in a non-union grocery. Minimum wage and a basement suite with one tiny window that wouldn't open." She sniffed, rubbed her nose with the sleeve of her sweater and turned her face toward the sea. Her voice wound tight with bitter emotion.

"When William Gatos came and looked me up, it was like some knight came into my life, you know. Oh, Billy was so sweet then. He was a few years older and seemed so ready for life. He had a union job at the pulp mill in Port Alberni. Making $17.95 an hour. Billy had already bought some land just outside town and was going to build a house there. He took me to restaurants where they had real candles in the chandeliers. Brought me flowers. I think probably I loved him then. At least my feet always seemed extra light when he came around and the hours we spent together felt like they were special. Sometimes when we were together my chest felt so full I could hardly breathe, like my heart was swelling up. Ever feel anything like that?"

I smiled sadly, nodded.

Tassina continued. "And he was Greek. Dark as papa." Her voice sounded brittle now, like china cracking at the edges. "What a wedding it was. People from everywhere and no more talk of going to Greece. And no questions even when Eleni came along so quickly. I was a good girl. I was married. I was going to be a mummy. Make papa a granddad. So if the math of months didn't add up, this could just be comfortably ignored."

She spun the wheel a little so that we would pass well outside the circle of a trawler's nets. The trawler was working close to shore. A man near the net drum waved and Tassina returned the gesture. A silence descended between us. I could think of nothing to say to distract Tassina from her memories. In the stern, Eleni appeared to be retelling the story of her trolls to Fergus. He caught my eye, his expression that of an old war veteran facing an eternal, soul-grinding campaign.

I thought of Tassina at 17 and of choices made. Seventeen was a dim memory to me, nothing stood out clearly from that year. At 18, I had been training to be a soldier. By 19, I was in Cyprus. There had been no basement suites in Victoria, no menial jobs. I was a remittance man's son and there was always the privilege of position and the money that came from my father's remittance cheques.

"You know, Elias, I started mucking around with the Sierra Club and eventually the Sunshine Warriors as a way of sticking a finger in Billy's and papa's eyes. That was the level of my commitment to saving the forests. In time, though, it changed. I really did start to care." She looked back at Eleni and her eyes softened. "Hard not to care, isn't it? We have to save something for her."

I nodded, while wondering if I really cared. Did signing a few petitions count? Did maintaining a membership at Mountain Equipment Co-op constitute waging war on the behalf of nature's survival? Perhaps the hefty donations I made to the Sierra Club were more meaningful?

"There's the pier," Tassina said. Extending out of some brush edging the shoreline was a battered wharf built out of old railway ties. Tattered tires cut in half were spiked along the sides of the ties to provide a bumper for boats to buffet against. A couple of single-mast sailboats were anchored just off shore, a twelve-foot zodiac was moored to the wharf itself. It appeared some of the Sunshine Warriors were home. Tassina grinned at me. "Don't worry, that's all the self-reflection I can handle in one week all over with in one big outburst." She nodded at the ice chest sitting outside the cabin. "There's some wine in there. On the way back let's drink some and talk about the weather. Deal?"

"If you like."

"I like," she said and powered the boat toward the pier. "The Zodiac's Lawrence Rafferty's. Looks like you get to talk to the big tamale himself today," Tassina added with a laugh.

Chapter Nine

Wooden steps led from the pier through a thicket of cedar and arbutus trees to a long straight stairwell that swept up a rock face to the Sunshine Warrior's clubhouse. Spongy with rot, the original stairway had been repaired here and there by nailing a new plank into place or replacing a decayed support with fresh untreated boarding. The original stairs were possessed of an air of professionalism, corners cleanly squared, joins snugly dadoed. By comparison the renovation work was embarrassingly amateurish, the boards cut unevenly and splintered at the joins by ill-hammered nail work.

Whoever the craftsman had been who made the stairs was also probably responsible for building the cabin that now served as a pseudo drop-in centre for ecological activists having a penchant for direct action. Constructed from cedar logs, the cabin was a shrine to fine workmanship. The massive logs used to build the house showed the lack of symmetry and perfection in the surface that comes from hand peeling of the bark. Each log interlocked precisely with its mates, every window was perfectly aligned despite the difficulty of cutting the logs, varying in thickness, so this could be accomplished. The work of constructing the house had been done some years ago and the cedar had aged to a lovely weathered grey. Its roof was equally dated and again none of the hand-split shakes showed signs of lifting or warping.

A stone fireplace with precisely smoothed mortar lines had been built off the cabin's north wall. Greasy looking grey smoke emanated from the chimney and drifted eastward on the sea breeze to hang in the boughs of the western hemlock and cedar giants that surrounded the house's small clearing. It was as pretty a setting as I had ever seen and I wondered that no one had ever mentioned this house to me before.

Which was the first thing I told the man with greying blond hair and beard who came out the front door and down a stone step to greet myself, Tassina, Eleni, and Fergus. The man turned his pale blue eyes back toward the house and looked at it in the manner of someone who, having come to take something for granted, has suddenly realized the error of this disposition. His face was thin beneath the beard, cheeks sunken and hollow. The man's body was lean, every bone starkly visible beneath a black T-shirt and threadbare denims. He pushed stray strands of hair away from his face and showed me a mouthful of crooked teeth.

"Lawrence," Tassina said. "This is Elias McCann. He's the Tofino coroner. Doing an investigation into Ira's death."

"Ira?" Rafferty said vaguely. A small shudder ran through him. "Dead?"

I interjected before Tassina could explain in the precise, short sentences she seemed wont to use when talking with Rafferty. Trying to be brief, I informed Lawrence Rafferty of the circumstances and timing of Ira Connaught's death. I didn't tell him about my murder theory and was thankful Tassina also chose to keep mum with this information. As I answered a few questions of Rafferty's, I began to sense from Tassina's expression that she wasn't fond of this leader of Sunshine Warriors.

As for myself, I was just glad his hands and body were of less than normal size. No need to add Lawrence Rafferty to the suspect list. After a few minutes, Tassina took Eleni inside the cabin to see the Warriors who lurked within. Rafferty and I walked over to a sundeck built to catch the light that filtered through a gap between two trees. The deck afforded a fine view out over the ocean. It was late afternoon, the sun starting its drop toward the horizon. In a few hours there would be a spectacular, fiery sunset for the day's heat was lifting a bank of clouds out on the ocean's far horizon that would add texture to the sun's descent into the sea.

Facing the view, we sat together on the edge of the deck, feet resting on wild grass. Rafferty pulled a pouch of Drum tobacco and a packet of cigarette paper from his jeans. By way of gesturing with the pouch in my direction he offered me a smoke. With a shake of my head I declined. The silence sat comfortably enough between us as Rafferty built a sloppy cigarette and twisted the ends closed. It took five attempts to get a Bic lighter to fire and set the tobacco alight. He inhaled deeply, coughed, and stared through a haze of smoke at me with his ravaged-looking face.

"When did you last see, Ira?" I asked.

Cupping the cigarette in his hand he considered for a long moment. The smoke twined away from the cigarette in a weak trail. "Two, three days. Three, I think."

"Here?"

A nod. A long drag, followed by a short coughing spasm. "He came over to get some things," Rafferty said at last.

"Railroad spikes?"

Rafferty grinned. It was like looking at the teeth in the sun-bleached skull of a dead coyote. "Going to be missed," he said. "Best there was."

The sun was warm. I took my Filson off and set it to the side of me that was away from Rafferty's spark-dribbling cigarette. "Ira have any enemies?"

"Man, we all got enemies." Rafferty grinned again. "Ain't a logger around cares much for any of us."

"How many are you?"

The grin turned sly. "More than enough for the job. More than enough."

"Your job being to prevent the forest companies from logging Clayoquot?"

Rafferty nodded. "That's the job for now. When we win that battle there'll probably be a new job needs doing."

The tone of Rafferty's words emanated a kind of world-weariness that unaccountably rankled me. I stood up and faced him. He looked up at me with eyes squinting against the sunlight that poured over my shoulder to strike his face. "So who would want to see Ira dead? Who in particular?"

Rafferty shrugged. His eyes, however, failed to meet mine. "Like I said, could be any logger.

Maybe they caught him. Or tracked him. They've tried that before."

"You knew Ira well?" I asked, shifting directions.

He considered the question. "Well enough. Been working together for five years here." He chuckled. "Guess, in that time, you get to know someone a bit."

Rafferty was starting to become wearisome with his helpful-appearing evasiveness, but I persisted. "Anything make him different than the rest of you? Anything that would single him out?"

The cigarette dissolved, bits of burning paper transformed into ash and fell into Rafferty's lap. He brushed them away ineffectually with a scrawny hand. "Natives," he said softly.

"Pardon?"

Rafferty looked up at me, squinting again against the sun. "He was real interested in the aboriginal land claims issue. You know, how the Tla-o-qui-aht tribe and the others in Clayoquot want their claim to the land settled before any logging is allowed in the Sound. Ira thought if we worked with the Natives there was a better chance of stopping the loggers. He wanted to radicalize them, get them taking direct action against the logging companies. Even talked about maybe how they could arm themselves and throw up blockades around the area. You know, like the Mohawks at Oka did a few years back. Said the government would back down then, give up on the whole thing. He believed the government wouldn't risk bloodshed between the Natives and whites so some forest companies could get logs." Rafferty shook his head in what seemed a suddenly angry gesture.

"You didn't agree?"

"Hell, no," he said sharply. "The Clayoquot tribes all got enough problems to deal with without becoming the spearhead for direct action." He glanced up at me apologetically. "Don't get me wrong. The aboriginal peoples have to be involved in the final decision on land use in Clayoquot, but we can't risk deflecting the struggle by changing it into a race relations situation. It's better for all of us, if on the whole, the Clayoquots are seen only to be involved in the peaceful side of resistance." Rafferty's voice had lost its lethargy, become strident and imbued with conviction. He sounded like a politician who had his lines down pat. The transition unnerved me. It was confusing.

I interrupted. "Was he talking with the Tla-o-qui-ahts? Or the Ahousahts? Any of the other local tribes?" Besides the Tla-o-qui-aht and Ahousaht tribes, the Clayoquot Sound region was populated by the Hesquiaht, Toquaht, and Ucluelets. Most of these bands are opposed to any harvesting of timber in the Clayoquot being undertaken by anyone but themselves. They have also laid claim to much of the land and want financial or territorial compensation from the provincial and federal governments for past violations of their sovereignty over the region. If the forestry companies had to wait until these claims were all addressed by the governments, or sorted out in the courts, not a tree would fall in Clayoquot in any of our lifetimes. It was a nice thought, but woefully unrealistic. What made it even more unrealistic was the fact that the Natives were themselves debating whether logging would bring prosperity to their peoples — assuming they would be the people doing the tree falling for the forestry companies. The

Native tribes remained as divided internally on this issue as the whites.

"Ira had his following among all the tribes," Rafferty continued. "There were some of the younger ones starting to talk about guns and spikes. I tried to get him to see reason, you know. Get him to leave the Natives be, but he kept going out to the villages and talking up direct action. Showing them how to do things. Did you know Ira had been in the US Army?"

I shook my head. I was surprised and it must have showed because Rafferty fairly cackled with glee at my expression over this bizarre revelation. "Yeah, that's how we all responded. Damnedest thing, eh? Old Ira was even down in Honduras with the Contras as some sort of weapons specialist or something. For a while he was into the whole Uncle Sam scene. That's where he got radicalized, he used to say. Saw all this shit down there and then came home and saw no one cared, no one was going to do anything about what was going on in Central America. So he bailed out of the army and came up here and got involved in the good fight." For a second Rafferty's eyes glittered like hard chips of graphite. "If I'd let him, he could have really showed the forest companies a hard time. Explosives, the whole nine yards."

"But you didn't let him?"

Rafferty stood, walked past me and stared out at the skyline. His voice became the politician's again. "There's a line you walk in direct action. Don't go far enough and no one takes you seriously, nobody notices. Go too far, like some of the Earth First people have done in the past or the Sea Shepherd Society is always threatening to do, and you lose popular sympathy. What we do won't get anyone killed."

My chest tightened. I felt like I was circling in on a possible key. "And Ira wanted to do things that might result in people getting killed?"

Rafferty waved a dismissive arm. "It was all talk." He grinned, trying to look disarming. His eyes remained hard chips, belying the smile at his mouth. "Ira didn't have the means to do anything. And I doubt he would have if he could. He was a devout Catholic, you know?" Rafferty giggled. "Ain't that a hoot. I mean this eco-freak, wilder than any of us, and he was off every week to confession and always praying for salvation and guidance. I always wonder how the priest handled his confessions? Wonder if Ira told him all that he was up to?" Rafferty shook his head in wonderment, started strolling back toward the cabin. Several men with flowing hair and a couple of women with even longer hair stood outside, apparently watching us talk. At least three of the men were as big as Ira had been. I examined their hands as we approached and felt defeated. The big men stood side by side watching our approach. They reminded me of suspects in a police line-up.

Rafferty quickly introduced me to this gathering of Sunshine Warriors. Each one grinned or waved in acknowledgment as Rafferty spoke a name. All the names and faces dissolved into a melting pot of outdoor healthiness. Their skin was weathered and unmottled, eyes clear and untroubled, bodies hard and trim from fighting the good fight on behalf of the planet and future generations. They were all blond men. I had hoped to see one who was darker, recognizable from the picture I had taken from Ira's boat that was still in my pocket. He was not here, though. Only these specimens of wonderful, uniform health, who bore names like

Clayton and Jason and Troy, Jasmine and Willow. I wondered how the emaciated-looking Rafferty had come to be their implausible leader.

After asking them all a few general questions about Ira's whereabouts on the days before his death and receiving vague answers that either showed they didn't know or were very good at lying from behind healthy, untroubled faces I asked after Tassina. They said she had already gone down to the boat. So Fergus and I headed for the stairs. Rafferty accompanied us to the landing.

As we reached the stairs, I noticed two men standing on the pier below. They were engaged in what looked to be a heated conversation with Tassina. Looking more carefully, I recognized Joseph Samuels, my Native ambulance attendant friend. Standing beside him was a shorter man with broad shoulders that stretched the fabric of a crisp blue denim jacket. His face was concealed by a tall black Stetson. The sun, starting to lay low in the west, glinted hard off the water so that the pier was obscured in a dazzling haze.

I must have spoken Samuels's name aloud for Rafferty said, "Samuels owns some land over near here. He's building a cabin on it. Uses our wharf sometimes."

At this I noticed there was another small boat tied to the pier. Like Rafferty's, it was a rubber Zodiac. An eight-footer with an oversized outboard motor hung on the back. I took Rafferty's hand, which was surprisingly hard and coiled-feeling, said good-bye, and thanked him for his help.

As I descended the stairs, I heard Tassina's voice rise sharply. Samuels put a hand on her arm but she shook it off and said something harsh again. I could see Eleni cowering inside the wheelhouse. Plopping the Filson on my head, I hurried my descent. Fergus trotted awkwardly down beside me, as if he too had sensed an air of violence and threat in the events unfolding on the pier. I was still well away from the pier when Tassina started prodding Samuels in the chest with a closed hand. Samuels cupped Tassina's hand in his own, like an outfielder might casually catch a fly ball in his mitt, and used her own leverage to push her away from him. She staggered, almost falling back into the crab boat.

Instead of going to her aid, Samuels spun on his heel and jumped down into the Zodiac. The short man leaned toward Tassina and said something in a voice, its menacing tone carrying all the way up the stairs to where I was rushing downward. Then, holding his Stetson carefully in place on his head with one hand, he followed Samuels into the boat. I lost sight of the pier as I descended the last stretch of stairs that passed through the woods verging on the water's edge.

The sharp crank of a rope pull starter was followed by a cough and a deep throttled roar of an outboard engine firing up. I came out on the pier in time to see the Zodiac bank sharply away, throwing up a wall of spray in its wake. The man with the Stetson sat in the front, one hand still clutching the hat down so its brim concealed his face. Samuels was at the stern, one hand on the engine's tiller, his closely clipped hair beading with spray coming back from the bow. He kept looking forward, so couldn't have seen me wave and the engine would have drowned out a shout. So I did neither, just watched the Zodiac cut around the shore until it turned out of sight.

"What was that all about?" I asked Tassina after Samuels disappeared.

Tassina's eyes were furtive, darting to and fro guiltily. "Nothing," she snapped. "It was nothing. Let's go, okay?"

I shrugged, nodded. We climbed into the boat. As Tassina passed Eleni in the wheelhouse she stroked the girl's hair comfortingly. "It's okay, sweetie," I heard her whisper. "Nothing to worry about."

After we cast off, and the boat was running smoothly back down the channel toward Tofino, Tassina hooked a loop of rope around a wheel spoke to ensure the boat maintained a semblance of the course she had set. Coming out into the stern, where Fergus and I were sitting, she asked me to open the wine. While I did that, she sliced cheese, smoked ham, and tomatoes and started making some sandwiches with slices of thick sourdough. She made four. One for each of us, although Fergus carefully removed the tomato from beneath the bread of his portion and dropped it aside before wolfing down the rest.

The wine was a good chardonnay from the Okanagan Valley. Tassina drank three glasses very quickly, one right after the other. But she wouldn't talk about the argument with Samuels. When I pressed her a bit, she said. "We used to go out together when I was young. He wanted to start up again. I'm not interested. That's all." Her voice was sharp and she glared levelly at me with brown eyes that evinced altogether too much innocence to be easily believable. I thought about it, though, and wondered if I was starting to become slightly paranoid; beginning to see lies and deception at every turn in my quest to find out who had killed Ira.

Perhaps for that reason I neglected to ask Tassina about the man who had accompanied Samuels.

"What's Rafferty's story?" I said instead, by way of defusing the tension building between us.

Tassina shrugged. "He's the brains behind things. Plots the strategies, sets targets. That sort of thing. Likes to be in control. Ira pretty well went his own way, but the others are really loyal to Lawrence. They would probably do anything he ordered."

"You don't like him."

She grinned. "How did you know that?" Another glass of wine went down the hatch. "There's another bottle in there," she said.

"Sure?"

"Come on, Elias. Don't be a party pooper." We were all sitting in the stern section, balancing on the old wooden versions of crab traps. I opened the other bottle of chardonnay and filled her glass. Tassina grabbed the cork from my fingers and tossed it overboard. "Now we have to drink it all, eh?"

I grinned, tried to look like my heart was in it. "So why don't you like him?"

She pulled the grey wool sweater over her head, leaned back and stretched. Her black T-shirt, which advised it was from the Seattle Hard Rock Cafe, was taut against her breasts. Tassina looked beautiful. The wine had softened her, taken the tension from her muscles. I thought it would be easy to make the mistake Samuels had supposedly made. It would be easy to want to start something up again with this woman if you had once gone some distance with her or to start something entirely new if you were just meeting her for the first time. "So why don't you like Rafferty?" I repeated.

"You're not easily distracted," she said with a lazy grin. I didn't contradict her.

Tassina rooted in her jeans' pockets and dragged out the lighter and crumpled Winstons. She lit the last cigarette in the pack with a flare of fire from the lighter. "Rafferty's always on the sidelines. He talks a good line and puts together some good tactics. But he's never been on a barricade and most certainly has never spiked a tree."

"A good general, then."

"A prick."

I raised an eyebrow by way of enquiry.

"I mean it, Elias." She jabbed a finger in my direction. I thought of her jabbing a closed fist at Samuels, who had caught it easily inside a big hand. "Lawrence is the kind of guy who is going to get someone hurt someday."

I remembered Rafferty talking of the need to walk a fine line in direct action. Not far enough and no one notices, too far and people are alienated. That had been the gist of his politician's spiel. I swirled the white wine in my glass, took a sip. "He seemed to know how to walk the line."

"Yeah? A year ago he sent two Warriors to sugar the gas tanks of some road building equipment a forestry company had parked up in the hills. The equipment had been trapped there when the protest barricades went up further down the road. So the company couldn't go in and bring the equipment out. Rafferty decides to fuck the equipment up with some sugar. Tells everyone there's nothing to worry about, no guards with the equipment. The two guys go in that night and turns out there's some big bastard standing guard on the equipment who turns a pit bull loose on them. One of the guys had his leg·torn up good before the guard must have got scared and called his dog off."

"I never read anything about that."

Tassina laughed. "Who was going to report it? Were we going to admit to vandalizing the equipment? Was the forestry company going to confess to using attack dogs to defend its machinery?"

"Do you know who owned the equipment? Who posted the guard?" I was having a troubling memory of a large pen out back of a construction site office building — remembering the insane rage of the pitbull.

Tassina emptied another glass of wine. Further back in the stern, Eleni was curled up asleep on an old sleeping bag. Fergus sprawled on his side next to her, his lungs filling and emptying slowly with air and his paws twitching in sleep. I watched them both enviously. The day had been long and the little bit of wine I had drunk was combining with the afternoon sun to make me drowsy, slow thinking.

"Some guy from Ucluelet, I think. Guy named Doran or something." I shook off the drowsiness and suggested another name. "Yeah, that was it," Tassina said definitely, "Dauphin. Dauphin Logging Company. A real winner, that guy. Was at the barricade each day shouting and yelling at us, demanding the cops arrest us and throw away the keys. Big bastard. He kept leering at me, gave me the creeps."

Little more than an hour before sunset, we sailed up to the Tofino government dock and tied on behind Ira's old scow. Tassina was a bit wobbly on her feet but otherwise seemed no worse for the wine. Perhaps it had even done some good as she seemed more cheerful than at any other time that day.

Cradling a soundly sleeping Eleni in my arms I carried her down below for Tassina. Under the wheelhouse was a tiny cubicle with a narrow line of windows facing toward the bow. Only a thin band of light trickled in through the window slits. Two cots were positioned on either side of a narrow walkway. Each had a sleeping bag and pillow on it. Just off the cabin doorway was a two-burner range. The range was a propane model, the kind lit with a match. Where a propane leak detector had once been wired into the wall above the cupboards electrical wires with bare ends hung. It all looked unsafe and typical of the boats built for, and financed by, those who work boats rather than use them for play.

I lowered Eleni down on the cot that was littered with teddy bears and troll dolls that were larger than the menagerie Fergus had been introduced to earlier. Tassina put Eleni into a pair of pink pajamas decorated with what seemed to be small blue Smurfs wearing boxing gloves and tucked her inside the sleeping bag.

In a sleepy voice, Eleni asked me to say goodnight to Fergus and I promised to do so. Tassina insisted I give Eleni a goodnight kiss. Feeling huge and clumsy in the tiny space, I gave the little girl a peck on the cheek. She opened large black eyes and asked, with what seemed something akin to panic, if she'd ever see Fergus again. I assured her I would bring Fergus around soon for another visit and she grinned, turned over on her side and seemed to fall instantly back to sleep.

Tassina and I went topside. I stepped up on the dock, Fergus jumping up beside me. Tassina stood with her hands on her hips, chewing thoughtfully on the corner of her lip and looking up at me. "Any idea who killed Ira?"

"No, Tassina, none at all. Sorry."

She shrugged, looked for a moment like she wanted to say something and then shrugged again. "Goodnight, Tassina," I said.

As I walked away she called out. "Hey." I looked back. "Do you think you could come by tomorrow?" She shifted awkwardly, put her hands in the back pockets of her jeans, like a kid thinking about confessing something secret. "Something we maybe should talk about."

"I've got time now," I said, although I felt there was little time at all.

"No, it'll wait until tomorrow. I'm really tired. Come by in the morning? Maybe for early lunch?"

"Sure. About eleven okay?"

She nodded. I told her I wouldn't be able to stay long. We left it like that.

Chapter Ten

Tassina and Vhanna shared two common traits. Both were victims transformed into survivors. Abused by a husband and repressed by a tradition of Greek male mastery over women, Tassina had rebelled to claw out her own identity. A tentative identity as yet, but one I felt was bright with promise.

Driving the Rover down that ever-familiar road leading from my inlet home to Vhanna's oceanside residence, I thought of these two women and what they shared. But they were also different. Where Tassina's rage simmered just below the surface, routinely erupting in anger and sometimes misguided action, Vhanna's interior spirit, the part of her that was wounded and which perhaps sought comfort, seldom tremored an eyelid or pinched a visible nerve. Often when I traced a finger down Vhanna's spine the muscles on either side felt corded, tensed like a whip ready to crack. At no time had I ever seen those muscles unleashed in an unrestrained fury. Vhanna kept a vice grip on her emotions, refusing to allow the disturbance within her soul to rise to the surface.

I know, of course, that Vhanna's past has left a large psychic scar upon her soul. She has endured a great deal more suffering than most North Americans can imagine. In April, 1975 Vhanna was probably a happy-enough ten-year-old living near the agricultural sciences college in the Phnom Penh suburb of Chamcar Dang. Her father, Yuan, was a Chinese rice trader. Lin, her Chino-European mother, had studied classical piano in Paris until she met and married Yuan, who was at the time a young student of economics at the Lycee. In more reflective moments, Vhanna occasionally speaks of her early childhood. She will talk of walking down the road each morning to the private school, of studying French and of the details of Cambodia's proud, ancient history and society. Of coming home to the sound of piano music spilling gently from the open windows of the small, elegant French colonial home. Of evenings spent sitting with her father and mother while the dinner table was cleared by the servants. Of how redolent fragrances from the garden drifted up to where they sat on the balcony. She quietly alert. Yuan lazy and chatty after a day spent juggling ledgers at the warehouses. Lin moving with a grace that left Vhanna feeling clumsy and inadequate in her child's body. It is during similar evenings, when the wine has flowed easily and we are twined so closely that our voices are but a whisper of thought, that Vhanna has related these memories of a happy Cambodian life.

Of the events following April 17, 1975, Vhanna has never spoken to me. I know she will probably never allow my entry into that part of her soul. This is, I think, a landscape firmly shuttered away from the light of her consciousness. It is also a landscape that holds what I often believe is Vhanna's darken-

ing psychological plane. I fear some day that darkness within her spirit will extend outward to cover
her entire soul and consume her.

Here is what I know about the time following April
17. Lars Janson, who ultimately adopted Vhanna
and brought her back to Tofino, stitched together
this much of Vhanna's story by meshing together
details drawn from the accounts of innumerable
refugees and the few details surrendered reluctantly
by a ten-year-old girl who crossed the wasteland of
Chuor Phnum Dangrek from Cambodia to the
camps in Thailand.

On April 17, the black devils of the Khmer
Rouge, wearing their telltale red-and-white checked
scarves, triumphantly entered Phnom Penh. Like so
many others, her parents took refuge behind the
locked doors of their home and waited for the storm
of violence and retribution to pass over the city.

A week after the newest wave of conquerors had
entered Phnom Penh, a group of teenage Khmer
Rouge boys, wearing black pajamas and scarves,
broke into the house. In the shadows behind their
backs, Vhanna recognized a maid who had been with
the family since her birth. This maid pointed and ges-
ticulated to an older man dressed in the same garb as
the boys wore. The boys' eyes, Vhanna felt, were
those of the dead; their pupils vacant and cold as
those of any corpse. Wielding their rifles like clubs,
the boys bullied Vhanna and her parents into the
street. Yuan was forced to kneel and his hands were
tied behind his back with steel wire. Then the boys
wrapped a strip of wire so tightly around his skull
that it came between the eyelids and pupils making it

physically impossible for Vhanna's father to hide his eyes from the horrors they planned for him to witness. Vhanna was also forced to her knees and her eyes were wired open in the same manner as her father's. Only inches away from Yuan and Vhanna, the boys proceeded to rip Lin's clothes off, throw her to the ground, and then brutally rape her one after the other. During the gang rape, the old man who appeared to be the boys' commander stood beside Yuan and calmly lectured him on the criminal acts of commerce he had committed that necessitated the family's re-education.

When the boys were all finished with Lin, Vhanna was pulled to her feet and her clothes torn away. But, Lars believes, the old man stopped the teenage killers from either raping or beating her. I'm less certain of this. Such merciful behaviour seems all too out of character for the Khmer Rouge.

When Yuan was completely shamed by having to helplessly witness the rape and beating of his wife and his daughter's being stripped naked before him, one of the boys forced a plastic bag over Yuan's head and cinched it tight around his throat. Tied as he was, Yuan could not resist. Vhanna and her mother were forced to kneel before Yuan and watch as he struggled to somehow find oxygen inside the bag which, despite his attempts to blow it away from his mouth, slowly, inevitably sealed in against his mouth and nostrils as the air inside it was consumed. He soon crumpled to the ground, twisted violently about in a futile effort to rid himself of the bag and finally died in a horrible shudder.

Given the black pajamas of peasants to wear, Vhanna and Lin joined the columns of hundreds of thousands of Phnom Penh residents who were marched into the countryside in one mass exodus from the capital city. The despised urban dwellers were all to be re-educated into the glories of agrarianism, which would render Kampuchea independent from the rest of the world. From the ashes of old Cambodia, Pol Pot, the megalomaniac Khmer Rouge leader, planned to build a grand nation. As the massive population of Phnom Penh departed the city on foot in one seemingly endless column of humanity, they left behind a city populated by thousands of dead. Every street was carpeted with the dead, left behind for the rats and other scavenging animals that soon claimed the city for themselves. Over the next few years an estimated three million Cambodians would perish during Pol Pot's mad reign.

Unknown to the guards overseeing the column's march, Vhanna and Lin carried away with them one vital, and absolutely contraband, vestige of their past. A small, secret pocket Lin had hastily sewn into Vhanna's black pajama pants contained mother and daughter's Cambodian passports and birth certificates. If we lose these, Lin told Vhanna, nobody will know who we are. Vhanna swore on her father's memory that she would die before she would ever lose the documents.

Somewhere during the endless trek north to the planned retraining camps Lin and a small group of desperate prisoners conspired to escape. Thirst, starvation, and exhaustion were taking their toll on the column. Each day hundreds of people fell out of line and collapsed on the roadside. Those who could not go on were either shot by the guards or left for dead. When darkness closed in, the column would lurch to a halt and the people collapse in the road. Sleep came only fitfully. The night was pierced continually with the screams of those who, for reasons known only to the Khmer Rouge, were dragged from the column to be raped, tortured, and executed. On one such moonless night, the small group slipped away, escaping their dead-eyed teenage guards.

For weeks the group of men, women, and children wandered through jungles, crossing roads and rice paddies only by night, climbing ever higher into the western mountains until finally they were well beyond the lower farming regions and struggling their way through ever-thickening forests. They sought a trail that would lead to the safety of Thailand. Through pounding rain or under a searing sun they struggled onward. As they walked, Lin forced Vhanna to memorize a series of numbers and an address. She told the young girl that this information was as important to remember as it was to protect the documents. Summoning the last reserves of concentration that her increasingly exhausted and hungry body could deliver, Vhanna confined the numbers and address to the recesses of her memory.

Starving, desperate for water, their feet masses of blisters, their bodies fed on by leeches and their clothes reduced to tatters, the small group struggled ever closer to Thailand. With each passing day their number dwindled. The old failed first. Then the other children began to lag and eventually fell ill or succumbed to starvation, until Vhanna was the only child left. Soon those women and men with injuries started to fall. As in a dream from which she might be able to startle herself awake, Vhanna saw her mother stumble, fall, and prove incapable of regaining her feet. Lin's skeletal fingers felt like brittle claws as they shakily reached up and brushed Vhanna's cheek. One of the few remaining men lifted Vhanna's near helpless body in his arms and carried her away. She tried to struggle, begged to stay with her mother. But the man would not listen. Over his shoulder Vhanna saw Lin lying on the trail, her legs twisted awkwardly. She wanted nothing more than to go back and help her mother straighten them out, to make her more comfortable. Lin's eyes locked with Vhanna's, but Vhanna was unable to read whatever message her mother was trying to pass to her daughter. Later, Vhanna believed the message undoubtedly concerned the need to remember the numbers and address, to keep safe the papers hidden in her secret pocket.

Eventually Vhanna found herself alone. The man died somewhere along the way a few days after they left her mother behind. Where the rest of the group had gone, Vhanna could not remember. Perhaps she had become separated. Perhaps they all died one by one. Vhanna survived by living like a wild rat. She clawed grubs from the earth, sucked water off leaves dripping with night's dew. Always, no matter how tired or hungry she was, Vhanna kept moving. Moving. Ever moving. The mountains were her goal. The high mountains toward which they had been fleeing. It was the goal the adults had set and talked of incessantly. Vhanna wound her way up animal tracks and trails perhaps cut by humans, working ever deeper into the heart of the mountains. At night, she burrowed deep into the brush and tried not to whimper openly when the snarl of tigers carried on the wind, or a wild boar crashed through the nearby brush, or the rustling sound of what she feared were deadly snakes or scorpions passed within inches of her body. Through the night, Vhanna recited the numbers and address to herself between periods of furtive sleep. Sometimes she would use the moonlight to look at her mother's picture in the little booklet she carried. She wished that she had a similar booklet by which to remember her father. At first light, Vhanna would be back on the trails, climbing. She climbed into the very clouds themselves and began to descend again. On a morning soaked with mist and menace Vhanna stumbled out of the jungle onto a road and fell with perhaps her last ounce of physical strength at the feet of a group of men tinkering with a rusted, broken down bus that overflowed with passengers and their possessions.

Lars Janson found Vhanna six weeks later in a refugee camp near Ban Kruat. Lars and his wife Frieda had come to Thailand from Tofino with the intent to teach the Thais modern forestry practices. But watching the huge teak and yang trees of the tropical rainforest being felled one after the other overwhelmed Lars with a sense of tragic remorse at his role in introducing clear-cutting to this ancient land. Quitting his job, Lars and Frieda joined the Red Cross and went to work in the refugee camps that were springing up along the Thai-Cambodian border. On a routine day, Lars was unloading heavy sacks of rice from a truck and tumbling them inside a storage locker when he noticed a small lair dug in behind some rice sacks. The hiding place contained a can of brackish water and some rags that served for a blanket. Amid these meagre belongings sat a small girl with the bloated belly and large eyes and head of the near-starved. Why she had left the dormitories to live here alone Lars never knew. That she was near dead was certain. Lars picked her up in his arms and carried the girl's limp form back to the hut he shared with his wife. Slowly Lars and Frieda nursed the little girl back from the edge of death. About them, other children died from malnutrition and there was nothing more the couple could offer them. But for one girl they could offer the extra rations from their own food to reverse the deadly course of starvation that was claiming so many of the Cambodian children.

As a young man, Lars had sailed with the Swedish merchant fleet, learning numerous languages in foreign ports. French was one of those languages. A patient man, he would sit on the stoop of their small hut, smoke his pipe, and talk to Vhanna in French and rudimentary Khmer. The little girl sat across from him, her eyes fixing on his and never darting about. She would study him with an almost unnerving intensity that left Lars wondering what answer she sought to find in the depths of his pupils. Lars asked Vhanna no questions. Instead he talked about himself, about Frieda, about the oceans he had traveled when he was young, of their home in Tofino, of Swedish legends and folklore. He told jokes, spoke of adventures, described animals, evoked images of the lush rain forests of Clayoquot and the native people who had inhabited them before the coming of the European explorers and settlers. He related the tales of Beowulf and the gods of the lands of fire and ice. Like a statue, Vhanna sat across from him, legs crossed like a little Bhudda, breathing gently, eyes wide and unmoving, hands in her laps.

Just when he feared nothing would reach through to this little girl, that nothing would wash away the visions running like crazed demons inside her skull, Vhanna looked at him differently. He saw a light in the eyes, felt her presence in a conscious way. She looked at him keenly and spoke a series of numbers, each carefully articulated. *"Cinq, deux, quatre, sept, neuf, cinq, une, huit,"* she said. Her French pronunciation was much better than Lars's. Asked again, she repeated the figures precisely and in the same order as Lars hastily scribbled them down. This time, too, she added what was obviously an address, an address ending with the words Hong Kong.

Only when this information had been related did she finally accede to tell Lars her name and the name of her father and mother. Reaching inside her frayed and worn pajama bottoms Vhanna tugged out two booklets and hesitatingly allowed Lars to look at them. Speaking very seriously and formally in French she told him to be careful as without them she would have no name and cease to be a person. Through all this time Lars and Frieda had been worrying their way through mounds of red tape, paying bribes, doing what had to be done to adopt Vhanna Chan, whose name Lars had only just now learned from the passports and birth certificates in his hands. Lars and Frieda were determined to take Vhanna home to Tofino so as to save her from this hell of a refugee camp.

A few days later, Vhanna told Lars of her experiences following the Khmer Rouge's invasion of the Chan household. She spoke in short, precise, emotionally detached sentences, as if telling a story about somebody else entirely. When Vhanna finished her incredible tale, she refused to speak of it again. After being once refused, Lars accepted her wish and never again asked about her experiences. Neither would he allow Frieda to pry. The day they got the papers permitting Vhanna's adoption they left Thailand for Hong Kong. The address proved to be a bank, the numbers an account filled with American dollars. Vhanna's father had been a prudent man who, apparently recognizing that some form of disaster approached, had carefully moved the majority of his wealth out of Cambodia before the fall occurred. Perhaps he had meant to take his family out before the Khmer Rouge invaded Phnom Penh. Whatever his intent, all that was left to Vhanna was a bank account containing a small fortune.

Even with the passports proving her identity, it took many months to get the bank to free the funds and allow Lars to transfer them into an account in Canada. The money was placed in a trust for Vhanna. This trust enabled Vhanna to attend university after her eighteenth birthday for the years necessary to get her MBA. This money, too, allowed her to buy land and build a house overlooking Tofino and to establish Artemis Adventures Inc. If it were not for her reluctance to trust banks and other institutions Vhanna would easily have been able to fund the adventure company without the share capital provided by a remittance man. But to make the venture a safe one to assume, Vhanna sought a thirty percent investment from me, which I willingly gave. I've always thought this was the closest Vhanna could come to offering me a commitment or to accepting one from me. As business partners we are wed for as long as the business endures. There is a touchstone there. The relationship between investors is for its duration seriously undertaken and becomes a matter of honour that requires each to do the best they can by the other.

Lately our always somewhat strained relationship has had to survive a new pressure. Vhanna has started tentatively talking about Cambodia. Not the past. Certainly not her personal past. Rather, she has started to speculate in very brief moments about how the country is becoming safer, how the Khmer Rouge may be finished, with the road opening for democracy, and how peace may emerge finally.

I know what she's thinking, even though she has not put her intent into words. Vhanna wonders if there might be family still living in Cambodia. She toys with seeking them out, with going back into that world of the killing fields in hopes of finding connections to her past.

It is impossible for me to sanction this emerging plan of action. I understand her wish to reclaim her family and roots, but I cannot believe it is a safe mission to undertake. The madness that creates killers like the Khmer Rouge doesn't just fade away. Just as the madness that led to bombs exploding in Nicosia that morning is still as virulent in Cyprus today as it was then, so too, the killers of the Khmer Rouge will haunt Cambodia's reality for generations to come. The hatred is too keen, too self-feeding. For Vhanna to go into Cambodia is to risk her life. I cannot abide this possibility. So far I have been successful in talking her out of this embryonic plan, but I know that once she decides to act there is nothing that will turn her back from this course. I fear, too, that she will refuse to have me at her side during this quest. If this were not the case, I would certainly accompany her wherever she must go. But I know she will want to go alone. And I know that I will not be able to stop her from pursuing this dangerous mission.

Vhanna. Pulling into the driveway and shutting off the Rover's engine, I was struck by the impossibility of my feelings for this woman. I wanted to reach inside her and caress her soul, soothe it and take away the pain of her childhood, allow nothing but my love for her to touch her heart. But I could no more take away or alleviate her past than I could prevent a small girl from bleeding to death in Cyprus. It was a fool's errand to seek such a goal; the ultimate in self-delusion to believe I could ever have such power. Yet I feared for Vhanna.

The sun flamed orange into the sea, passing spectacularly down through a veil of cloud rising up from the water. Again I had climbed the security wall and set Jabronski's alarms ringing. But I found the cellular phone lying untended on the chaise lounge next to the desiccated bonsais. "It's me," I said when Jabronski answered, "nothing to worry about." I could hear the sound of a car engine roaring in the background so I knew the security guard was already in hot pursuit toward the house.

"Does she want you there?" he barked and then laughed harshly. "Shit, Elias, this is the second time today you've got me running."

Unfamiliar with such toys I fumbled with the phone, seeking the off button. Jabronski's laugh pursued me until I found the right switch. The cellular I like less than Vhanna's bonsais. The trees are merely tortured growths; a phone that works wherever you are is an obscene entity spawned by the imaginations of those with a fondness for 1984-like technological dictatorships.

I returned to the wall and opened the gate from the inside to let Fergus into the inner court of Vhanna's yard. He had stared at me in puzzlement as I climbed over the wall. Now he trotted about the deck looking for some trace of Vhanna. At last he glanced through the railing to the beach below, froze, pointed with tail wagging, and looked up at me with eager eyes. I nodded permission and he led the way down the zigzag staircase to the beach.

Vhanna was far out on the water-packed sand below the tide line. Fergus started to move toward her, but I snagged his collar in one hand and forced him to sit patiently and quietly beside me on the bottom step. Overhead gulls soared on the wind, their loud screeching calls providing the only sound to compete with the slow rolling of the ocean waves. Silhouetted against the setting sun, Vhanna appeared only as a dark shadow moving in the dream-like slow dance of the Tai Chi adept. She wore a black nylon-lycra sport top that left her shoulders and waist bare, and matching shorts that extended to just above the knee. The clothing moved on her like a second skin. Her hair was unbound and swayed to the rhythm of each movement.

A cool wind blew in from the sea and I wondered how she could dress so lightly when I was glad of the comforting warmth provided by my Filson jacket. But then I suspected she had been out here on the sand for some time working through the 108 movements of the Taoist Tai Chi that can be endlessly varied to provide an infinity of combinations. Vhanna faced the sea and was perhaps unaware of my presence. I knew also that, if she did know I was sitting here, she would not acknowledge me until she had ceased the set. Vhanna has an extremely focused singularity of purpose that often resembles a stubborn streak running as deep as a vein of gold ore. It's just one of her many traits that I love.

I was content to wait patiently and enjoy the breeze, the ocean view, and the view of Vhanna moving like physical music across the sand. Fergus quieted and I released his collar, knowing he wouldn't race forward without permission. The sun sank lower, like a torch sizzling into the ocean. Sandpipers scurried along the edge of the tide; sometimes running, other times taking nervous flight. Fergus glanced eagerly from the birds to me but I shook my head and he remained at my side, his flanks rising and falling rapidly with excited breath.

Just as the last remaining crescent of sun slipped beyond the horizon, Vhanna's slow movements of stretched arms and legs erupted into a flurry of sharp kicks and jabs as she switched from the slow rhythm of Taoist Tai Chi into the more ancient movements known as Tai Chi Combat. What had before resembled gentle ballet was suddenly transformed into a violent form of shadow boxing that utilized arms, legs, feet, and hands in a chillingly efficient show of violent force.

Weighted equally with every Yin force, it is said, there must be a balancing Yang force. Taoist Tai Chi and many other Tai Chi disciplines, with their emphasis on restrained, slow grace, constitute the expression of Yin. In opposition to this, Tai Chi Combat techniques unleash the Yang nature of the Tai Chi adherent. This, so Vhanna has explained, allows the self to exist in harmony within the practice of the Tai Chi discipline. More than seeking harmony, I suspect, Tai Chi Combat allows Vhanna to push the practice of this martial arts form to its maximum potential and implementation. The thought that she can apply all her Tai Chi skill to defend herself physically is something that naturally would appeal to Vhanna. It also must seem eminently sensible that any martial art worth learning should have application in the directions of combat.

Yin and Yang in balance, at least in a style that Vhanna appreciates.

Watching the fluid, lightning motion of her body I reminded myself never to get into a physical fight with Vhanna. Whirling in a blur of hair, fists and legs she suddenly came to a halt with legs spread, one fist forward, the other back, facing me. I watched her draw a long breath deep into her chest and release it slowly as her body relaxed and straightened.

Fergus glanced up at me and I nodded. Feet churning sand with every stride he raced to her. Hands thrust deep into coat pockets I followed at a more restrained pace I hoped would appear nonchalant. My heart, however, was beating a bit too quickly and my skin felt slightly clammy with apprehension.

When I reached Vhanna she was bent over petting Fergus, who was sitting with his head down so her hands could more easily get in behind his ears. Whichever ear she rubbed he leaned toward her until his body wavered off balance, at which point Vhanna would switch sides to straighten him back up. She glanced at me, her face expressionless, a light sheen of moisture beading her forehead. In the fading light her eyes were dark, unreadable pools. "How long were you there?" she asked.

"Not long."

She stopped scratching Fergus, picked up a stick and threw it far down the beach in one angry snap of her arm. Fergus started after it, hesitated, glanced back at me imploringly and then sat back down on his haunches, looking sheepishly toward Vhanna. "We've had a long day," I explained.

"It's okay, Fergus," Vhanna said, kneeling down by him to give a few more ear scratches. She turned her back on me and looked out at the darkening ocean.

"I think you were right," I said at last. My chest seemed constricted, making my voice sound huskier than normal. She glanced back at me, questioning. "I think Ira was murdered." Carefully I explained what my day's investigation had yielded about the manner of Ira's death. I didn't tell her about my visit to Ucluelet or going with Tassina to see the Sunshine Warriors. Nor did I mention yet the search of Ira's boat.

"What will you do now? Will the police take over?"

"Danchuk doesn't care about Ira. He cares about his senator." I removed my hat, ran nervous fingers through my hair. "I think I have to keep looking into this."

She stood up, came over and looked up at me. "Is that why you came here? To tell me this?"

I nodded, then shook my head in denial of the first gesture. Slowly, I replaced the hat. Digging into my pocket, I removed the photo taken from Ira's and passed it to her. She took it delicately by one edge and removed it from my hand in such a way that our fingers didn't touch. Vhanna gazed at the photo for a long time. I thought of the image. Thought of Vhanna standing in the middle of the smiling faces of the Sunshine Warriors with Ira at her side and a dark-haired man with a wild beard standing behind her, his arms circling her, his hands tucked into the pockets of her kangaroo sweater, she leaning back into his chest. Ira's hand rested on her shoulder and she was looking up into his face with a small smile on her face. "What does it mean?"

Palming the Polaroid inside her hand, in much the same way as I had hidden it earlier from Danchuk, she stared up at me defiantly. "It's nothing. They were friends of mine."

"When was the picture taken?"

She shrugged. "I don't know. Well, probably in 1993."

"And him? The dark guy?"

"Another friend, that's all."

"A Sunshine Warrior?"

Vhanna shook her head. She told me he was a friend of Ira's who had come up from the United States to help out.

"How well did you know him?"

"Well enough," she snapped, then hesitated. Her voice dropped to a whisper. "That's not true. I didn't mean that. Elias, what do you want from me?"

Your love, I almost said. "I need to know where he is now."

She brushed her hair back from her face. "You don't suspect Starling, do you?"

"Starling?"

"That's his name. Barry Starling. Everyone just calls him Starling though. He knew everything about this kind of thing. About how to mount passive resistance."

"Always passive?"

Her teeth flashed. "As passive as Ira anyway."

I thought of spikes. Of a man who wanted the Clayoquot tribes to rise up in armed insurrection. A man who knew about dynamite and guns and had been trained in their use in Central America. "Do you know if he was in the army with Ira?"

She claimed not to know about that. Nor had she apparently known about Ira's military service.

"Where's Starling now?"

"I don't know. After the arrests started, I pulled back from it all," she said. "They kept wanting me to join them at the barricades." She hesitated, I sensed her worrying her lip with her teeth. "I couldn't be arrested," she said softly. "They didn't understand."

I imagined Vhanna being put in the small, locked paddy wagon by burly policeman; imagined their hands touching her roughly. Then I thought of a small girl who had escaped from Cambodia and the horrors she had seen and endured. The others would think she feared arrest for the effect it would have on her business. For that, they would slowly ostracize her. She would never tell them the truth of her fears. "I know," I said.

She glanced up at me quickly and a little regretful smile tugged the corners of her mouth. "Yes, you do." Vhanna leaned down to give Fergus another stroke. "Is there anything else, Elias?" Her voice was formal now, businesslike.

I shook my head, said I should be going. The photo was still clasped in her hand. I thought of asking for it back, but decided not to bother. The photo only offered complications. Whoever Barry Starling was he had come and then gone away. For a few moments in between, the man had had his arms about Vhanna Chan and inside them she had perhaps found some happiness. Her expression in the picture had certainly been one of happiness. Probably that was why she was making no move to return the picture. Vhanna said she wanted to stay on the beach a little longer and offered no invitation for me to stay with her. So I left her there on the beach. Reluctantly, Fergus followed me up the stairs. From the top of the stairs, I looked back. Vhanna was far down the shoreline, a shadow fading into the gathering gloom.

Chapter Eleven

I considered stopping to ask Tassina about Barry Starling but decided to leave that until our pre-arranged meeting in the morning. The day had been long, frustrating, a journey down many winding paths leading nowhere. Fergus and I were weary, stomachs rumbling with hunger. Time to call it a day; to sift through what we had learned, to rest, replenish, prepare for tomorrow.

The cabin was dark. I had neglected to leave the yard light on. Out of the deepening twilight sky only Venus cast a cold, steely light that offered no illumination. Fergus and I climbed from the Rover and made our way carefully to the cabin.

The interior struck me as unusually forlorn. My father's furniture and books filled it to a point of clutter. Unshuttered windows gazed inward like black eyes. When I switched on the foyer light the cedar paneled walls appeared to absorb its glow, leaving everything shadowed and dreary.

Since moving here, after Merriam's death, my feelings toward the cabin have swung like a pendulum in rhythm to my emotions. At times, the cabin is a warm sanctuary, a place of calm and serenity. Other times, like this night, it was as if the cabin reflected the emptiness and futility of my life.

In evenings such as this I pondered ridding the place of Angus's wonderfully preserved Edwardian furnishings, painting the walls bright colours, opening the ceiling and installing skylights; filling the space with light to ward off spiritual darkness. After Merriam's death, I never returned to sleep in the home where we had lived together. I stayed in a hotel until I found this cabin. When I sold the house I also disposed of all the furniture. I kept only a few personal things. Things like the quilt she had finished sewing just before she died, paintings of sporting dogs working in the fields that had hung in my den, books, the Parker shotgun. Sergeant Bellows offered to return the Remington over-and-under, but I told him to get rid of it and assume he did so.

When I moved into the cabin I determined to start fresh. But, for some still-undefined reason, I traveled to the Comox Valley and my father's house. Watched over by a neighbour, the house had stood dormant since his death. The fields were planted with alfalfa and harvested by the neighbour in exchange for his vigilance. Somehow I had never got around to disposing of the furniture or selling the property.

During that visit I arranged for much of the furnishing to be delivered to the cabin. His fine library of classics, outdoor writing, and essays on the literary arts I boxed and included in the delivery. I convinced myself that my motivation was purely pragmatic. It made little sense to buy new, cheaply constructed furniture when these finely crafted antiques were there for the taking.

Occasionally, though, as was the case this night, I pondered the wisdom of my decision. As a means to starting life anew, to shake away some of the guilt, I had purposely cast away the possessions accrued during my life with Merriam. Having done that, however, I surrounded myself with father's trappings. Was there not the risk I might become like him? Might I, too, become a man existing outside of modern time? A man who wrote love letters to a woman who had long ago abandoned him. A man who, from the day Lila left, sought seldom the company of others and who, until his death, lived almost invisibly in self-imposed exile from the world.

As I went about the tasks of feeding and watering Fergus in the small kitchen, these thoughts walked my mind with troubled footsteps. It was a path I try to avoid venturing down. But this bleak night, after a futile day, I seemed powerless to stem such contemplation. While Fergus dug into his dinner with relish, I half-heartedly cubed a small Salt Spring Island lamb roast, chopped onions, carrots, potatoes, rutabaga, and mixed them together into a thirty-minute stew to cook on the range top. I chose a red Merlot for the sauce, and blended in fresh rosemary, anise, and oregano.

By the time I had all this browned, mixed, and simmering rapidly, Fergus had gobbled his dinner. He wandered into the living room and stretched with great satisfaction on the rug before the fireplace. When I came in to set a fire he was already fast asleep. I envied him. It would be hours before exhaustion pushed me into that escape from troubled thoughts.

As the evening wore on I sat before the fire sipping Glenlivet, staring sightlessly at the slowly blackening coals. In all of the day's inquiries I could find no thread of truth that led me closer to the identity of Ira's killer. Suspects I had galore. Yet they were all tenuously connected, the linking threads gossamer thin. In the end, every lead was severed, the line of reason cleanly broken.

And, as if I were trapped in Yeats's "widening gyre," my thoughts churned and twisted up a funnel spiraling away from the quest for Ira's killer into my own troubled longing to resolve the differences between Vhanna and myself. Our conversation on the beach had been the most stilted and forced of the day. So many things I had wished to tell her, but the words had refused to come. I had kept them shut inside, feared to release them. To speak further of how I felt for her, to have forced yet another confrontation of the heart, might have only served to push her farther away. So we had talked of the business of Ira's death and the mystery of the photo. We had communicated nothing of import to each other. I sensed her drifting away on life's sea, as a ship with a broken anchor line is carried away by unseen currents. Standing on the shoreline, with no boat to man for pursuit, I knew not how to draw her back. Was there any reason she should want to return, resist the pull of the current?

As the last coals burned down to cooling embers Fergus rose from his slumbers to walk with workmanlike determination to the door. I let him out into the night, cleared the table and rinsed the dishes. By then he had returned and I followed him up to bed. Lying in the darkness, Fergus sighing and stretching in his wicker bed across the room, I could easily conjure the physical sensation of Vhanna twined against me. Such an image was a mistake, of course, rendering sleep even less likely than before. So reluctantly I forced thoughts of Vhanna away and tried to determine what direction my inquiry should take in the morning. To these hopeless seeming thoughts I finally drifted into uneasy sleep.

The marsh beneath my feet was mushy, each step slipped deeply into black oozing muck and had to be dragged free. Running was impossible. Stumbling was the best I could do. And that was no good at all. I needed to run. The Parker shotgun was heavy in my hands, the hammers pulled back, primed to fire. Fergus raced far ahead, his barks piercing and urgent. A gun fired, so close the concussion rattled me. Yet I had not fired the shotgun. I couldn't have, because the struggle to walk forward consumed my every effort. Fergus barked louder, returned to me, pawed with urgency, refused to stop when I pushed him away.

I twisted up from the bed and this time the explosion heard was definitely real, not the manufacture of dream. The second "crump" was deeper, throatier than the first; it had also been real and had penetrated my sleep, I was now sure. Again windows rattled. Fergus stood by the bed, front paws beside me, barking to waken me. I jumped up and raced to the window.

Against the night sky, a fiery orange glow rose from behind trees near the waterfront. My stomach clenched, the sour bite of fear filled my mouth. I yanked on clothes. Still buttoning my jeans and doing up the shirt I stumbled down the stairs. Fergus hurried at my side but I shouted for him to stay as I pulled on some boots. Running across the yard, I reflexively pulled on my coat and hat against a chill I could not feel. I jabbed the key into the ignition switch, flicked it over to prime the engine, jabbed the starter button and pumped the gas. The Rover spluttered, turned over, coughed. Swearing, I yanked the choke out and pushed the starter again. The engine turned, wheezed asthmatically, fouled, and died. Gas vapours thickened inside the cab.

The night sky was brightening beyond the trees, a foul orange pall bordered with black smoke. Scrambling from the Rover, I flung my coat and hat inside and ran down the road, my heart pounding. Even as I started out, I realized it was too far by road. I would get there too late. Probably I was too late already. I dived down a narrow path through the wild roses, hurtled a neighbour's fence and cut across his open yard. Someone snapped on a light and my shadow stretched far ahead of me, running madly. A dog barked. Ignoring the property owner's puzzled shout, I lunged over another fence and into a screen of dense brush. Vines tore at my face and hands but I bulled through and found myself on a gravel driveway.

Seconds later I reached the road above the wharf and stumbled to a halt. Gasping for breath, I looked down at the dock. The crab boat was ablaze from bow to stern, fiery smoke whipped out across the water on the breeze. Sirens wailed somewhere off in the night and began closing rapidly. But not fast enough. I ran for the dock, pressed into the ungodly heat wave coming from the boat. It was almost like pushing against an invisible wall as I fought my way toward the burning vessel. My cries to Tassina, to Eleni, were drowned by the raging crackling of the flames slicing through the vessel's aged timber. There was nowhere on the crab boat's deck that wasn't ablaze. Every inch of deck was burning, there was nowhere safe to jump aboard and try to get to the cabin. The fire was greedy, the wood dry and old. Hanging loose, as if torn from one hinge, the cabin door tilted wildly; a black shadow being swallowed by fire. The heat was hideous. I could feel my skin starting to blister. The hair on my wrists shriveled and smoked. I could hear it sizzle. I retreated, lungs sucking desperately for oxygenated air.

I stumbled clear just as several men, staggering beneath the weight of their bulky yellow suits, face shields, oxygen masks, and hoses snaking from the fire truck pushed past me. Shouting and yelling, they braced in position well away from the boat's deck and started to spray suppressive foam into the blaze. The white stream seemed pathetically trivial as the fire sucked it into its gut.

Dazed, rebelling against the certainty of what I knew, I wandered about the parking lot calling out Tassina and Eleni's names in a voice so raspy it seemed not my own. I told myself they might have got clear, might have escaped the first explosion, been off the boat when the second blast set off the propane and diesel fuel that despite the firefighters' efforts now burned the vessel down to a charred ruin. Tassina didn't answer, no dark-haired child emerged from the shadows. At last I slumped onto one of the railroad ties bordering the parking lot and stared dully at the cooling blaze on the water. Around me people flowed into the area. Volunteer firemen careened past the policeman who stood at the intersection in his Halloween festive orange- and black-striped coat waving a flashlight to let them in. His efforts to deter spectators from entering the parking lot were half-hearted at best and the place was soon jammed with half of Tofino.

I watched a Jeep Wagoneer with Dauphin Logging scrawled on the door panel lunge into the yard, saw the huge figure of Phil Dauphin tumble out and run toward the wharf. He was pulling on firemen's clothing and I noticed a sticker on the back window of his jeep that read: Ucluelet Volunteer Fire Department. There were many men like Dauphin arriving to scramble from trucks and race to help with the fire.

Despite that, I wondered what had brought Dauphin to Tofino and why he would respond to a fire alarm here. But I could not hold the train of thought. I huddled in the dark, out of sight, tracing back again and again over the sounds that had dragged me up from a troubled sleep.

At some point, Vlassis Mavrikos came out of the crowd like a whirlwind, his arms brushing aside the hands of a few men seeking to restrain him. He was a whipcord of a man with black, wiry hair worn in an old-fashioned pompadour. Tonight he wore black knit dress pants and a sleeveless white undershirt. His feet were bare and his face darkly shadowed with a day's growth of beard. Two firemen intercepted him as he tried to get by them to reach the boat. Moving awkwardly like astronauts in their fire suits they blundered back to the fire trucks with Vlassis bundled between them.

I walked over to the trucks. One of the firemen recognized me and nodded his head. I couldn't tell who he was as his face was hidden behind a soot-covered face shield. Taking Vlassis by the arm I led him away from the trucks to a spot where Ira's listing scow formed a visual barrier between us and the smouldering crab boat. Vlassis followed me as meekly as a child might. His hands hung loosely at his sides.

He gazed up at me and I saw the bright gleam of a desperate hope in his eyes. "Where are they, Eli? They are safe?"

Vlassis is the only person in the world who calls me Eli. He has done it since I first met him and it seems to constitute some kind of kinship on his part between us. For a moment I thought of what to say. Was there not some hope? Could they not have been gone? At friends? Gone back to William Gatos? Gone anywhere? But I knew they had not. Vlassis knew this too. Still I said, "We don't know yet if they were aboard. It'll be a while yet."

Even as I offered this crumb of optimism I saw the ambulance moving slowly through the crowd, its lights flashing on and off. But there was no siren, no sense of urgency in the speed of its approach. It parked alongside the fire trucks and Samuels climbed out of the passenger side, Lou Santucci banged the driver's door behind him. They huddled with several of the firemen. Then Samuels stepped away from them all and stared toward the boat. His hands tightened into fists and loosened repeatedly, spasmodically. Big hands, powerful hands.

I had released my grip on Vlassis and without the support he slumped down onto one of the railroad ties. He sat there with his arms draped between his legs. His head hung down and I could hear him sobbing softly. In between each sob he said a single word. Eleni. Over and over he whispered his granddaughter's name. A couple of Greek men with their wives came over and sat with him. I took the opportunity to slip away.

Samuels and Santucci had opened the doors to the ambulance and dragged two stretchers out of the back. They wheeled one down the wharf, two firefighters brought the other. Mayor Tully and Danchuk emerged out of the crowd. Side by side they walked down the wharf, following the stretchers. Danchuk was wearing his black and orange striped Halloween coat, Tully a dark squall jacket. Tully is a short man, but his head was several inches higher than Danchuk's.

I followed after, although it was not something I wanted to do. The evening was suddenly eerily still. The boat still smoked but there was no sound of flames devouring wood, no embers crackled. Behind us half of Tofino stood, but not a murmur of voices carried on the breeze. The thump of our footsteps on the marina deck seemed loud and threatening.

Four firefighters moved awkwardly within the wreckage of the vessel. One of them was working with a long handled pike, prying away a section of the cabin housing. With a final yank he pulled the charred wood away, letting it collapse overboard into the murky water. A man, smaller than the rest, muttered to the others, gestured for them to stand back. He gingerly lowered himself through the space the man with the pike had opened.

For a few seconds he was lost from view and we could only hear him rustling through the gutted interior. The cabin roof had caved in when the supporting timbers had been burned away so it would be hard to move about inside. I was conscious of my heart beating very loudly, my breathing was shallow. Mayor Tully looked over at me and nodded a grim greeting. Samuels followed his gesture. He was wearing an ambulance attendant's uniform with the little cap pushed far back on his military-style haircut. I returned his greeting, but his eyes seemed to look right through me. In the light they were black and impenetrable as stone. The firefighter holding the pike coughed, cradled the long pole in his arms. He pulled off his helmet and with a gloved paw wiped sweat thick with soot sludge from his face and hair.

The helmeted head of the small firefighter appeared in the opening to the hole leading into the cabin. A short huddle took place. An arm gestured out of the cluster of firefighters and Samuels stepped across carrying black bodybags. My breath hissed out. Until then, I hadn't realized I was holding it.

What happened afterwards passed by me with nightmare quality. Two firefighters wrestled something out of the hole. It was a bodybag containing a bulky object they took to one of the stretchers. After they laid the bag on the stretcher, Samuels carefully covered it completely with a blanket. The firefighter still in the cabin then handed a smaller body-bagged bundle out to another man's waiting arms and this was placed on the other stretcher and similarly covered by Samuels.

Behind us I heard a soft keening that had to be coming from Vlassis. It was an unearthly sound, like that of a soul falling into Hades. As it continued a chill seeped down my spine and settled in the pit of my stomach. The two stretchers were wheeled by us and I found myself suddenly gathered up inside another huddle of firefighters that this time included Tully and Danchuk. One of the firefighters pulled his helmet and attached faceshield off. It was Jabronski, Vhanna's security service man and Tofino's volunteer fire chief. He looked tired and old tonight, the crinkly skin around his eyes that usually gave him a kindly appearance, merely added to his haggard appearance. "They were probably gone within seconds of the explosion," he said softly. "Both still in their bunks."

"Who were they?" Danchuk snapped, as if Jabronski were a felon being interrogated.

I saw Jabronski's shoulders rise tightly and then slowly relax. "Don't know," he said. "Vlassis Mavrikos owned the boat." He gestured toward the parking lot. Vlassis's weeping spoke for itself.

"Anything else? Know what caused it?"

Jabronski shrugged. I had the sensation he wanted to brush Danchuk away like he might a midge or a gnat. "First impression is that the propane for the stove leaked and got set off somehow. Stove's all blown to shit. The propane blowing would have set off the diesel fuel. One big boom and then the fire finished everything."

At this explanation, Danchuk looked about with what appeared to be satisfaction. His mouth tightened noticeably when he saw me and his eyes looked even meaner. I gathered he hadn't noticed me before. "I'll go talk with Mavrikos," he barked and started to walk away.

I reached out, caught his shoulder and brought him to a halt. "It was his daughter, Tassina, and her little girl, Eleni. We talked with them this morning, remember?"

He shook my hand away and straightened his coat until all the orange stripes were back in line. I figured this gave him time to prepare his answer. "You sure they were still on the boat? Sure that's them?"

Tully intervened. "Dental records will prove it, Gary. I'll make some calls in the morning and find who has their charts. It doesn't sound like anybody should be talking with Vlassis about this right now. Let's leave it for now, okay?" He was as smooth as the politician he was during mayoralty elections.

Danchuk glowered at me. "Been a long time since we saw them here. Early morning."

"I was with Tassina until about sunset. She put Eleni to bed just before I left. I don't think she was going anywhere tonight."

"What were you doing here?" His eyes were like a ferret's peering down the hole of something he planned to kill.

As soon as I had opened my mouth I regretted it but it was too late. Silently cursing myself, I said, "Just a visit. Nothing special." I thought of Samuels on the pier below the Sunshine Warrior's Flores Island clubhouse. But Samuels was back by the ambulance and I doubted my story to Danchuk would reach him. Also I sensed he wouldn't want to explain why he had been on Flores Island any more than I did. Thinking this I realized Samuels and I needed to talk.

Danchuk glowered at me for a long moment and then shrugged. "Check the dental records during the autopsy anyway, mayor, ah, doc, ah." One foot stamped as if against the cold and he pivoted on a heel like a soldier doing an about-face. For a moment Danchuk stood rigidly staring at the boat, his expression thoughtful. "US senator coming tomorrow morning and now this. Hell of a thing." I wondered if he meant the fire, the senator coming, or both. "Terrible accident," he expanded.

"If it was an accident," I said and immediately regretted yet again having spoken. There was nothing to do now but continue, though. I told them about hearing two blasts. Ended by saying that the first sounded like a dynamite explosion, not fuel or propane going up.

"You'd know the difference?"

I nodded. "You get to know the sounds," I said, thinking back to Cyprus and a summer full of bombs — a cornucopia of types of explosives. Each had its own distinctive trademark explosion, just as each caused death in slightly varied ways. I started to explain the difference between a dynamite blast and the exploding sound of a gasoline bomb but Danchuk gestured for me to be quiet.

"We don't have time for this, McCann. I'll have the boat cordoned off and we'll get a team in from Nanaimo to check it out some time tomorrow."

I should have let it go there but couldn't. The sense that time was running out and that the death of Tassina and Eleni was somehow linked to Ira's death was too strong. "We have to get to the bottom of this. We have to find out who is doing this killing."

Danchuk stepped toward me and there was such iciness in his manner that I heard both Jabronski and Tully step away from me as if I were about to draw deadly fire. I inclined my head, Danchuk reclined his. We locked eyes and I forced mine not to waver away from his gaze. He slowly, methodically started jabbing one blunt finger into my chest to punctuate every second word. "In the morning," he said as he jabbed, "I'm calling the regional coroner and he is going to tell you to back right off, McCann. Your job is to determine how death occurred. Yet all day I've been getting calls about you. About you asking questions. People wondering who you were to be asking these questions." His finger was jabbing harder each time and as he finished this sentence I caught his wrist in my hand, lowered his hand to his side and then gently released it.

For a tense second I thought he was going to swing a fist at me and I started to brace for the blow. Instead he suddenly strode off down the wharf, then halted abruptly after a few steps and whirled back. "Go home, Coroner. Stay there. No more questions. No more playing detective. And when I'm done with the senator. When he's nice and on his way then I want to talk to you about how Tassina Mavrikos and her daughter died and why you were with her for half the day today." I saw his teeth flash in a twisted grin. Then Sergeant Danchuk of the Royal Canadian Mounted Police strode down the wharf on stubby legs, brushed past the local newspaper reporter without so much as glancing his way, and walked manfully away — until finally the darkness swallowed even the brilliant orange stripes decorating his coat.

"Jesus, Elias," Jabronski said, "you sure know how to piss people off."

I nodded. It seemed a very insightful observation. The three of us trailed off the wharf. Most of the crowd had dissipated. Jabronski went over to talk with the reporter, who had a living to make as well. Tully said he was going back to bed and suggested I should get some sleep and forget about things. His voice had the tone of a kindly minister counseling a lost member of his flock. I told him I would and declined his offer of a ride back home. Away from the crab boat wreckage, the air tasted fresh and clean. I wanted to walk a while in it, to let the musky scent of salal and cedars replace the stench of a dying boat and two lost lives. Lives I inexplicably felt could have been saved if I had only been able to sift all I had learned today and find within that information the identity of a killer who knew how to make murder appear an accident. A killer, I was also convinced, who planned to strike again soon. But I had no idea where, when, or who would be the next victim.

Chapter Twelve

I followed the longer route via public lanes back to my house. There was no need for hurry. Attempting further sleep would be futile on this grim night. I kept visualizing Tassina as she had been in the stern of the boat on our return trip from Flores Island. Leaning back in her T-shirt, glass of wine in one hand, cigarette in the other. Her honey hair framing chocolate eyes and tawny skin. It was hard to equate the Tassina then with the small form the firefighters had carried off the crab boat in a black bag. Eleni I wished not to think of at all. Doing so scrambled too many images I found impossible to separate.

To think of Eleni brought forth remembered pictures of a little girl describing the traits of a troll menagerie to Fergus. But those visions soon jumbled and merged with a street full of smoke and flame in Cyprus. The dark eyes of a young girl in pain whose questions I could not answer. Images, too, of a small girl with shiny black hair, alone on a trail crossing the Chuor Phnum Dangrek escarpment. Too many intersecting threads of my life to face when I thought of Eleni, so best to try and blank out all images of her.

Something I did poorly at best.

Again, I returned to a house cloaked in darkness. When I opened the door, Fergus wasn't there, which was unusual. I tensed, shut the door softly behind me so I wouldn't be silhouetted in the starlight. Burglaries are rare in Tofino — but not unknown. Crime happens. But the kind of burglar who got past Fergus was one I preferred not to meet. At least not unarmed. The room was inky dark, but it was my home and I knew the placement of each item of furniture. Yet something was amiss, a current of air brushed my cheek where there should have been no air movement at all.

Stepping carefully and slowly across the room I reached the fireplace and took the heavy cast poker up from its rack. Doing so resulted in only the smallest of scraping sounds as metal dragged against metal, but it drew a low whoof of a bark from the deck as Fergus alerted to the stealthy noise coming from inside the house. I waited for him to come through the deck door to investigate. For now, as my eyes adjusted to the deep darkness of the house interior, I saw the sliding glass door leading to the deck stood open. That explained the air current. Fergus didn't come, but I heard his low rumble of warning again.

Replacing the poker in the stand, I imagined how his coat would be uniformly standing on end, his ears pricked, head leaning forward, four legs coiled tight and ready to spring. But he wouldn't move from his station. Not now; not ever, I suspected, without appropriate permission.

"I didn't hear you come in," she said in a voice that was little more than a whisper.

"That's fine," I said. An irrelevant and unnecessary comment, but all I seemed capable of at the moment. The silence stretched between us.

"I heard the sirens. Heard them fading away in this direction." Her voice softened even more, becoming almost indistinct. "I was worried, so I followed them."

"We're safe," I said. Again, it struck me that my words described the self-evident.

"I saw the trucks down at the wharf and I parked on the road but after walking half way down I changed my mind. When I got back to the car someone had double parked and blocked me in. So I came up here." She uncrossed her legs and stood up. Fergus swivelled his head to follow her every movement. I did too. Vhanna stepped over to the deck rail, turned back to me, back braced against the railing. She was entirely dressed in black. Jeans, denim shirt knotted at the mid-riff, calf-high Doc Marten boots. Her hair was pulled straight back from her face to fall in a plait down her back. With her back against the railing, Vhanna's face was shadowed, unreadable. "What happened?" she asked in the same soft voice.

I told her about Tassina and Eleni. I didn't mention the two explosions. Perhaps I wanted to hear her theory as to the cause of their death.

Vhanna, however, received the news without comment. She turned away, leaning out over the deck railing, to stare at the blackness of the inlet water and the glimmer of stars above.

I joined her at the railing. Fergus crowded up against her other side and we both cast our gazes into the blackness too. The breeze off the water was light and cool. I thought I felt Vhanna shiver ever so gently beside me. "This has to end," she said, so quietly I wasn't sure I heard the words or imagined them.

Then Vhanna was pressing against me and our arms wrapped tightly around each other. Our mouths met and I felt the fingers of her one hand twist hard in my hair. The other hand was pressing with equal intensity against the base of my spine. Both my hands cupped her face, my mouth drank deeply from Vhanna's. Dimly, I was aware of Fergus padding into the house with a disapproving rattle of his dogtags. I felt Vhanna's smile even as I grinned against her lips. "Silly dog," she murmured into my mouth.

"A good friend," I whispered back to her tongue. "Vhanna," I said somewhat more firmly, "I'm sorry."

She leaned back against my hands which continued to gently cup her face. Her fingers covered my mouth. "No. No words."

"But —"

"Shhhh." Vhanna stood on tip toe while pulling my face down to her and kissed my eyes delicately. Her tongue traced down to my lips. I lost interest in talking and let her guide me into the house. We climbed the stairs to the bed. I heard Fergus sigh and then a soft thump as he jumped up on the couch downstairs. He knew no one would bother to scold him for the transgression, but it was also a way of reminding us of his continued disapproval. Vhanna giggled. "He's such a prude." Her hand was in mine, small and fragile-feeling, like some precious porcelain.

We undressed each other slowly beside the bed, touching only as needed to pull clothes away. Vhanna pushed me down on the bed and straddled my hips. Her breasts were small, firm, widely spaced. In the darkness, her skin glowed palely. I pulled her down to my chest and she stretched like a cat along my body. We clung to each other, our mouths dancing across opposing faces. Our skin seemed hot and cool at the same time, elements of fire and ice; it felt almost as if we were blending into each other's flesh, merging spirits. "Vhanna," I whispered, as I rolled her over and pressed down upon her. The fingers of both her hands were in my hair, pulling my lips to meet hers. Our bodies met and blended together as closely as two bodies possibly can.

Much later, I woke from a sleep I couldn't remember drifting into. Feeling deliciously rested, I stretched, savoured the liquid feeling of all my bones and muscles. Only when I stretched did I realize I was alone in the bed. I sat up, momentarily disoriented, fearing Vhanna's presence had been only a dream.

But Fergus' bed was empty so I knew he was somewhere else in the house with Vhanna. I got out of bed, reached for my robe and found it missing. Taking an old one out of the closet I descended the stairs. The first glow of false dawn touched the sky inland and cast a soft illumination onto the deck. I found Vhanna leaning against the rail again, looking out at the inlet. The heavy green terry robe swallowed her, hanging down almost to her ankles, her hands lost inside the arms. It made her look small and vulnerable. There is a photo in *National Geographic* magazine of Vhanna standing on a massive rock alongside a Nepali river running hard with winter breakup water. In the photo she is wearing khaki hiking shorts and a white bush shirt with large practical pockets. Her hair is pulled back in a tight ponytail and her hands are on her hips;

her posture exudes a bold, unrelenting determination. The Vhanna I know never looks small and vulnerable. Small, yes. Vulnerable, no.

I hesitated in the doorway, noting the tightness of her cheeks, the pull of muscles around her mouth and eyes. As I stepped out on the deck she turned her head toward me and the worried expression drained away slowly, being replaced by a soft, satisfied smile. Yet, around her eyes the muscles didn't relax, the tightness remained.

"I couldn't sleep," she said. "I watched you for a long time. You were sleeping so peacefully I didn't want to disturb you."

I folded her in my arms, she leaned her back into my chest. Vhanna's head fit perfectly under my chin. Her hair slipped down inside my robe to dust my chest and stomach. I brushed my lips against the top of her head, pressed lightly down upon the hair there. "What's the matter?" I said.

She shrugged. "Nothing, just couldn't sleep." Vhanna is mysterious in many ways but she is not a good liar.

I thought about this. Let the silence draw out. With each passing second the tension in her back increased, each muscle tightening so that I could feel the motion in her shoulders as they rose little by little and pressed more into my chest. "Tell me," I said at last.

"There's nothing to tell."

"Yes. There is."

Her voice sounded tight. If I hadn't known her better I would have thought she was on the verge of tears. "How do you know?"

I smiled, bent down and kissed her cheek. "I know you," I whispered in her ear.

She didn't respond to that immediately. But after a moment or two she sighed lightly. "Yes, you do," she said. "As well as anyone."

Again the silence stretched, but this time it was comfortable feeling.

"It's nothing I know for certain. Just a sense I have." She paused. Her hands touched my arms, tightened on them below the elbows. I drew her in closer. My heart was beating and my mouth was dry. I didn't know if I wanted to hear more or not.

"Ira came to me a few days ago. He wanted my help."

I stepped back and turned her to face me. She crossed her arms, pulling the robe closed. For a second, she kept her head down and then she looked up at me, face calm and strong as usual. All traces of vulnerability were gone. Yet, just as always, the strength in her face was not something hard or cold. It was a strength that was simply there, indisputable, constant, capable and confident. Seeing that expression made me want to tell her again that I loved her but I forced myself to focus on the matter at hand instead. "I don't understand."

She chewed her bottom lip for a second, as she does when she's trying to cut through to the heart of a matter. As she does when she's looking at one of my business proposals for a friend about to become venture capital partner. Finally, she reached a decision and favoured me with a little smile. "This is what I know. Ira came and wanted to borrow the boat. He needed to go up island. Up Nootka Sound. Needed to get something the Warriors had stashed up there somewhere.

"I asked him what it was, but he wouldn't tell me. So I said he couldn't have the boat. We had a little argument about that. I figured he was planning to use the boat to haul some pot out of the hills or something. It was too big a risk to take. And he wouldn't tell me what he was after. After a bit he laughed and said everything was fine, that he'd get someone else to take him up or borrow a boat elsewhere.

"I couldn't understand why he didn't take one of the Warriors' boats, but he said he couldn't. He said he didn't want word getting out that he was going up there. I asked him again what he was after but he wouldn't tell me. We left it like that."

"Could have been anything. Grass, like you thought. Anything. I doubt there's any connection." I was starting to feel relieved. Vhanna hadn't been hiding anything. Her next words blew my relief away like a blast of wind running ahead of a gale.

"Tassina took him up there the next day."

"She said she hadn't seen Ira." She also said there was something she needed to talk with me about. That was why I had been going to see her in the morning. Was that what she wanted to say? That she had seen Ira. That they had gone up Nootka Sound together and brought something out of there. I thought of the two explosions I had heard, thought of Ira Connaught strung up in a tree after being strangled. What the hell was happening here?

"Do you have any idea what they were after?"

Vhanna shook her head. "But I know where they might have gone."

Chapter Thirteen

Salt spray whipped back from the prow of Vhanna's boat as it slashed through the oncoming ranks of deep, rolling swells. The sun was a brilliant ball of glare over the mountains and the sea glistened under its light. Morning found us already shooting the gap between Meares and Vargas islands. We traveled the same route Tassina and I had traversed a day earlier. Only this time we would go further. Nootka Sound was our destination. The throaty growl of the two 12-cylinder Detroit diesels in the stern of *Artemis* testified to our sense of urgency.

Artemis was a ludicrous boat. It was a forty-two-foot gin boat built in the 1930s so a Vancouver land developer could entertain prospective clients off the shores of English Bay with the city sparkling before them like some Oriental jewel. Once his marks were sufficiently booze-soaked, sun-drenched, and besotted with Vancouver's lush beauty, he would sell them a patch of land that was either sinking into marsh or on a hillside undermined by underground seeps and springs. Sir Johnathon Talbot, Esquire had been the land tycoon's name. He had been acquainted with my father, who had always had a kind word for the man who had fleeced many a British emigrant during the pre- and post-war years. Sir Talbot, as he was known, followed in the tracks of a fine heritage of Old Boys from the British public schools who had discovered the way to riches in a new land was to prey on the gullible from the land of old.

He was as sleazy as land developers of all times and places, but concealed his lechery under a mask of propriety that would have deceived a Swiss banker. But Sir Talbot had easier prey in mind than steely-eyed Geneva bankers. His victims were middle-aged clerks from Yorkshire and returning privates from regiments raised in places like Leeds. They never thought to call him anything other than Sir Talbot in the most deferential of manners, as if they sought his approval to enter this new land to which they came on hesitating feet. Sir Talbot took them out on the bay in the boat that then bore the curious name of *The Angel Queen*. Gin and tonics flowed, papers were passed, the pale faces of the men turned cherry red before the wind and liquor; pens flashed and names flourished. Sir Talbot always returned to harbour a wealthier man.

My father once told me Sir Talbot was a good old chap who failed to comprehend the seriousness of what his ventures meant for those he inveigled. Apparently, like all aging public school boys, Angus couldn't bring himself to indict a fellow member of the old school tie. So he turned a blind eye to Sir Talbot's deceptions and they remained friends until the knight, whose ascendance to peerage many considered suspect, faded into the darkness of that final night whilst sitting bolt upright in the pilot's chair of *The Angel Queen* during yet another deal closing. For several minutes the nervous clients from Hong Kong, for this was where Sir Talbot was in the 1980s finding a new vein of hopelessly hopeful customers to bilk, thought he had merely fallen asleep. Politely they waited. And waited some more, while, according to the legend that arose around the event, Sir Talbot's head lolled back and his mouth gabbled open in what could have been mistaken for snoring. It was some minutes after he ceased twitching and jerking in the chair that someone, perhaps the Filipino servant, cottoned on to the fact that Sir Talbot's state of rest was that of the eternal variety.

Due to the fact that Sir Talbot had passed away aboard the vessel, *The Angel Queen* developed the undeserved reputation of a ship accursed. More realistically, the 1980s signaled the onset of a period when the price of diesel fuel skyrocketed. She was a thirsty boat. Her two engines sucked up fuel with the abandoned relish journalists and remittance men demonstrate when faced with free champagne at a literary event or local opera opening. Such wasteful ways caused even a gin boat to be shunned by prospective buyers.

But the engines were not her only extravagance. *The Angel Queen* had been hand built with a white painted mahogany plank hull strong enough to hold the two mighty engines. Her decks and cabin were also warped from the finest Asian mahogany with outer walls coated in glisteningly smooth white polyresin paint and the trim varnished to a dark plum. Inside the cabin below decks, walls, cupboards, book racks, and doors were constructed of hardened teak. Brass trimming thick as a wrist reinforced the seals at the windows. She was equipped with every conceivable navigational aid known to the yachtsman of the

1980s and had feather-touch controls that were absolutely precise in their balance. Yet, other than for the occasional venture under the Lion's Gate Bridge for show, she had never in all her life at sea sailed beyond sight of Vancouver's high rises.

When Sir Talbot passed on, the boat was hoisted on blocks at a Vancouver shipyard. There it sat in ever-fading grandeur until two years ago when Vhanna mentioned in passing that she was thinking of buying a boat. I, spinning a good tale even better, told her of Sir Talbot and his vessel. Then I promptly forgot the matter. This being near the beginning of our relationship I was understandably diverted by thoughts of when next I would be able to steal a few exclusive and secluded hours of Vhanna's time. This distraction continues to plague me.

It was with some trepidation I later learned that Vhanna had journeyed almost immediately to Vancouver and sought out the boatyard. *The Angel Queen* was there on her blocks. Two weeks later the ship made the longest voyage of its prestigious career and sailed into Tofino harbour under a waxing moon. Vhanna re-christened her *Artemis* after the Greek goddess of the hunt, forest, and moon for which her adventure company is also named.

So it was on *Artemis* that we now hurtled across the sea, bound for Nootka Sound and the location to which Ira Connaught was taken by Tassina Mavrikos a few days earlier. It was a trip they had both returned from, but of which neither could now speak.

Within an hour of Vhanna's admission that she knew where Ira had gone, *Artemis* raced toward the dawn. It would be a long trip, taking us through the gap between Meares and Vargas islands, round the oceanside of Flores Island, past

Sydney Inlet, by Hot Springs Cove, across the
entrance to Hesquiat Harbour, curving about the
rugged headland there and down into Nootka
Sound. Somewhere near the mouth of Muchalat
Inlet, which pushes inland to the logging town of
Gold River, stood a cabin that had been Ira's goal.
There I hoped to find some clue as to what Ira had
brought back aboard Tassina's crab boat.

Artemis bucked like a stubborn mule as she
thrashed a path through the rolling surf. It was hard
to stay on your feet without clutching at any available handhold. Fergus cowered in the stern, looking
balefully in my direction. We are both possessed of
somewhat delicate stomachs when it comes to this
kind of pounding pace on open seas. Stumbling
from the galley, I kicked the door shut behind me
and, gingerly struggling to maintain my balance
while not dumping two coffee cups, climbed into
the pilothouse. I carried practical mugs. Plastic,
with lids you could drink through, and the garishly
lettered name of a gas-food bar on the side. I stumbled awkwardly up the short stairwell to the upper
deck where Vhanna held the wheel.

She wore a black Gore-tex squall jacket with the
hood thrown back and black nylon pants. Her hair
was tied back severely in a ponytail that flipped up
and down with every crashing roll through a broach-
ing wave. She stood with her legs set wide apart, her
back straight, small hands tightly grasping the
spokes of the wheel as she steered with casual skill
into the waves in such a way that we rode them
without any real peril besides the threat of slopped
coffee or tumbled remittance men and their dogs.

Vhanna looked, and was, a mariner at heart. Since acquiring *Artemis* she has become an able captain and navigator. Despite this, I continue to feel unsafe when we are out on seas that are running high.

I slumped gratefully into the seat next to the wheel and extended one cup. "I think this is yours," I said.

She took it, sipped, grimaced and passed it back. "Milk and sugar. Yuck."

I shrugged an apology and traded the milk- and sugar-laced cup for the black one. The coffee was good, hot and tart. Fresh ground organic beans from Nicaragua. We sipped it to avoid burning our mouths. The warmth played against our hands. Icy air, unwarmed yet by the rising sun, whistled over the windshield. All around us the sky was clear, brightening to a turquoise blue that would be painful to look at as it rose higher in the sky.

As if thinking this too, Vhanna slipped a pair of sunglasses out of an inside jacket pocket and shoved them into place. She glanced at my Filson as if trying to divine what was hidden in the pockets. "I forgot them," I confessed. I'm not fond of sunglasses. Perhaps this leads me to misplace them. Too often they seem a convenient screen behind which people can hide their eyes, denying a way of reading the story their expressions might truly tell.

Vhanna has no time for such contemplation and is of a more practical mindset. She demonstrated this now by tugging a bottle of sunscreen from another pocket of her jacket and tossing it to me. I caught it with my free hand and managed to spill no coffee in the process. Vhanna grinned in apparent appreciation of my dexterity. I studied the sunscreen tube and read all the warnings, exhortations and reassurances printed there. "Just put it on, Elias. Put lots on. Don't want your nose to rot off."

"I have a hat," I pointed to my battered Filson which I had tossed into a secure corner of the cabin to keep it from blowing away.

"Do as you're told for once, okay."

We smiled at each other over that, eyes meeting and a challenge exchanging. I removed the lid and squirted sunscreen into my palm, dabbed a little on my nose and cheeks. Vhanna scowled, but her eyes smiled as she set her coffee cup into a holder and switched the wheel to automatic pilot. I noticed that we had hit a patch of water where the seas were relatively calm and apparently her piloting was no longer necessary. It still seemed to me that the boat was rocking somewhat precariously. Vhanna took the tube of sunscreen and rubbed the lotion all over my face and neck, pausing at the end to push her tongue into my mouth. I cupped her bum in one hand and pulled her closer but she pushed away gently. "You're so devious. Just trying to lure me away from the helm."

"Wither goest though, goest I." Vhanna wrinkled her nose in distaste at my Elizabethan impersonation, turned back to the wheel and snapped off the automatic pilot. "We could leave it on and check things out below."

She gave the proposition due consideration. Even chewed her bottom lip a bit. "We'd have to stop the boat. There's too many driftlogs here this close to shore. Too many rip currents, too. And it's just too rough out here today."

We were rounding Flores Island already, but were too far offshore for me to see the Sunshine Warriors' clubhouse. I remembered Tassina and I speaking yesterday with Lawrence Rafferty. I remembered Tassina arguing with Samuels and the older man on the wharf and then refusing to talk about what was said. The sense of urgency came back and I cursed it. "You're right. We best keep going."

Vhanna gave me a wan little smile which I thought was perhaps tinged with genuine regret. Not being able to see her eyes the expression was hard to read. "Later," she said softly, as if it were her idea to keep going and a bribe was necessary to keep me on the scent of the hunt.

"It's a date," I said quite solemnly. With Vhanna and me, an opportunity passed by may never come again. There is always a sense that the future is an unpredictable tangle of intersecting strands of rope waiting to trip our best intentions and pull us apart. For now, we were united in common cause and our mutual passion bound. By tonight cause and passion might just as easily tear us in opposite directions. This was something I believed we both knew and, consequently, we were strongly tempted to hold the moments now and linger amid them. But Ira, Tassina and Eleni were dead. If an explanation for their deaths were to be found anywhere perhaps it waited in a cabin up Nootka Sound. So, instead of twining our arms around each other, Vhanna shoved *Artemis*'s throttle forward to full speed and the big boat reared even higher in the bow and slapped harder against the waves.

I clutched hold of the brass rail surrounding the upper cabin and hung on against the boat's bucking. In the stern, Fergus curled into a tight ball, eyes rolled back with discomfort, tongue drooping from his mouth as he breathed in sharp, anxious pants. I understood the feeling completely. Beside me, however, Vhanna faced each approaching swell with an impassive expression that was partially hidden by the damned sunglasses.

There was no wharf or dock where Vhanna thought the cabin was located. The only indication something other than forest might be located within the dark woods was a singular narrow track extending through the weeds from the treeline down to the water's edge. Vhanna dropped anchor well offshore and we lowered the small wooden dory hung crosswise on a pulley system at the boat's stern. Before lowering the dory to the water, I put Fergus in. Once the boat was lowered, Vhanna and I clambered down and joined him.

Vhanna took the bow, Fergus the stern, and I settled amidships to work the oars. It felt good to exercise my muscles and to hear a boat that moved quietly and smoothly through the water without the aid of an over-powered engine. The roar of *Artemis*'s engines echoed in my ears and I could still feel the pounding of the waves and the vibration of the diesels tremoring through my muscles. Fergus watched the approaching treeline like a conquistador coming in from the sea to conquer a rabble of natives. In his case, it was an expression of happy benevolence rather than villainy. But then, the shore was oddly empty of birdlife or other prey that might lend itself to flushing, so he posed little threat to any living creature.

I had expected to hear the hooting of blue grouse from within the thick woods, to see seagulls swirling overhead along the shoreline, and the occasional bald eagle nesting in the upper branches of trees overlooking the beach. But there was no sound at all. The forest waited quietly and its stillness was eerie to the point of malevolence. For a moment, I thought with regret of the shotgun that was safely buttoned away in its locker back at the cabin.

Just before the surf rolled us against the shore, Vhanna jumped with a long stride from the dory's bow, managing to land with dry feet on the sand above the tidal wash. Trailing the rope tied to the bow, she ran up the shoreline, turned, and began reeling the boat in hard while I dug the oars in powerfully so that the boat slipped as far up the beach as possible, settling with half its length on dry ground. Jumping out I grabbed one side and she the other. Together we wrestled the little boat up the shore until it was a few metres above the tide line. The tide was running out so there was little worry of the boat being pulled out to sea while we explored the forest, but Vhanna took the time to secure the line to a wind-twisted and dwarfed pine tree. It was a precaution I heartily endorsed. Not being a swimmer, the prospect of trying to reach *Artemis*, should the dory become lost, was something I would rather not have to face. Fergus and I walked across the sand to join her. It was warmer on shore and Vhanna undid her jacket. Underneath, she wore the black denim shirt from the night before. Also as before, it was tied at the mid-riff.

"It's through there," Vhanna said pointing up the small track. She added, with only a slight hesitation, "I think."

We followed a path that extended from the sand and mud beach through weeds and scrub to the forest edge. Despite the sun's heat on our backs we kept our coats on, knowing it would be far cooler under the forest canopy.

The trail wound through a low stand of scrub pines before plunging into a tunnel of blackness as it entered the rainforest. Much of this area had been logged decades before, but for some unknown reason this section of forest remained virginal. Huge cedars soared above our heads, their canopies blocking the light, so only thin tracers of dusty illumination reached the forest floor. The massive lower trunks were heavily encrusted in moss. In the shadow of these giants, little ground cover existed. The forest floor was bare, eternally damp and softly carpeted by moss and rot. Wherever a small gap in the canopy allowed light to filter down to the forest floor swordferns had sprung up. Their hard struggle for life and light was evidenced by the brown, brittle leaves that greatly outnumbered those that were green and healthy.

Once we entered the ancient forest the trail disappeared. Vhanna took the lead. She walked briskly as if she had some idea where the cabin stood. The silence was total. Fergus hugged close to Vhanna's side. He did not forage as he normally would have when presented with a new, unexplored wood. I stayed close to Vhanna as well, glancing tensely about. It was only the primeval feel of this place I told myself, not that there was anything real to fear. But I knew my true anxiety stemmed from the potential threat of humans more than any danger the forest might offer. It was as if we had entered the secret lair of those who had murdered Ira, Tassina, and Eleni.

Vhanna stopped suddenly and crouched, pointing ahead with one raised arm. Heart pounding, I bent down and sighted along her arm. There, to my relief, was no crazed murderer. Rather, Vhanna pointed toward a small cabin that stood in the deep shade cast by a clutch of giant cedars. Its walls were constructed of rough-planed plank boards, the roof was made of hand-split cedar shakes. The wood was old, aged to a dark grey by rain and weather. It looked deserted. "Why would he come here?" I asked.

"I don't know. I just dropped him off here once and he was only gone for a few minutes. He had told me there was a cabin. And I knew it must be close because of the short length of time he was gone from the beach."

"Let's take a closer look." The closer we got the more dilapidated the old shack became. Its roof sagged badly at one corner and the walls bowed inward as if the westerly winds had managed to reach through the protective wall of surrounding forest to stove in its braces. When we reached the cabin, I gently pushed the splintered wooden door inward. The hinges squeaked tiredly. A rotting foundation of raised logs kept the cabin well off the ground so I had to step up awkwardly to gain entrance. With Vhanna pressing against my back, we both slipped inside. The cabin was permeated with a foul pungent odour that, even though I could not place its source or cause, seemed hauntingly familiar.

Light filtered through knotholes in the boards of the wall. A larger shaft of light traced through a section of roof that had collapsed into a far corner. In the light's ray, I saw a stack of cardboard cartons about the same size as those containing grocers' vegetable tins. The boxes were stacked in a neat pile near where the roof had given way. As I moved toward the boxes warning stickers caught my eye. I froze in place, suddenly realizing the source and nature of the pungent odour.

Vhanna started to push pass by me, intent it seemed on inspecting the boxes. I put a restraining hand on her arm and squeezed it tight. She glanced at me, questioning. I motioned my head toward the door and carefully started withdrawing. Vhanna tugged toward the boxes, but increasing the pressure on her arm, I pulled her away. She started to speak but held her silence when I put a warning finger to my lips. Puzzled, she nevertheless allowed me to lead her quietly from the cabin. Even when we gained the outside, I kept my hand on her arm and drew her further back toward the cover of the trees.

Fergus milled about me in a puzzlement as deep as Vhanna's, but both silently accompanied me as we withdrew from the small opening surrounding the cabin. When we were about one hundred metres away, with several giant cedars between us and the cabin, I finally halted. Crouching down I gestured for Vhanna to bring her ear over to my lips. "The boxes are full of dynamite. It's old. Decaying. Soaked through with water that's leaked in through the roof."

"So?" Vhanna's answering whisper was impatient. I knew what she was thinking. Dynamite. I had told her of two explosions at the crab boat. One explosion could have been dynamite. Vhanna wanted to investigate the stored boxes.

"That smell. The pungent stench. Did you notice it?" I continued whispering. Vhanna nodded. "It's nitroglcerine, decaying nitro. When dynamite breaks down the nitro in it leaks out. It separates from the gelatin or cellulose base they put in explosives to keep the nitro stable. The nitro emits vapours. It's worse than propane or natural gas. A match. A shoe scraping against a board. Anything can set it off and the whole damn batch blows."

Vhanna stared back at the cabin. She was imagining it. So was I. We had been in the cabin. And we had got out. I took a deep breath, feeling the cold pit of fear in my gut. "I have to go back."

She shook her head. This time it was her hand that restrained my arm. I took her hand in mine and squeezed it gently. Her skin was icy. "There are things we need to know. It'll be all right." It was a stupid thing to say, but I said it anyway. We both knew there was no way of knowing.

"Why you?" she said. "Why not report it and have the police come and do it?"

"Take too long. And Danchuk's with his senator probably by now. He wouldn't come. We have to know, Vhanna. There may be answers in there."

"I'm lighter, smaller."

I squeezed her hand again and hoped my fingers wouldn't tremble. "Won't be long," I said and stood up. If I didn't do this quickly I might not be able to do it at all. Before starting for the cabin I shrugged my coat and hat off. Vhanna handed me a pencil thin maglite she pulled from yet another of her coat pockets. "You're like an outfitter's shop." I gave her a smile that was supposed to be reassuring but she didn't return it. I headed for the cabin before either of us did something that would make going through with this impossible.

When I reached the doorway I paused to turn on the maglite. The bright beam lanced into the cabin. I was wearing rubber-soled deck runners so there was little danger of friction from the shoes disturbing the explosive. But with damaged nitro it's all a toss of the dice. You might give a box a kick and it won't blow.

Then again just walking near the explosives can cause sufficient tremor of air to set the stuff off. In the army I had been trained to handle explosives. Experience had taught me the best way to handle the stuff was by not going anywhere near it.

As I warily entered the cabin the stench seemed worse, thicker. It tickled my nose, cloyed in my throat so that I desperately wanted to cough. I steadied my breathing, ignoring the scratchy feeling deep in my throat, and then moved stealthily across the room.

Before each step, I scanned the floor with the flashlight beam. As I neared the stack of boxes I noticed imprints in the dust that matched those in the corner. There had, I realized, been more explosives here before. Someone had removed them. Ira? That was something to think about later. Now wasn't time for the idle distraction of such speculations.

Close up, I could see several of the boxes topping the stack sagged and buckled rottenly. Water stains darkened the sides of the entire stack and the top boxes were black with it. The red explosive warning labels on each box reflected brightly in the maglite's beam. Here and there a black syrupy liquid oozed through box seams. The syrup dribbled down the box sides to form puddles on top of the lower boxes. It was a chilling sight.

Taking another slow breath I forced myself to move within a few inches of the stack. I ran the beam over the boxes until I saw a label that was visible and uncovered by the black oozing nitro. On the label were three rows of numbers set one above the other. These were identification numbers required by law. Each set of numbers was clearly evident. It was the last set of numbers I was interested in so I spent a minute memorizing these figures. Next to the label was a bright orange diamond sticker with a black classification code printed inside the diamond. The code was 1.1.D, but I didn't need to see that to know this was a case of blasting explosives. The leaking nitro and its stench told me that. Normally there would have been no odour but when nitro becomes wet it turns mushy and swells. As it swells the cartridge containers wrapped around it rupture. The nitro oozes out causing the cardboard storage boxes to stain and sweat.

I ran the beam over several of the other boxes and discovered the same orange diamond identification marks and the same series of numbers on the labels. Every box was apparently filled with dynamite. And the dynamite in all the boxes was breaking down because of the water leaking in through the roof. For twenty-five days it had rained virtually non-stop. I wondered if the explosives had been here throughout the storm or longer. I suspected they were put here months ago. The cabin was a deadly bomb. Whoever had stored explosives here and allowed them to become this sodden was at the very least a fool. The person might also be a murderer.

Slowly, I retraced my steps toward the doorway. I paused only once to check my memory of the numbers against one of the labels and got a match. Just before I reached the doorway I stepped on a plank that creaked ominously underfoot, a sharp groan of wood giving way echoed through the cabin as the board separated along a shrinkline. I stood waiting, my heart thumping. Sweat beaded my brow, ran down my face and stung my eyes. I was concentrating so hard I could hear the ticking of my wristwatch, feel the slightest brushing of a draft coming through one of the knotholes to touch my cheek. After a timeless moment I slowly transferred my weight so there was no pressure on the cracked board. I raised my foot ever so gently and placed it down again well clear of the damaged floorboard. A moment later I was at the door and gingerly stepped down from the cabin. Walking sideways, one eye on the cabin as if seeing it blow would give me some kind of a chance, I withdrew to where Vhanna waited in the shelter of a cedar wider than ten of her. Fergus sat tensely at her side. She picked up my coat and hat, bundled them under one arm, and at my nod followed me away from the cabin.

Keeping the tree between us and the cabin, we retreated, neither of us speaking, both walking as quietly and carefully as we could. I wondered if the animals and birds had sensed the danger in this place and that was why there were none around. It seemed a foolish thought but I could find no other reason to explain their absence.

When we came out of the forest and picked up the trail, I judged we were far enough away from the cabin to be safe. I stopped and wiped the sweat away from my face. "Do you think Ira came here for that?" Vhanna asked.

I told her about the imprints left by boxes that must have been moved recently. "Whoever moved them took them out from right next to the damaged explosives. My guess is the boxes the person took were okay. There was no rain getting in where they were stacked." Vhanna shivered, thinking no doubt about moving box after box with damaged explosives standing next to you, explosives just waiting for a reason to go off. I nodded. "Madness. Must have been bloody mad. Crazy. Could have blown himself to pieces." Dozens of other words were pouring into my mind. Words full of images of explosion and destruction, of insanity and evil. I took a deep breath, steadied myself, forced away the visions of streets full of smoke and flame, of cabins dissolving in rubble. I was alive. I was safe. I had gone back in there and come out again. That too had been madness. But it was a necessary madness. Perhaps Ira had thought the same when he went for the good explosives. If, I reminded myself, it had been Ira that took the explosives away.

"Let's get back," Vhanna said. When she put her hand in mine I held it tight and she returned the pressure. We walked down to the beach. The dory was still safely up on the sand, *Artemis* floated on a green ocean under a bright blue sky. Out of the dark, brooding forest everything seemed bright, fresh, and pulsing with life. It was very good to be alive. I hugged Vhanna briefly and let her scent replace the nitro's pungency. She kissed my cheek and went to undo the line tied to the pine tree. I pushed the dory down to the surf line. Fergus happily let me hoist him into the little boat. Vhanna and I pushed it off together, jumping in just before the boat slipped into the surf. I fought the oars for a moment and then we were moving free, heading toward the boat. I rowed hard. Vhanna stared over her shoulder toward *Artemis* as if urging us on. Yes, it was good to be alive. But, in a cabin shaded by giants, death still lurked for the unwary. And somewhere else someone might be planning even now to put to use the dynamite he had taken. There had been many boxes. The dust on the cabin floor had been disturbed in dozens of places. That much explosive could cause a lot of dying.

Chapter Fourteen

The *Artemis* skimmed across the foaming wave crests in pounding bounds that sent shudders through the boat and up my legs. Clinging grimly to the helm's rail, I watched the approaching ocean with fearful concentration. Vhanna's eyes were also riveted intently on the rolling swells. Every few minutes she spun the wheel and all forty-two-feet of vessel wrenched sharply to port or starboard. Seconds later I would see some debris rolling away in our wake. Mostly it was driftlogs, occasionally rusty barrels, tangles of fishing net, chunks of styrofoam, oil-stained yellow tarps; the usual flotsam cluttering a dying century's ocean coastline. The litter made traveling at this speed a risky business. I waited for Vhanna to misjudge the distance, fail to see a log or steel drum. Any second, I expected to hear the grinding crunch and ripping shriek of a wooden hull being wrenched apart.

I hated being helpless, nothing more than a witness, a hapless passenger. Then again, Vhanna was more adept at piloting the *Artemis* than I would ever be. For her part, Vhanna appeared utterly calm. She handled the wheel with a matter-of-fact efficiency that seemed to border on the edge of carelessness. Vhanna had tucked one arm of her sunglasses into her shirt's top button, saying she could see the colours and shapes in the water easier without them. The unwavering focus of her black eyes on the water hurtling toward our bow assured me she was not being reckless. Vhanna had freed her hair from the ponytail and it streamed out behind her on the wind created by the boat's passage. Spray slapped up and dusted us with a light mist as the hull bounced over the summit of each wave.

Vhanna glanced over at the chart spread out on the map table next to the wheel. "We're inside the cell net," she said.

Gingerly freeing one hand from the brass rail — to which I had been clinging for the past hour — I picked up the cellular phone mounted to the boat console. Distrustfully I glared at all the little buttons. "There's something wrong with these things, you know," I muttered. "Soon a person will never be able to just be out of touch. Imagine a whole world eternally on call. Won't matter where you are, the boss can come calling, making demands."

"Elias," Vhanna's voice was exasperated.

I sighed, punched buttons. I could have used the VHF much earlier on, of course, but I wanted this conversation to be private; unable to be monitored by prying ears — especially one set of ears. When Nicki, the dispatcher-cum-receptionist-cum-typist at the Tofino RCMP detachment, answered, I identified myself.

"You sound kind of far away, sugar," she said. Ever since I accepted the coroner's position and Danchuk's enmity toward me became quickly evident,

Nicki has called me "sugar." For some reason she relishes my difficulties with Danchuk. She also has made it clear that we are allies in a common struggle against the force of Danchukness, wherever and whenever this nemesis might appear. It's an alliance I carefully nurture, for it gives me a friend within the enemy's court.

By any standard, Nicki is a daunting woman. Standing close to six feet, boosted always by at least a couple inches of stiletto-spiked heel, she's all shape; firm flesh jutting out in all the right places, shoulder-length brunette hair, and a penchant for clothes that fit like skin. She smokes Camels, sucking them right down to the filter tip. At Rossiter's every Friday night, she drinks Tequila with a lime twist, and, in the same venue, delights in teaching the German and Japanese tourists how to line dance. Nicki grew up in Tofino and has been at the RCMP office as long as anyone cares to remember. Single, she jokes no man can keep up with her for more than a week or two. It's a perfectly believable explanation devoid of much boast. For the past five years, she and a slender Haitian woman called Lacy, who works the bakery service counter, have shared a small cabin not too far from mine. Rumours abound, of course, but neither Nicki nor Lacy bother to either deny or validate the interpretations surrounding their relationship. It is true they touch each other often in sensual ways but it is also true that such intimacy is natural to both of the women with any friends they meet, male or female. Sometimes I think Nicki has hugged and kissed me more than Vhanna ever will. It's not a course of thought I care to pursue.

After explaining that I was calling from the *Artemis* and we were way the hell and gone out on the northern ocean, I asked, "Is his nibs there?"

As I had hoped would be the case, Nicki reported he was off at the airport awaiting the senator's imminent, but also delayed, arrival. With him was all the rest of Tofino's small force of Mounties and a number of fresh arrivals from Nanaimo and Victoria. "He may be away in body, sugar, but he's present in spirit. Radio never stops and it's usually him wanting an update of the plane's arrival time. His honour, Senator Jack Sloan is late. This has made your friend and mine more nervous than the March hare."

Before she could get into further details I interrupted. There wasn't time to share Danchuk stories. I told her what I needed.

"Hmmmm, he gets wind of this," Nicki said cheerfully, "I'll be in deep doodoo. You ain't exactly the flavour of the month, you know."

"Am I ever?"

"Good point. Okay, shoot, sugar." I recited the numbers from the labels on the explosives, making her read back the last of the three numbers that had been on the water-damaged explosives. "Give me a few minutes and call back," she said and broke the connection.

I returned the cellular to its console bracket. Vhanna glanced at me inquisitvely. "Should know in a few minutes," I said.

"Sure, sugar." Vhanna's grin was all mischief as she turned her concentration back to the water.

I stared at the sun, checked my watch. Time was flying. It was already near noon and we still needed answers. Without answers, there was no way to calculate our next move. I felt the time trickling like sand through my fingers, sensed there was too little to hold.

Glumly, I looked down to the aft deck where Fergus sprawled in a gloomy, untidy bundle. One bloodshot eye caught mine and rolled abjectly toward the heavens, but I could only offer a reassuring smile. It was easy to tell his stomach was as queasy as my own.

Jerking the phone up, I punched Nicki's number. She answered on the third ring. "Jeez, sugar, you don't give a gal any time at all. Always in a hurry and then on your way." I allowed her wit a tight chuckle and then waited wordlessly, impatiently. "God, no fun today. Everybody's got their asses just screwed tight, eh."

"Give, Nicki."

After a long, world-burdened sigh, Nicki filled me in.

"Damn," I muttered. "Look, send a message up to the Gold River detachment will you?" Quickly I gave her the map coordinates for the Nootka Sound cabin that I had taken earlier from one of Vhanna's topographical charts. After telling her of the cabin's volatile contents, I said, "Don't mention anything about me giving you this, okay?"

A long silence greeted this news. When Nicki spoke again she was all business. "Is there something we should know about this?"

"I don't know yet. Nicki, I wouldn't ask you to do this if it weren't important."

Another silence. "Yeah, I know. But if his nibs finds out my tits are going to be in the wringer, you know. You ain't supposed to be messing around in things. He was on the blower to the regional coroner and anyone else who would listen this morning to nasty commentary about you."

"Look I don't want to get you into trouble, Nicki. If you have to tell him I understand. But we both know he's not doing anything to find out what's happening here. And he's just looking for an excuse to stop me from looking at things further."

This time the silence seemed to span hours. I stared out at the water racing toward our bow, let the spray carried on the wind dampen my face. "I'll tell Gold River it was an anonymous phone call on this line, so there's no question about why the source wasn't automatically registered by 911."

"Thanks, Nicki."

"See you in the salt mines, sugar." Nicki rang off without a good-bye, leaving me a crystal clear message that she wasn't happy with the burden I'd put on her shoulders.

"So?" Vhanna asked when I hung up.

"Dauphin Logging Company. Dauphin was the end user on every box of explosives. According to the records he had to file with the police to take delivery of the dynamite, it was all intended for road construction. No record of any thefts of explosives from Dauphin either."

Vhanna dropped the throttle to full slow. The *Artemis*'s bow dropped into the swells and the boat wallowed gently in the current. We both stared out at the distant mainland. We were still well north of Clayoquot Sound and its currently untouched forests. Here, in land ruled by the forestry corporations, the clearcuts stretched across the mountain ridges like so many ground zero sights blistered into the landscape. Only trees clinging to steep slopes that the logging crews couldn't access survived as a memory of the great woods that must have blanketed the land before the foresters came. "It doesn't make sense," Vhanna said at last.

"No," I agreed.

* * * * *

It took us half the time to drive from Tofino to Ucluelet in Vhanna's red Mazda Miata convertible roadster that it would have taken me in the Rover. At her house, Vhanna changed into a natural cotton-coloured shirt, loose-fitting black Levi's and Oxford-style black Doc Martens. The sleeves of the shirt were rolled up to just below the elbow, the shirt knotted at the mid-riff. Her hair streamed in the wind. Every time I glanced her way I realized again how lovely she was.

Vhanna took the little two-seater through the corners as if she were racing in the Le Mans, hands and arms maintaining a perfect ten to two o'clock racing posture, except for when she dropped her right hand to the gear shift to execute rapid up or down double-clutched shifts. I watched the surrounding country pass in a blur and let myself relax and enjoy the way the road flowed under the car's wheels.

I prefer an unhurried driving pace, so it made sense for Vhanna to do the driving. The press of time made Vhanna's pace the sensible one. I'm a stroller, preferring to stop often to smell wild roses, watch hawks soar on thermals, stretch out on a moss-covered meadow dusted with wildflowers for a lazy daydream. Vhanna, by contrast, hastens toward every destination, pushing safe limits to the edges. Often, she seems to me to be a blur of motion, moving almost too fast to be noted and contemplated upon.

Yet even in her life-pace there is contradiction. The slowness of her non-combat, traditional Taoist Tai Chi regimen, the many hours she will spend fussing over the tormented bonsai plants decorating her house, long stretches of complete quiet spent contemplating the ocean and the sun setting into it. Often, sharing the silence on her patio, I wonder at Vhanna's thoughts — but seldom does she offer to let me inside her mind.

In these moments, I sometimes wonder if she drifts back to Cambodia and her childhood. Just as I often consider that the speed of her more normal pace reflects defiance against the forces that sought to destroy her life and which carried off her entire family. Is it not natural for survivors like Vhanna to concentrate as much experience and sensation into every waking moment as possible? Is it not natural to seek to live life intensely and immediately, pushing to the very edges of oblivion to remind yourself that you live, feel, breathe the sweet air of life? Is it not a question of either living like this or going to the other extreme — withdrawing from the world and cowering behind locked doors out of fear of unseen forces bursting in upon you to cause you harm? Vhanna, I think, has adopted the better approach. Still, I sometimes ponder how deeply the scars inflicted upon her must extend down into her soul and know there is no way either she, or any of us, can continually salve away with a flurry of living the permanent marks carved upon the tissue of our hearts.

These are thoughts, of course, I never voice to Vhanna. Not anymore, at least. Long ago I learned she has short patience for such soul searching and reflection. Vhanna finds this kind of navel gazing annoying and pointless. She tells me life just is and all we can do is live it as well as possible, find what pleasures and meaning we can, and not surrender to death without a fierce fight.

About the time I was drifting through to the end of these thoughts, the radar detector started beeping its frantic warning. Vhanna dumped a gear and threshold-braked sharply so our speed fell away from 140 kilometres per hour to the legal limit of 80. We crested a hill and saw, stretched out in the other lane, a long line of RCMP patrol cars protecting three black stretch limousines. "Ah, Senator Sloan arrives," I said, as we crept by the cavalcade heading toward Tofino from the local airport. Each police car carried at least two uniformed officers and behind the smoked windows of the limousines the shadows of people in both the front and back seats were visible. Danchuk's police Blazer rode point, so it was his radar that the Miata's detector had picked up. Presumably, he had it switched on just to warn oncoming traffic to slow down as I couldn't imagine he would abandon the cavalcade to pursue a speeder. Then again, perhaps he had simply forgotten it was on. I liked this idea.

"The senator," Vhanna said, "will be lucky if he can see a tree through the forest of security."

"Do you think they always lay on so much security for a senatorial junket?"

Vhanna shrugged. She had been somewhat taciturn since we set out from her place. At first Vhanna hadn't wanted to come at all, saying that she had to get ready for the senator's welcoming banquet to be held in the evening at the community centre. For a woman who could transform herself from the role of a safari leader into elegant hostess of a formal ball in the time it took me to pour a glass of Glenlivet this seemed an odd concern. Even more unusual was her suggestion that I should take the Miata myself. I declined because I needed her driving skills as much as the car to make the trip quickly.

As we slipped past the last police car, Vhanna stepped down hard again on the pedal. Seconds later, we were hurtling down the road at our previous clip. I slouched down in my seat and listened to the wind rushing over the windshield and the whine of the tires on the road. It struck me that Fergus might have enjoyed going this fast, letting his ears stream in the wind behind him. We had left him on Vhanna's patio. After the horrors of the boat ride, he was quite content to stay behind. But Fergus was a landlubber at heart who loved cars and might find pleasure in one that went so fast — especially if Vhanna was at the wheel.

Soon we had to slow for the outskirts of Ucluelet. Minutes later Vhanna turned into the workyard of Dauphin Logging Company Ltd. The mud that had been in the drive the day before had dried out and the Miata bounced through the hardening ruts all the way up to the office building. As before, throughout the yard there were a number of overalled men working on equipment and I felt their eyes on us as we passed by. I found my mouth dry, a dryness that licking my lips didn't rectify. Dauphin's Wagoneer was parked outside the building, Vhanna pulled the Miata up alongside it. From behind the office, the dog started howling angrily as we got out and walked to the front door.

Vhanna said she would wait in the car but I noticed some of the men down by the equipment were starting to drift up toward the office building. That, and the continued threatening howls from the dog behind the office, made me refuse to leave Vhanna outside while I had a face-to-face with Dauphin. Reluctantly, she agreed to accompany me inside.

I decided the best tactic was to be direct, so I opened the door and walked straight in. The foyer contained a few bent chairs with various legs and arms broken or tenuously attached to the chair frames. A metal desk with a fake laminated wood top faced the doorway. Cluttering the top was an old-fashioned rotary dial phone, rolodex, and a manual Olympia typewriter. An ashtray made from a minia-turized logging truck tire with a metal tray where the wheel would be was piled high with lipstick-stained butts. Packed around these obviously permanent office fixtures were hundreds of pieces of paper — order forms, invoices, bills, reports, time logs, and other documents that defied quick interpretation. Judging by the totals on the bottoms of some of the bills and the sums on the invoices, money came in and went out of Dauphin Logging Company at an alarm-ing rate. A good number of the bills bore the kinds of brightly and heavily stamped threats that accompany third and fourth notices.

All of this I took in as we walked slowly across the room, past the desk, and up to the closed door behind. I gave the door a loud knock with my knuckles. Vhanna was still in the foyer and over my shoulder I saw her giving the desk closer scrutiny. He who leaves his affairs lying so visibly out in the open is easy prey for the eternally curious.

Hearing a guttural grunt from behind the door, I accepted the apparent invitation and walked inside, finding myself staring across a replica of the desk outside. Even the papers seemed the same. The only difference was the logging truck tire ashtray. This time it was piled with butts lacking lipstick stains. Dauphin's large head rose up slowly and his eyes fixed on me like a raptor contemplating its next meal. "Coroner," he said. Then he grinned and, accompanied as it was by the piercing gleam in his eyes, the flash of teeth proved a rather unpleasant expression. After a second, I realized Dauphin no longer looked at me. Rather he had fixed his grinning expression over my shoulder toward where Vhanna now stood in the doorway. "Well if it ain't Ms. Artemis in the living flesh."

"Mr. Dauphin." Vhanna's tone was that of someone identifying something insensate, like a piece of granite or a glob of red clay.

Dauphin leaned back in his high-backed leatherette office chair, which groaned beneath the weight, and locked his huge hands and fingers behind his head. He wore a blue and white cowboy shirt, stained heavily with sweat beneath the armpits. The room was hot and stuffy despite the whirring of a small air conditioner hanging haphazardly from one window.

"I have some questions," I said. Among them was what the hell was going on between Dauphin and Vhanna? The air was charged with an atmosphere of malice that made no sense to me.

Dauphin's eyes were still fixed appraisingly on Vhanna, slipping up and down her body with obvious licentiousness. "What brings you here, Ms. Chan?" His voice was drippily sweet, but tinged with a hard edge of threat.

I spoke before Vhanna could get a word in. "She's with me and I'm wondering what you can tell me about some dynamite."

That had the desired effect. Dauphin's hands came from behind his head and he sat bolt upright, his meaty paws placed flat on the papers cluttering the desk. "What'd you say?"

I told him about the dynamite we had found and where we had found it. It didn't take long to tell the tale, but by the time I finished Dauphin was struggling to recover some of his earlier calm. He had leaned back and tossed one blue-tooled cowboy boot up on the desktop. In his right hand he held a pencil that he diddled up and down while looking again at Vhanna with a smirky grin.

"Ain't mine," he said when I finished.

I read him the end-user number. "It's yours, Mr. Dauphin. Care to tell me how the dynamite got there?"

He pointed the butt of the pencil at me in a vicious jab. "This ain't your business, Coroner. Ain't none of your business. I complained to the cops yesterday about you and they explained how you didn't have any jurisdiction to be asking these questions."

I had expected this, counted on it even. Now I planted both my hands on the edge of the desk and leaned over him, glaring straight into his eyes. They held mine and didn't blink. "You can talk to me now, Dauphin, or you can talk to your friends at the police in an hour or two after I leave here and call them. Your choice."

"And if I talk to you, you just walk away and that's the end of it, eh?"

I shook my head. "No, but you won't have to talk to the police today." Glancing at the bills and invoices cluttering his desk, I said, "You'll have a little time. I would think you could use a little time well. Don't you?"

He leaned back even further so that the chair seemed in danger of toppling over. His eyes drifted back to Vhanna. "How do you fit in, doll?"

"Just along for the ride," she said. Again her voice was totally flat.

"Ever see that boy again. What was his name?"

"Starling. His name was Barry Starling."

"Yeah," Dauphin said and grinned. He looked back at me. "She ever tell you about that?" Dauphin chuckled at my obvious puzzlement. "Found her and him at one of our equipment storage sites up in the hills. He was doing a little sabotage by pulling coils and other things off the engines. Ms. Chan here was smart, jumped in her Jeep and was gone like a shot. But that meant she left the long-haired geek behind. We had a little fun with him and sent him on his way. He got the message. He blew town." He turned his eyes on Vhanna again and this time his eyes were cold and hard. "Should have stayed, too. We could have shown you a real time."

"That's enough Dauphin." I was fighting to control both my temper and confusion. Vhanna and the man in the Polaroid, the American who had known Ira, sabotaging logging equipment up in the hills? It made no sense, but Vhanna wasn't denying it either. Whatever that was all about, however, had no relevance to the dynamite. For now, finding out about that was all that mattered. "Dynamite, Dauphin. Cartons and cartons of the stuff. All with your user number on it. How did it get there?"

"Fuck you," he said, but his voice was heavy rather than angry or threatening now. It almost seemed like his shoulders had slumped and the air had gone out of him. The transformation from threatening bully to this deflated blow-up doll was startling. Even more surprising was that I couldn't sense what I had said to bring the change about.

"The dynamite?" I said more softly than before.

"Shit. Fucking shit." He lowered his foot from the desk and sat up straight, leaning across it, elbows resting on the paper, suddenly earnest eyes fixed on mine. His big open palms gestured in a shrug toward the papers on the desk before him. "See these. Bills. More fucking bills everyday. It never quits. A new transmission for a skidder runs into the hundreds, brake drum for a logging truck is as dear as a Robson Street penthouse whore. The bills just don't stop. But the timber's gone. Gone until we can get into Clayoquot. And when we go in there fucks like her and that Starling will be doing what damage they can." He glared at Vhanna, but I thumped the palm of my hand lightly on the desk and his attention swerved back my way. With that, the fight that had started to rise in him deflated again. "I gotta make ends meet. Gotta come up with ways to keep the debt collectors and the banks off my back. Only language they speak is dollars, Coroner. Give them some money and they'll back off for awhile, give you room to breathe."

"You're telling me you sold the dynamite?"

"Give the man a cigar."

"Who to?"

Dauphin gave me an ironic smirk. "You really sure you want to know, Coroner?" I nodded. He shrugged. "I sold it to Ira Connaught. Twenty thousand dollars worth. Delivered it to a beach in Nootka Sound. He was waiting there for it."

"When?"

"Last fall. Just before winter rains set in. He paid in cash. American dollars to be exact. Old currency, no matching serial numbers. The money paid off a lot of outstanding bills. Wouldn't have made it to now without it."

"Tell me how it worked," I said.

It was a bizarre tale. To believe Dauphin I had to accept that Ira somehow learned of the logger's financial troubles and approached him with an offer of cash for explosives. Despite the fact that Ira and Dauphin were enemies in the battle over the future of the forests, Dauphin decided to sell him the dynamite. He had some on hand and purchased more in three batches, jigging up phony work orders from the forestry corporations for road work to justify the need for the purchases. Dauphin Logging was a big company so although large purchases like these were rare they were not altogether unheard of. The explosives were transferred to Ira in the fall and Dauphin got his money. He had no idea what Ira intended to do with the dynamite and had not heard from the Sunshine Warrior again. He also neither knew nor cared where a chronically unemployed and basically penniless Ira had come up with so much money.

"Couldn't believe it when the Greer boys came and told me they found him dangling from a tree up in the bush," he said at the end. "Real fucking coincidence." Even as he finished, Dauphin looked like he regretted the last words.

"Why a coincidence?"

Dauphin paused a long time, eyes shifting about the room. Finally he sighed. "It was the Greer boys who made the delivery for me. They picked up the explosives, too."

"So if something went wrong you could pretend you didn't know anything about the deal?"

"Something like that," Dauphin replied with a smirk. "Might still work out that way."

"But you've told me."

"So?" Dauphin was looking smug in a way now that was again threatening.

"I'll set the police straight if you lie to them."

This time his grin was like a tiger's before it leaps on the back of its prey. "Don't think so, Coroner. Just realized the only witness you got is Ms. Chan and I don't think she's gonna want to talk about any of this. Are you, doll?"

"I'll be in the car, Elias," Vhanna said softly and walked out of the room before I could say anything.

"Got any more questions, Mr. Coroner, or would you like to just fuck off now."

I spun back on Dauphin. "What are you trying to pull, Dauphin?"

The big man laughed, a bellowing guffaw. "Not trying, Coroner. It's already pulled." He gestured to the door. "Go run along now. She'll explain it to you." The grin dropped and the eyes turned mean. "Lot of the boys out there know what she was doing up there with the equipment. Don't think they'll be too happy about her being here and just letting her drive off. Besides she's damned pretty for a slant-eye."

I started to say something, but the urgency of fear made me walk quickly out of the office instead. There would be time enough later to sort Dauphin out, I thought.

Outside, I found Vhanna standing beside the driver's door of the Miata. In a circle around her stood four beefy men. Rick and Chuck Greer were among them. Obviously, they had returned from their alleged hunting trip up into the mountains. One of them, either Rick or Chuck, was suggesting Vhanna go into the workshed with them. As he talked he passed a socket wrench back and forth from one hand to the other. Vhanna had her sunglasses on and her face was unreadable but I could see the warning in how her feet were poised and the way her hands were ever so slightly tensed and hanging freely at her hips. She looked like a cobra in that moment just before it uncoils in a lightning swift deadly strike. If one of the men moved any closer all hell was going to break loose. Even with Vhanna's Tai Chi combat skills there were four of them and only two of us. Not odds I much favoured.

"Mr. Dauphin said I might find you boys out here," I called out in a hole-hearty-fine-fellow-well-met voice as I came off the step and waded through the line of men to get beside Vhanna. "Said he wants you inside right now to draw up a deposition on the dynamite purchase and delivery you made last spring. Seems there might be some problem with it." The two Greers both glanced at each other in confusion and then back to me suspiciously before looking at the open doorway of Dauphin's office. While this was going on I opened the driver's door and motioned for Vhanna to get in. She slipped in with the deft speed of a jewel thief and the engine started with a whir. Shutting the door on her, I leaned toward the group of men and whispered softly so they had to bend over to hear me. "Just between me and you, boys, looks like you might be in deep shit. But Mr. Dauphin will tell you all more."

One Greer nudged the other and they headed for the office as fast as their long legs could carry them. Now there were only two of the others left, Vhanna was in the car, and I was between them and her. They glanced at each other, then at me. I shrugged to let them know it was their choice. The bigger of the two elbowed the other and jerked his head toward the workshed. Muttering obscenities back and forth between them, the two men sauntered off as cool as they could, so I'd know it was their decision and that I hadn't bested them. I hurried around to the other side of the car and climbed into the convertible's passenger seat without opening the door. "Get us out of

here and then we need to have a talk." I looked
straight ahead as we drove over the rutts and left the
workyard of Dauphin Logging Company.

"Elias," Vhanna said as the car passed through
the gates.

"No. Not now," I answered more sharply than
I meant to. In silence we drove north out of the
town and back onto the highway toward Pacific
Rim National Park.

Chapter Fifteen

Vhanna wheeled the Miata into the beach's parking lot. In silence, we hiked down to the sandy shore. The mid-afternoon sun was warm and the sky a brilliant aqua dotted with the sharp white of circling gulls. With the tourist season not yet underway there were few people around. From his perch atop the wind-twisted branches of an old hemlock a solitary bald eagle glowered down upon us with an implacable eye. The eagle's presence reminded me of Dauphin. My anger at the man burned with an almost white heat.

I had rolled the sleeves of my denim shirt up and left the Filson hat tucked behind the passenger seat. Slipping off her Doc Martens and white socks, Vhanna followed me down the length of broad white sand. She held the shoes with her right hand so they were between us. Walking with my hands plunged into my jeans pockets, I didn't look directly at her until we were well down the beach.

"Tell me about Starling," I said finally.

We covered several more feet before Vhanna answered and when she did her voice was almost lost to the breeze and rolling of the breakers striking the beach. "It was after Merriam died. A couple months later. Ira introduced us. We talked and there was something about — I can't explain," she said tightly.

"Try." We stopped. Faced each other. The few metres separating us seemed to have expanded into an uncrossable gulf. I wanted to touch her, to say that none of what Dauphin hinted at mattered, that only we mattered and nothing else. But I knew, too, this wasn't the case. Everything about Starling and his relationship with Vhanna mattered.

Vhanna regarded me icily for a moment. Then she tugged the sunglasses from her breast pocket and put them on, concealing her eyes. "When Merriam died," she said in a low monotone, "everything got confused. I...I didn't know what I felt. And, then, Starling came along. We could talk." She placed a hand on my arm. "Not about Merriam or us, but about other things. About Artemis Adventures, the country, the environment. Anything we wanted to discuss. When we were talking I didn't have to think about Merriam, didn't —" She shrugged, stopped. Her fingers fell from my arm and her thumb hooked into a belt loop on her jeans.

"And what Dauphin said?" My voice sounded strangely thick to my ears, clotted so that the words escaped as a harsh whisper.

"One day we went up into the hills for a drive. Starling said he wanted to show me something special. He directed me to where there was some logging equipment stored. It wasn't guarded at all. Probably because it was parked well, down a really rough logging road, not much more than a skidder track through the brush. Starling started vandalizing the equipment." Vhanna began walking again, her pace fast, hands kept tight to her body. I matched her pace. "He started getting really wild. Tearing things off the engines. He was running from one vehicle to another and back again, jumping up into the seats and crawling around on the engine cowlings. I stayed by the Jeep. I kept telling him to stop it and get away from the machinery."

She stopped and turned back to face me. Vhanna pulled the sunglasses from her eyes to meet mine. "That's when Dauphin and the Greers showed up. They were in a four-wheel drive pick-up. They must have seen Starling on the equipment because they roared right past the Jeep up to where he was. Starling jumped off a skidder and started to run by the truck toward where I was but Dauphin jumped out and hit him with something. I think it was a tire iron. He went down hard, face first and didn't move. Then Dauphin and the other two men started coming toward me. They were all carrying tire irons. Dauphin was laughing and calling to me."

As she talked, Vhanna's voice had become more distant, as if she were looking down a tunnel that stretched back into a past much more distant than anything experienced by her here on Vancouver Island. "I just drove off. They ran and tried to cut me off but I gunned the engine and Dauphin had to jump to get out of the way. I saw him roll through the dirt just clear of the front fender. One of the others threw the pipe he had and it smashed the windshield on the passenger's side. I got out of there."

I remembered the smashed windshield. At the time Vhanna had said a rock thrown by a truck had broken it. "What about Starling?"

"They worked him over pretty badly and left him there. After I got away, I circled back in the Jeep using other roads to get in. Just before nightfall I found him. He had several cracked ribs and a lot of bruises, a couple of teeth knocked out. I brought him out to the hospital. He made me drop him at the emergency ward entrance and went in by himself. He didn't want me involved further." Vhanna turned toward the ocean, ran a hand tightly through her hair. "I didn't want to be involved further, either."

"He explained his injuries as being from an accident or a fall or something?" I asked. Vhanna nodded. "And you never reported Dauphin's assault on him because that would have implicated you both in the sabotaging of the equipment." Again she nodded. "After Starling recovered, he left town?"

"Yes. A couple weeks later."

"Where did he go?"

Vhanna shrugged. "I don't know. Back to the States, I think. He hoped to link up with the Earth First people down there. Get into the thick of the eco-war."

"More terrorism?"

"It's what he thought we had to do. The only way to stop the corporations and governments destroying us all for short-term economic gain was to fight back. He was insistent about that — about how this was the new war."

I grimaced at the dogma of the words. "And you?"

"I don't know, Elias. Do you?"

It was my turn to shrug. "I don't see violence as the answer. Usually the wrong people end up getting hurt." I thought of Tassina and Eleni. Had either deserved to die? Was that what they were? Casualties in the eco-war? "There's one thing I don't understand." There was more than one thing, but this was the most puzzling part. "Why did Dauphin think that what happened back then would preclude me from telling the police about his selling the explosives to Ira?"

Vhanna pursed her lips and when she looked at me her face was haunted, her skin pale. "You report him and he'll tell the police I was involved in the vandalism."

"But he can't prove it."

She gave me a small smile of patient indulgence. "Would it matter? I'd still be questioned by Danchuk. Word would get out. My reputation would be smeared. The reputation of Artemis rests on my integrity, my ability to take people close to danger and bring them back again safely. Would anyone believe I could do that after my name was linked with something like eco-terrorism? Would I be able to get insurance? Even the environmental movement would turn against me and my company. It could put me out of business. Dauphin realizes that."

And with the Greers acting as supportive witnesses, Dauphin would be believed enough to do the damage. Certainly Danchuk would give him a forum within which to make his accusations. Dauphin couldn't explain away his selling explosives illegally but he would do his best to take Vhanna down with him. The man was shrewd. He had understood intuitively that I wouldn't allow that to happen. So the secret of his dynamite sale was safe — for the moment. By the time the police in Gold River found the cabin and traced the rotting cartons back to him, Dauphin would have jigged up some paper trail lie or cooked up an alibi. Perhaps the Greers would be set up to take the fall for him. Whatever happened there was a good chance Dauphin would elude prosecution.

"I need to think," I said. Without waiting for an answer, I walked down the beach alone.

My pace was fast, driven by confusion, despair, and anger. I felt betrayed. While I had been struggling with guilt and sorrow over Merriam's death, Vhanna had been seeing Starling, talking and laughing, driving through the forests together on their way to trash logging equipment. I remembered those weeks after Merriam's death all too well. Everything had been chaos. I was torn with guilt, with the sense that somehow I had driven Merriam to suicide. In my mind it was often my finger and not Merriam's that pulled the trigger of the shotgun that night. I had needed Vhanna desperately but at the same time had not been able to go to her. I could not bear to be with her. Had it been our relationship that had finally caused Merriam to pass through the veil between her tentative hold on sanity so that she chose to plunge into the darkness of death?

Vhanna had not come to me, either, and I had read in that act the message that she could not deal with my sorrow and was unable to help me. Perhaps my hope that she loved me was illusory, foolish. Why should she love a remittance man? Vhanna was full of vital life, questing for experience. Increasingly, I seemed to exist in stasis, a vacuum in which time passed but was of little importance. Fergus and I hunted. I read my father's books and listened to my music. To create the impression of usefulness I invested small amounts of my ever-growing remittance-generated wealth into the businesses of my friends. But that wasn't a vocation or a reason for being. I was a sham, a man without purpose, just as the remittance men of old had been without purpose, just as my father's life ultimately had no motive or reason. Surely, I thought, Vhanna must realize these things and want nothing more to do with me?

A large drift log tossed upon the beach during winter storms drew my eye. I walked over and leaned my back against its smooth washed and sun-dried wood. The ocean surf rolled in slowly, breakers tumbling into the sand with low booming rumbles. Gulls soared and swooped above the water, shorebirds skittered on long legs across the sand. Far down the beach, Vhanna walked in the opposite direction. She looked small, fragile.

For the first time since Merriam's death I realized how self-indulgent I had been during that time. It had never occurred to me that Vhanna, too, might have been confused. She, too, might have been touched by the cold hand of guilt. Maybe she hadn't sensed my need for her and had interpreted my withdrawal as rejection. Could she not have thought that I blamed her for our relationship and for the possibility that this had contributed to Merriam's decision to take her own life?

Was I not doing the same thing now? She had met Starling and found someone there who she could talk with about things that did not concern responsibility for a suicide. With him, Vhanna had not had to dwell on pain and guilt. Perhaps she found with Starling a means to set aside her own feelings of guilt or self-loathing. She had been the lover of the husband of a woman who had killed herself. How natural that she should feel guilty and in some way responsible.

I had never considered this possibility. Instead, I had withdrawn, making no effort to contact her. I had huddled down within myself and dwelled on my grief and my guilt, giving no consideration to her feelings and grief. I had been a fool. And now I was compounding that act by appearing to reject Vhanna yet again for finding companionship with another man.

Had they been lovers? Did it matter? Vhanna was her own person. If there was anything I was certain of it was that I didn't wish to own anyone else, or to be similarly owned by them. I would hope that they would not deliberately set out to cause me harm or hurt and I would do the same by them. Beyond this, there should be no further restraints or prohibitions on behaviour and so there could be no guarantees. I had lived in a marriage in which love and romance had been subjugated beneath a blanket of expectations and restraints. My heart had slowly grown cold and hardened during my life with Merriam. I wanted nothing to do with that kind of relationship again, even if that meant I should never again know the security of an apparently permanent relationship.

Such appearances are false anyway. Relationships evolve and mutate, transform to keep pace with our own growth. What I sought now was a relationship that acknowledged this fact. With Vhanna I had known great disruption of the heart, had longed for her when we were apart, grieved the distance between us when we quarreled; but through all of that I had known love that was as intense as it was liberating and uncertain. Yes, I feared Vhanna's feelings were not of as deep a vein as my own, that she was more ambivalent about our relationship and love. There was that risk, perhaps some day I would lose her to Starling, some other man, or a cause I could not comprehend. Until that day came, though, I was determined to keep our relationship alive and burning bright with a vital flame.

Down the beach, Vhanna was now a mere speck of darkness against the whiteness of the sand. I started after her, walking quickly. There was much to talk about, much to make her understand.

As I closed on her, I allowed my thoughts to stray to the investigation into Ira's death and the explosives I was convinced had been used by someone to kill Tassina and Eleni Mavrikos. I knew now where the explosives came from, knew from Dauphin's confession that there must still be many more unaccounted cartons of dynamite that had been removed from the cabin. But it was a closed circle. The explosives led to Dauphin and Dauphin led back to Ira who had been murdered in a manner that simulated a suicide. There was no reason to believe anyone else was involved. And there seemed little sense to the theory that Dauphin was guilty of killing Ira and then blowing up Tassina and Eleni. Perhaps he had motivation to kill Ira, perhaps the Sunshine Warrior had threatened to expose him or in some other way posed a threat. But Tassina? What threat could she have been to Dauphin? They had, however, known each other and Dauphin had been on the wharf the night Tassina and Eleni died. And, of course, it appeared Tassina might have used the boat to transport Ira and his explosives somewhere. But where? Did Dauphin know she had done this?

The more I thought about, it the more I could imagine Dauphin and the Greers killing if it was to their advantage. They were brutal, violent men. Dauphin was also a desperate man trying to keep a sinking business afloat. Who knew what crimes the combination of desperation and his own violent nature might lead him to commit. Yes, there was a good chance that the road leading to Dauphin was in fact leading to the final destination. If Dauphin was the killer, then what should I do about it? I had no proof that would stand up. To report his confession of selling the explosives illegally would result in Vhanna being compromised for the vandalization of the logging equipment and might lead to the dire consequences for her business that she had mentioned. I couldn't do that to her. Dauphin had understood this in the way that bullies so often anticipate another person's Achilles Heel. And in the end, my knowledge wasn't worth anything. In no way did it prove Dauphin a killer — if indeed he was.

I found Vhanna sitting on a log at the head of the trail that ran up to the parking lot. She was looking out at the sea, her sunglasses masking the expression on her face. I walked up and carefully removed the glasses so I could see her eyes. "I love you," I told her. "And I'm sorry for how I behaved after Merriam died. I was selfish. I know you don't like to talk about the past or worry the future, so I'll just say that you are the most important person in my life and I'm grateful that you are here."

Vhanna looked away from me and her eyes blinked rapidly for a few seconds. When she turned back there was a small smile tracing around on her lips. She took my hand in hers and squeezed it, I stepped forward and drew her against me, felt her face press against my chest and her arms tighten around my back. We stayed like that for a long time — until eventually she slowly pushed away from me. When Vhanna's eyes met mine they were clear and bright. "We'll get him, Elias. We will."

"You think it was Dauphin?"

Vhanna nodded. "Who else could it be," she said with assurance.

Who else indeed? I thought and wondered why I still felt a shadow of doubt.

Chapter Sixteen

I picked up Fergus and the Rover at Vhanna's place and drove into town. Vhanna needed to get ready for the banquet for Senator Sloan. We agreed she would drop by my place in a couple of hours so we could attend the affair together. I hardly felt like a banquet, especially one at which Danchuk would be in attendance, undoubtedly decked out in the ghastly splendour of his scarlet serge Mountie dress uniform. This was no time to be banqueting. There was work to do, answers to find; answers that certainly were not to be uncovered while sitting around a table in the community hall. How many speeches must be endured before the plates of dry chicken breast covered in tasteless sauce and accompanied by broccoli and bland, overcooked rice were brought around? The speeches would be a mishmash of platitudes, as every side of the Clayoquot logging controversy was expressed in polite style. This banquet after all was being hosted by the local Chamber of Commerce, which was composed of business people ranging from radical environmentalists to radical pro-logging supporters. Each would have to be allowed some chance to fulminate from the podium. Either restraint would be maintained throughout or the whole thing might degenerate into a brawl.

Faced with such a hideous vision, I had tried convincing Vhanna that a quiet evening meal at my place with candlelight and wine would be far more enjoyable. She countered that, while this would certainly be preferable, such a course of action was not socially responsible or acceptable. As a member of the business community who supported a ban on further logging in Clayoquot, she reminded me, Vhanna had to attend to show the senator that the environmental position met with strong business support. More compellingly, she was going to be the man's guide around the Sound the following day, so they should meet. Also, of course, a few photo opportunities emerge if the media also attended the banquet frolics. Glumly, I acquiesced and agreed to accompany her. But I did elicit her promise to slip out a back door with me the moment the meal and speeches ended.

The sun was starting to set as I passed Father Welch's Volvo parked alongside the local fitness centre. Fergus scowled and grumbled under his breath at me as I parallel parked behind it in a spot that caught the shade of a tree. "I know you're hungry. Won't be long," I said, banging the door shut and donning my hat. Glancing over my shoulder I saw Fergus look sadly in my direction for only a moment before slumping down, below the window level, to curl up on the seat. These past couple of days had been exhausting for the poor fellow. I determined to make it up to him as soon as I could by taking him for a long day's walk in the woods, or even just spending a day at home with a good book and some music. That would be a fine idea for both of us. Our lifestyle was usually much less frenetic than this.

To one side of the club entrance was a long counter set close to a wall full of shelves containing various muscle building supplements that came in jars, huge plastic containers or freeze-dried packages. Behind the counter a young woman with blonde hair tied back in a cheerleader style ponytail wore a broad toothy smile, a tracksuit and a nametag that read "Stacy." The rest of the room was full of cardio-exercise machines which, at this time of day, were mostly unused. Yet an equal number of male and female diehards of varying ages were striding along on treadmills, stairclimbing, cycling, cross country skiing or rowing with sweaty intent. I told Stacy I was just visiting a friend, signed the guest book to keep her smile in place, and ascended the stairs to the weight room.

The pounding beat of one of the current teenage dance divas washed in waves through the long narrow room that was cluttered with a bewildering array of machines possessing levers and bars that could be pulled this way and that. Before a row of benches stood dozens of one and two-handed barbell weights. I looked around the room, searching for Father Welch, and saw what might be his figure seemingly attached to a diabolical torture device that fit padded steel braces on his shoulders that linked to a bar adorned with a series of large circular weights. I counted five on each side of the bar. The figure's feet were braced against a wide steel plate, hands gripped thin upright handles set to either side of the padded braces pushing down on the shoulders, and the entire device was tilted on a forty-five degree angle. What I took to be Father Welch was moving the massive weights on his shoulders along slides built into the frame that encased the entire device from a sitting position to full body extension and then slowly lowering himself back again to a sitting position. Up, down, up, down. This went on for the entire time it took me to walk from the entrance to the far corner of the room where the machine stood.

On the way over, I passed two teenage Native boys and a girl from Opitsaht, which is across the inlet. They all wore black muscle shirts, nylon pants, and runners with the laces undone. The girl had dyed her hair red and a white Molson Canadian ball cap was twisted so the bill stuck out sideways from her head. All three were doing single-handed arm curls with dumbbells that looked too heavy for their respective sizes. I knew the girl and one of the boys to be brother and sister; the other was the girl's boyfriend. They sometimes stayed at my nextdoor neighbour's rather than taking the school water taxi back to Opitsaht. They were good kids but little interested in school, far too interested in partying and the wonders of sex. We exchanged greetings as I walked past with the kids not breaking their rhythm for a second.

The apparition in the torture device was indeed Father Welch. A Father Welch with legs that shivered and spasmed with each upward and downward motion of the massive weights. His face was a fine ruby red and there was a possibility his eyes were going to pop from the sockets if he persisted in this self-torment. Each of the large round weights on the outer edge of the posts read forty-five pounds. Quick arithmetic told me that added up to two hundred and twenty-five pounds a side or "45 lbs." in total. Plus he was hefting his own substantial weight up and down with each movement. I figured Father Welch probably weighed in at about two hundred and forty pounds of bulging muscles and all-too-little supporting fat.

"Ever hear of the word hernia, Father?" I said loudly enough to be heard over the upward crescendo of the teen diva who seemed to be entering into some form of delirium about how everything was all right and okay and she would carry on anyway. It seemed a good motto by me, but I wished she could pursue this goal a bit more quietly. Father Welch glanced my way once with swelling eyes and then, staring back at the ceiling, continued as he had been for several more up and down pumping actions. Finally, he pulled the levers in so they snapped into brackets fitted next to the slides. This allowed him to remove his shoulders from under the pads without having the massive weights crash down on his back to cause permanent spinal damage. When he stood up a little of the red colour drained away from his face. He wore black shorts that hung loosely around his heavy legs and a red muscle shirt faded almost white-pink and pocked with holes presumably rotted in by sweat. He scoured his face and grey hair with a large white cotton towel before flipping it over his shoulder.

"You're at an age where you should be taking better care of yourself. Keeping the muscles strong and limber," he said with the mock tone that an aerobic talk show host or evangelical fitness guru might adopt. "Two workouts a week. One focused on the upper body, the other on legs and back. A routine for the abs each time and twenty minutes cardio downstairs would make you a new man. Improve your outlook on life, too. Make a better person out of you." He pointed at the machine. "This is a great one, an Apex Hack Squat. Want to see what you can lift?"

Ignoring the challenge in his voice I politely declined, but the Father was barely listening now. His eyes were fixed on something across the room. "Tanya, don't curve your spine like that. You'll hurt your back," he shouted. I saw that Tanya, the Native girl, now had the backs of her legs hooked against a padded brace, stomach resting on another padded brace set on a stand before the one for the legs and dangling with her head down toward the floor. Arms crossed over her chest she then snapped her torso up so it was on a straight line with her braced hips and stomach and then slowly lowered herself back down. This time her back stayed straight and Father Welch called his approval and then grinned at me from under his moustache. "Nothing like a little exercise to keep teen hormones from starting to rage out of control." Father Welch's smile faded and he looked serious. "Too many bloody funerals, Elias. Too many."

I nodded. "You'll be doing them all?"

"Yes, Vlassis came to see me this afternoon. He's taking it very badly. Can't say I blame him, either. Are there any answers, Elias? It's hard comfort you can offer a man when his daughter and granddaughter are dead and no true cause is known."

"Sorry, Allan. Nothing's certain yet. It's still being investigated." I hesitated, wondering how to continue. "Allan I need to ask you something."

"So ask."

"Ira Connaught. Did you hear his confession?"

Father Welch looked away, walked to where the free weights stood in their racks, lifted one absently in a large paw and started doing bicep curls. The weight had a little decal with the number "55" on it, presumably its weight. "Elias. That is between Ira and me."

"I understand, Allan, I do. But it looks like Ira was involved in something, something that was heading toward violence. Tassina, Eleni, Ira, what happened to them all is interrelated somehow but I can't fit the pieces together to make sense of it. Did he tell you anything that would help?" I held up my hand to signal him to silence. "It isn't over yet. Unless we find some answers soon I think more people are going to die. If you know something, if he told you anything at all that might help find out what's happening, you have to tell me."

"No, Elias, I don't have to tell you anything." The priest's voice was flat and hard. He kept pumping the weight, eyes fixed hard on me. "Confession is inviolate. You could get a court order and I wouldn't tell you what a man said in the confessional. You know better than that."

"Damn it, Allan." The kids down the way all turned, expressions growing curious and attentive. I lowered my voice to a whisper. "You were right, Allan. Elias didn't commit suicide. He was murdered. I'm sure of it. And I'm also sure that Tassina and Eleni were murdered as well. But I don't know why or by whom. Anything you can tell me about what Ira was doing or thinking at the time might help."

Father Welch lowered the weight and dropped it back on the rack as he considered this for a moment. "You're asking me a simple question as to the state of mind of a parish member. Drawing upon my sense of Ira, from the things we discussed outside the confessional, I would have to say that Ira Connaught was troubled, worried about something that he had become involved in and now had second thoughts over. I think he was seeking to stop whatever it was that he had got mixed up in."

"If he told you what that was in confession would you tell me?"

"No, Elias, I wouldn't. I couldn't. It would be wrong."

"And if more deaths are the result of silence?"

Father Welch's big hand closed powerfully on my wrist; a vice of pressure that closed just to the point before pain began. "I've told you what I know, Elias. And I'm very close to committing a grievous sin in doing that. Understand that?"

I thought about it for a moment. "I understand, Allan. And I appreciate it." I touched the brim of my hat with a finger and said good-bye.

"Go with God, my son," Father Welch said with usual irreverence.

"Always, Father," I replied, as always.

"Reprobate," he said to finish the ritual between us and turned toward where Tanya was starting to imperil her back again as she snapped up in too much of a curve from her dangling position. I descended the stairs, waved to the still smiling cheerleader behind the counter, and fled the shrill of teen divas, the heavy panting of people running nowhere on treadmills, and a priest. A priest who was my friend and who looked bizarrely like a World Wrestling Federation villain but who would not disclose the secrets of a murder victim gleaned in the confessional.

The fire investigation team had surrounded the wreckage of the Mavrikos boat with various inflatable floats to keep it from settling under the water. Yellow police barrier tape ran along the side of the wharf to enclose both the burned hull and Ira's listing boat. The tape warned everyone to not cross over it. I wondered if

Danchuk's stringing of the tape to encompass Ira's home meant he was starting to seriously consider the autopsy evidence suggesting the Sunshine Warrior had been murdered. Or was he just covering the bases by trying to look diligent.

I stepped over the tape and boarded Ira's boat. When Danchuk and I had searched the boat earlier we hadn't known about stolen dynamite and had no evidence proving Ira's death a murder. Perhaps another search would turn up some fresh clues and I wasn't going to waste time trying to get Danchuk's approval or cooperation.

For the next 30 minutes I combed the drawers and cupboards of Ira's rat's nest of a home and found nothing of value. There were a couple large manila envelopes jammed with more Polaroids taken during the hot Clayoquot summer of demonstrations, including a couple of the Midnight Oil concert held at the infamous Black Hole clear-cut near the logging access road into the area. Vhanna's back was recognizable in one of the frames and the dark-haired bulk of the man next to her might have been that of Barry Starling. Other photos showed some of the arrests of protesters at the blockade that had tried each morning of that summer to stop the logging crews going into Clayoquot to do their work.

I sorted through the photos at the galley table, spreading them out over all the old newspapers that cluttered its top. Although I examined each carefully they offered up nothing but a jumbled chronicle of demonstrations and blockades. Finally I returned the Polaroids to their envelopes and stuffed the bundle back in the cupboard where I had found them. It looked like it was time to go and I had found nothing worthwhile. One last time, I ran my eyes over the interior of the boat, seeking signs of a hidden cupboard, a corner that I had neglected to inspect. My eyes grazed over the newspapers, passed on, and then shifted back. Excited now, I dug into the papers, shifting from one to the other. Working quickly, I sorted them by date running from oldest to most recent. Then I started going through them. The old stories from the summer about the protesters and the arrests I set aside. Instead I focused on the stories written since things on the demonstration front had quieted down.

The first of these stories was a *Victoria Times-Colonist* front section. On page six was a small story about Senator Sloan's anticipated visit to Tofino. It was dated August 15. The next date was August 22 and again there was a story about Senator Jack Sloan's investigation trip to Clayoquot. On August 24, Ira had clipped a story from the *Province* that had a logging company spokesman accusing Sloan of being an anti-logger, pro-environmentalist coming to stir up world opinion against the provincial government's decision to permit some of Clayoquot to be logged. A September 12 story from *The New York Times* contained a quote from Sloan saying he was going to Canada on a fact-finding mission and the proposed logging of Clayoquot was an international issue now and so his trip was appropriate and proper, despite counter-claims by the British Columbia government.

Furtively, I moved from one paper to another. All the clippings, all the papers from the summer to the most recent contained a story on Sloan's planned visit. The final story was from a recent *Times-Colonist*. In the copy was the precise date and expected itinerary of Sloan's visit. This night's banquet was mentioned and his subsequent plans to fly into Clayoquot by helicopter and tour both logged and natural sites of the forest. Again, the story contained a number of quotes from pro-loggers protesting his planned visit and from environmentalists welcoming his arrival. The story had been published the day before Ira's body was found.

Setting the paper down, I stared out the small window at the hills beyond the inlet. The light was fading rapidly from the sky. Pieces clunked together in my mind, but the jigsaw puzzle image they constructed was jumbled and confused. There was a screaming lack of logic to the whole thing. I decided that all I could do was brood on the details more; perhaps, if I thought about it long enough, a logical pattern would emerge.

Vhanna would soon be at the house waiting for me and Fergus had yet to be fed. I spread the papers out on the table so they looked untidy again. Although, as the coroner working the case, I had the authority to conduct my own investigation I rather doubted the rules allowed me to search property without a police officer in tow. It was best, then, to leave things more or less as Danchuk had last seen them. Taking one last glance around to ensure that there were no glaring signs of my intrusion I walked out into the falling dusk.

When I opened the cabin door, Fergus proceeded with haste and determination to his bowls. Vigorously he lapped down the stale water there and then looked at me in silent accusation. I apologized for neglecting his needs and ran some fresh water into his bowl. He gulped this down noisily, while I dug out his dry food and poured a heaping serving into the food bowl. I added some quickly cubed cheddar cheese over the top even though the custom is that he only gets this for lunch. It occurred to me then that Fergus had gone without lunch. For that matter so had I. After slicing myself a couple of thick chunks of cheese and opening a bottle of pale ale, I noticed the light on my answering machine flickering incessantly.

Vhanna had bullied me into buying the machine when she spent a weekend in Skagway trying to phone me and never getting an answer. She had just finished a white-water rafting trip down some hitherto barely traversed Alaskan river and thought I might like to fly up and spend a few days hiking with her in the mountains. It was a good idea and I would have gone — had she been able to contact me. Unfortunately, that weekend, Fergus and I had gone camping as part of a failed grouse hunt.

As I punched buttons that made the tape in the machine run this way and that, in what seemed a baffling sequence of movements, I thought about how Vhanna and I really should spend more time together by getting away on trips. Perhaps I'd raise the idea with her after this dreadful banquet was over.

A deeply resonating bass voice boomed out of the machine at me. "McCann, this is Dr. Harris. Call me at my home number. It's imperative we talk." Harris provided his number.

"Shit." Fergus glanced up from his food and his head cocked. "Danchuk, you little prick," I muttered as I used the stub of a pencil to scratch the number down on a slip of paper. It was obvious what was going on. Danchuk had phoned Carl Harris, the regional coroner and my superior, and complained that I was exceeding my authority.

I dialed Harris's Nanaimo home number and listened to a long voice mail recording procedure which instructed me to push the three button of my touch-tone phone if the matter was urgent. Although tempted to dodge him by leaving a message on the non-urgent variety I pushed the appropriate button and in seconds Harris's voice was thundering down the line at me. There were no pleasantries. "McCann I'm damned tempted to suspend you and ask the provincial coroner to dismiss you. What the hell are you playing at?"

There was no use telling Harris that Danchuk wasn't doing his job and that I suspected there might be more killings unless some answers were found quickly. "It's my job to determine cause of death," I said. "I've been investigating the circumstances surrounding the three deaths here in an attempt to get all the facts relating to that cause so I can come to a logical and full conclusion as to the cause of death in each incident. For some reason that seems to be upsetting Sergeant Danchuk."

Harris hadn't mentioned that the complaints were from Danchuk but I figured it was time to take the gloves off on that front. In the end, did I really care if I was fired as coroner? It wasn't a job I had particularly wanted. In fact, I didn't really want any kind of job. I was a remittance man after all and had no need of work, nor a desire to do good works of any kind.

"It isn't just Sergeant Danchuk, McCann. I've had complaints from a Mr. Dauphin and a Mr. Rafferty."

Rafferty? Why would Rafferty complain? I asked Harris what the two complaints were about. Dauphin, typically, reported that I had been down to his office harassing him and asking leading questions. Rafferty's complaint was more interesting. He had told Harris about my visit to the Sunshine Warriors' clubhouse and how Tassina had been with me. Rafferty had told Harris that he felt I was too close to the various people who died in Tofino these past two days to be objective and suggested another coroner should be put on the case. "I think he's probably right, don't you?"

I told Harris I disagreed completely. Yes, I had known Tassina, but there were few people in Tofino I didn't know. The same was true for anyone who would be appointed coroner. I argued that all small towns suffered from this problem.

Harris cut me off in mid-sentence. "McCann, it's like this. You are to cease further investigation into this matter that in anyway strays from your legal duty to determine cause of death. That does not extend to why or who caused the death. Those are police matters. Your concern is cause of death and cause of death only. I have Doctor Tully's preliminary report where he speculates that Connaught may have been strangled into unconsciousness and then hanged by the perpetrator. That's a sufficient preliminary cause of death, so there is no need to continue further investigation into that case. Doctor Tully and Sergeant Danchuk have also provided me with information that says Tassina and Eleni Mavrikos died when the boat they were on was the subject of an explosion and subsequent fire. The two died of injuries resulting from that explosion and fire sequence. That, too, is a sufficient preliminary finding of cause of death. Further investigation is up to the police in both cases. You will conduct no — hear me — no further investigations into either incident without the presence and cooperation of the local police. If you do, McCann, I'll suspend you so fast you won't know what hit you. Understand?"

I told him I understood perfectly.

"Good. I think that's all that needs to be said, right?"

I agreed that nothing further needed to be said and we both rang off. "I understand," I mumbled as I went upstairs to dress for the banquet, "but I didn't agree to stop." I would just have to proceed more carefully.

Chapter Seventeen

I had only just finished changing when Vhanna arrived. We both made brief apologies to Fergus, who turned his back upon us completely and crawled wearily up on a corner of the couch. I left a couple of lights on in the living room for him, turned on the yard light, and we departed. Vhanna wore a natural white cotton button-up shirt with large safari-style pockets, a short straight black skirt, black flat-soled dance-style shoes and dangly earrings that I had given her. They were Kwakiutl engravings of eagle spirits on a flat, irregularly shaped silver disk. Holding back her hair on either side were matching eagle spirit silver berets that had been another gift. The silver pieces glistened in the night and seemed to accentuate the slenderness of her body and the dark flash of her eyes. "You look wonderful," I said. "Sure you don't want to stay home and spend the evening waltzing to the new Tish Hinojosa CD — romance to a little Tex-Mex."

She laughed and pointed at the Rover. "Onward and upward, Elias. You should get out more. You're in danger of becoming a hermit. What do you do when I'm away?"

"Wait for you," I said more seriously than the mood called for.

Vhanna shot a tight look my way but then her face softened into a glimmer of teeth. She squeezed my hand. "You're impossible." I nodded. Her arms went around my neck and she tugged my face down to her level. Standing in the small yellow pool beneath the yard lamp we kissed. Vhanna felt small and delicate. As always, I resisted the urge to squeeze her as tightly as I wished to, fearful of causing some injury. After a long time Vhanna leaned back, her eyes meeting mine and smiled. "Should we go?"

I shook my head and then nodded. "The Rover?"

She laughed. "Yes. It'll look so much more eco, don't you think?" The Miata was parked in the shadows cast by a small grove of cedars that bordered the open yard. It was where Vhanna had first parked when she came here after I bought the cabin. Merriam's death was still fresh in the community's mind and the little cove of trees was invisible from the road that passed by above my property. If ever there had been, there was no longer need for such discretion, but the habit persisted.

I opened the passenger door and Vhanna climbed with nimble grace unfettered by her skirt into the Rover's high cabin. After I climbed in the other side Vhanna took my right hand in hers and gave it a tight squeeze. "Thanks for coming. I appreciate this, you know." With a shrug I pushed the starter button. The Rover shivered to life and with a clunking of gears I pointed its snout toward the Tofino Community Hall and the banquet to honour US Senator Jack Sloan.

*****

There was a notch in the parking lot between a Mercedes sedan and the upward slope of the hill angling up from one side of the parking lot. The Rover backed neatly into the snug space. By backing in, the radical angle was on my side and Vhanna could easily escape without demonstrating any of her rock-climbing skills. Having no such skills myself, I scrabbled out behind her on the passenger side. The parking lot was jammed with a cornucopia of vehicles that reflected Tofino's evolving economic and social nature. Battered four-wheel-drive pickups were flanked by glistening BMWs and old Volkswagen Vans painted in psychedelic shades right out of the 1960s. A young man looking like he had fallen out of a university calendar photo of an MBA class treaded on delicate toes of Italian leather loafers through the maze of muddy potholes. From one of the VW vans emerged a man with shoulder-length hair, beard, and a tie-die purple shirt worn untucked over white bell-bottomed jeans. Both men were approximately the same age. The two joined hands and proceeded into the hall together. Vhanna tucked her arm through mine and we followed this unlikely couple inside.

For the august occasion of meeting an American senator I had gone to substantial effort, thinking that Vhanna would appreciate such a gesture of good grace. Instead of jeans, denim shirt and Filson coat, I wore navy canvas slacks, a washed blue twill shirt, a green and blue mixed-colour Ecuadoran cotton tie, quickly scrubbed brown leather Chukka boots, a scarred and worn-but-well-preserved brown leather bomber length jacket that had been with me since Nicosia, and my old Filson hat. Vhanna kept smiling at me with warm eyes so I knew she was pleased with my efforts. "As soon as the banquet's over," I whispered in her ear before passing our tickets to the checker.

She squeezed my arm. "We'll run faster than the wind," she murmured back. Her lips brushed my ear. Wilma Effortson, the Chamber of Commerce's long-suffering clerk, tried to blot the back of my hand with a bingo dobber filled with garish red ink but I turned us both quickly away from the table. Wilma, upside-down dobber dribbling little red blots on the table, pursed her lips into her favoured disapproving glower. Then her mouth hardened into an embittered-seeming line as the MBA and hippie couple cheerfully extended hairy hands for dobbing. I paused at the next table to buy a ring of drink tickets from Jabronski.

"Thought you'd be on security tonight," I said.

Jabronski grimaced as he handed me a fistfull of ticket stubs in exchange for $20.00. "All these guys with ear plugs and then the damned Mounties in red. Aced me out of a good night's work and some decent money. No bouncer services, no alarms, no security guards. Shit." Jabronski grinned up at Vhanna. "Speaking of which, I was thinking maybe some electrified barbed wire along the top of your fences might stop this stalking problem you're having."

Vhanna grinned at me. "Some stalkers are better than others. We'll let it go for now."

Jabronski hooked a finger my direction and waggled it in a come hither gesture. I bent down so he could speak to me without being overheard. "Stay clear of Danchuk. He wants to squeeze your balls. Strutting around like a fucking little rooster tonight."

Promising to keep low, I guided Vhanna to the bar and ordered myself a scotch neat and Vhanna a white wine. The wine came out of a cardboard box and the scotch was Johnnie Walker Red. It promised to be a long, grim evening.

Scattered around the hall were a number of scarlet-coated Mounties. Equally obvious, in blue suit jackets with grey pants and little plug earphones stuck in one ear, were the U.S. security service types. Wires from the plugs ran from their ears down into their shirt collars. This, I gathered, was supposed to make the plugs inconspicuous. Perhaps their tiepins were secret microphones. Somewhere, I imagined, a communication van serving as a command centre must be parked. With such a diverse crowd milling around I wondered how the secret service types decided who needed watching. Would you worry more about the MBA man? Or the hippie? What about the familiar looking Indian elder in jeans and Stetson over by the coffee urn? Or how about Dauphin, wearing a brown cowboy suit and whose wife was clinging for dear life to his arm as she balanced on perilous heels.

No sooner had I noticed Dauphin than there was a commotion at one of the fire exits fronting the hall. A small convoy of blue suit jackets and scarlet serge gusted through the doorway. Surrounded by this colourful array was a man in a grey suit jacket, matching pants, a white shirt and a darker shade of tie that looked suspiciously old school. Senator Jack Sloan's hair was government grey, his eyes steel blue, his teeth sanitized white, and his body had the kind of fit trim that comes from daily consultation with dieticians and exercise instructors. Following in his wake was a group of serious, stern-eyed advisers. They were all dressed in slightly more dour shades of blue and grey suits than the senator wore. I noticed that none of their clothes fit as perfectly as the senator's. The aides filtered out quickly toward some of the surrounding tables. Sloan, meanwhile, was guided to the head table, where he started grasping palms of various Tofino notables. Among this group was the Indian elder in jeans and Stetson. I suddenly realized he was the older man who had been in the Zodiac at Flores Island when Tassina had quarreled with Samuels. Perhaps tonight I could find out who he was and what that argument had been about. I looked around the room, searching for Samuels. It was beginning to look like coming to the banquet might have been a good idea after all.

I didn't see Samuels. Instead, my attention focused on Sergeant Danchuk, who was standing awkwardly on the periphery of the main group, looking anything but resplendent in his scarlet serge. The jacket stretched tautly across a rotund belly giving the impression that the buttons were likely to burst at any minute. Little puckering folds of fabric seemed to sag off his shoulders and the arms of the jacket appeared far too long for his arms. The blousing of the pants above the knees had the effect of making his legs seem shorter than was even usually the case. As with the jacket, excess material rolled down unnaturally over the high-topped leather boots, which fairly gleamed with polish. His wide-brimmed dress hat straddled thick eyebrows. The effect was rather like that of dressing up a chimp for a vulgar vaudeville parody of the boys in red.

Hearing Vhanna take a sudden sharp breath, I thought she might be overreacting to Danchuk's ludicrous appearance, and turned to make an appropriate witicism. But suddenly her hand left my arm and she walked away. Her steps carried her in the direction opposite the RCMP sergeant who bore both of us nothing but ill will. Bemused, I watched as she slipped through the throng of people beginning to jockey for positions around various white tissue-covered tables. Vhanna emerged from the centre of the crowd next to one of Senator Sloan's men. He was a tall fellow with wide shoulders and close cropped black hair that set off a thin angular face. His dark blue eyes were fixed on Vhanna. A tight smile pulled at one corner of his mouth to give him a slightly mocking expression. As she walked up to him the man opened his arms and she slid into them, putting her own arms around his back. They hugged like people who had never expected to see each other, although I noticed the man's eyes were still trained on the room about him in what seemed a searching manner.

Leaning back against the bar, with careful nonchalance, I drained my scotch and signalled the barkeep for a refill. I tossed a drink ticket on the bar and didn't meet his eye as he filled the glass. When I looked up again, I saw Vhanna signalling frantically for me to cross the room. Standing side by side as they were, the man and Vhanna looked terribly natural together. In one hand Vhanna held her wine glass, her other was tucked inside the man's arm.

After taking a long, slow breath I walked across the room to meet the man I now recognized as Barry Starling. A very well-dressed and groomed version of Barry Starling, who I had to assume was now in the employ of a US senator. The world was beginning to seem awfully small, after all. Just a little too conveniently small for my taste.

* * * * *

"So after I left here last year," Starling was saying, "I went to California hoping to get involved with Sea Shephard or a group like that." He smiled self-deprecatingly and put a small forkful of pale chicken breast dripping with sauce into his mouth. We were sitting at the end of one of the tables near the front. Vhanna was beside me. Starling and I faced each other across the narrow expanse of white tissue and small dinner plates of food. Earlier, we had toasted Queen Elizabeth II and President Bill Clinton. There had been no toast for British Columbia's Premier, who had approved logging of Clayoquot, but I supposed decorum didn't require his mention and his star was fading much faster than that of either the Queen or the sex-scandal beleaguered president. Starling was explaining to Vhanna how he had left Tofino a failed eco-terrorist only to emerge as an aid to one of America's up and coming senators. The group of men and women seated down the long table from us were debating which were the best inlets for clam digging. I would have liked to pretend theirs was the more interesting topic but found myself as intrigued by Starling's story as Vhanna appeared to be.

Starling had withdrawn from Tofino after the run-in with Dauphin because he saw little more to be achieved here. Being American, if he stayed and manned the summer's environmentalist blockades of the logging roads into Clayoquot, all that would be accomplished was his arrest and probable deportation back to the US. He said the attack on the equipment proved to him the futility of direct action. Sabotage wouldn't make the loggers stop. Perplexed and demoralized by these realizations, Starling had set off in search of an organization to work within where he could fight for the environment via quasi-legal channels.

He had thought to do so by joining one of the semi-radical environmental groups such as Earth First or The Sea Shephard Society, but the first had gone underground and the second didn't seem to have any logical strategic plan that Starling could endorse. Disillusioned, he did what many lost souls opt to do — Starling went home to Excelsior Springs, Kansas. And the rest was history because who should he meet there a month later but his old high school buddy and now senator, one Jack Sloan. The senator was home for that most American political event known as a corn feed. It started out as small talk about where Starling had been recently and before he knew it they were deep into a short discussion about environmental policies and the government's role in protection. It was, Starling said, a discussion that was carried on for several weeks afterwards by letter, phone, and fax until one day Senator Sloan asked if he would join his staff by becoming his environmental policy assistant. It was a dream come true for Starling, a chance to be involved in something that would have real impact.

"So was it your idea for Senator Sloan to come see Clayoquot?" I asked. Perhaps there was an edge to my voice as Vhanna gave me one of her out-of-the-corner-of-the-eye looks, which are usually accompanied by a frown. The frown was there this time as well.

Starling grinned, but I noticed again his eyes seemed to be looking past my shoulder, as if he still exepcted to see somebody else. "No, not at all. I mean, I would have loved to get him up here, but he raised the idea. Jack is really concerned about the old-growth timber. Clayoquot has got a lot of American press."

I supposed it was logical that somebody from Kansas would have real concerns about preserving old-growth coastal forests. We are all of one planet as the slogans go. I tried to surmise whether my concerns about pesticide saturation of farmland and diversion of natural water sources in the Great Plains would prompt me to fly to Kansas, but perhaps it was an unfair comparison. Out of consideration for Vhanna I didn't bring up this line of thought.

Instead, I sipped some lukewarm white wine and tried surreptitiously to see a wall clock. Surely this dinner would end soon and I could take Vhanna out of here and return to the evening we had planned. Across the room a tall, gangly figure with long blond hair slipped past a couple of tables and slid quietly into a vacant chair. It was a moment before I recognized the figure as that of Lawrence Rafferty. I had never before seen him in a sports jacket. Of course I've hardly ever worn one myself and so could hardly talk. Still, a moderately dressed-up Rafferty was a surprising sight. I wondered what would have brought him here this evening. It seemed an odd place for someone dedicated to direct action. But, then again, Starling was here and an aid to a senator to boot, so anything seemed like it could be explained this evening. Except why Ira Connaught, Tassina Mavrikos, and Eleni Mavrikos were dead. There were no answers to these questions to be found here.

All the suspects were present, though. Samuels was sitting with the elder in the Stetson. Dauphin was forking down hardened chicken amid a table of forestry officials. Rafferty had just ducked into the room. Starling, who had for a brief moment flickered into my mind as a suspect when I saw the size of his hands and heard his story from Vhanna, sat across from me. Hands. I was surrounded by a town full of big-handed men. Surrounded by men, like Rafferty, who were surrounded by followers with big hands. Trying to determine from the size of men's hands who killed Ira was as useful as trying to hold a cloud. Why even Father Welch fit my one descriptive identifying trait for the killer. So, I supposed, did I. The regional coroner, I reflected gloomily, was right: my investigation was stonewalled and other than describing how three people had died nothing more could be achieved.

Certainly, I wasn't going to prevent the stolen dynamite from being used in whatever way someone was planning. If there was anyone out there planning to put the stuff to use at all. Perhaps the connection between Tassina and Eleni's death and that of Ira's was just the product of the mind of a remittance man looking for some kind of life's purpose. Seeking to save the day. To dazzle and impress Vhanna with my intuitive skills and hear the admiration in her voice that was so evident in the words passing now between herself and Starling. She had asked me to solve the mystery behind the murder of her friend Ira and I had unearthed nothing but more unanswerable questions. I had achieved nothing but possibly prompting a murderer to kill again in order to silence Tassina. Had that been what it was all about? Did Tassina have information that might have identified the killer? Was that what she wanted to tell me the next day? If I had not meddled, would Tassina still be alive? Questions that could probably never be answered. Questions I knew I would ask myself for years to come. I stared dourly at my plate of half-eaten food. When a server came by a moment later to pick up empty dishes, I signalled her to carry mine off.

"You get used to this kind of food on the political circuit," Starling said cheerfully. "After eight months of this I think I could eat anything."

It was a straight line that was almost too good to pass up, but I let it slide. "You joined the senator's staff in the summer, then?" I said instead.

"Yeah, around late July."

And about three weeks later Ira Connaught started collecting clippings of Senator Sloan's planned trip to Clayoquot and approached Dauphin to buy some dynamite. A coincidence? Obviously so. With his preppy short hair and suit, the thought of Starling being involved in murder was preposterous. Besides, he couldn't have been within a thousand kilometres of here at the time Ira died.

A clinking of spoons on glasses at the front of the room brought us all to silence. "Oh no," I muttered. Vhanna squeezed my knee. The accompanying sympathetic smile made my heart lift. Perhaps there was luck in this evening for a remittance man after all.

Mayor Tully, looking much more the small town politician than a doctor of medicine this night, made some neutral and absolutely irrelevant introductory comments. Then Senator Sloan rose to the podium. A gaggle of reporters, some accompanied by crews swinging around mini-cams, pressed suddenly forward and garish spotlights filled the hall with an unnatural glare. I sipped lukewarm coffee. The server had put a small dish holding something that looked vaguely like a vanilla-coloured cleaning sponge smeared with thick red gel before me. Neither Vhanna or I touched it, but Starling dug in with happy abandon.

The senator's speech was mercifully short and full of innumerable qualifiers. He was not here to interfere in Canadian politics. He sought only to get first-hand knowledge. All of us have a responsibility to preserve the planet. He had an open mind on the practices of Canadian forestry companies. Everyone, he was sure, could see ways that environmental protection could be improved. It was his hope that this visit would help foster a spirit of understanding and mutual cooperation between Canada and the US. At the end, everyone clapped. Who could take offence? A second later, I had my answer to that. In one corner of the hall Dauphin and the foresters glowered. On the other side Rafferty and a clutch of earnest-looking souls scouled.

There were several thank-you remarks from various Tofino and Ucluelet luminaries and then the evening was called to a mercifully quick end. Starling was on his feet, insisting that Vhanna and I meet the senator now instead of waiting until morning when the tour was scheduled to begin. Before I could say anything, Vhanna agreed. Taking her arm, Starling led the way and I trailed along a few steps back in their wake. We had to wait, of course, for the media to finish and this process took about twenty minutes. By the time they were through, the senator's forehead was beaded with little droplets of perspiration. Once the reporters started putting away equipment and dismantling microphones, Starling stepped up to Sloan with Vhanna's hand still grasped in his arm. "This is Vhanna Chan and her friend —" he paused, searching. "Sorry. Elias McCann. Ah, he's a local." Starling stumbled again, his tongue flicking over his lips as he searched for words. "Mr. McCann is the local coroner and a Tofino businessman," he finally blurted.

Vhanna shot me a threatening glance, so I didn't contradict Starling's gracious description of my various vocations. I hadn't really planned on clarifying things anyway. I rather doubted the senator would understand what a remittance man was without a long, convoluted explanation. Or perhaps he might prefer a briefing paper. He looked the type who would prefer briefing papers to oral reports. After Starling's introductions, palms were gripped and sincere words of greeting spoken.

Then Senator Sloan looked at Vhanna thoughtfully and said. "I enjoyed the article on you in *National Geographic*. Diane, my wife, wants to go to Alaska or the Yukon with your company and go white-water rafting for a month. Sounds cold and dangerous to me. Not like what I'll be in store for tomorrow, I hope." This last was said with a glitter of teeth and a crinkling of the eyes.

Vhanna gave a small laugh as false sounding as the senator's chitchat and assured him everything would be perfectly safe and comfortable. Then she said in a more direct tone that she hoped his wife would go to the Yukon with her. "It should be a good trip. We've been going into Tatshenshini River for several years but now that our government has decided to preserve it the area is a good counterpoint to Clayoquot. Why they saved one and not the other is an interesting subject."

Sloan smiled. "Yes, well, often it's hard for us outside of the inner circle of a government to understand the reasons behind some decisions. So we have to look things over carefully ourselves and draw our own conclusions. Which is why I'm here." Sloan paused, looked appropriately thoughtful. When he spoke his voice was soft, so I could barely hear it and his attention was completely on Vhanna. "Actually, Ms. Chan, I'm glad Starling told me about you. He mentioned you several times after I sent him up here a few weeks ago to set this trip's details into place. It was his knowledge of you and Clayoquot that helped me decide that I really must come and investigate things directly. Without you to take me back into the real heart of the Sound I'm not sure what the use of this visit would be. You are really well-acquainted with the country aren't you?"

Vhanna nodded, her expression showing traces of puzzlement in the tightness around her mouth. That Vhanna was familiar with Clayoquot was an understatement. She had probably tramped almost every square foot of the place from the ice and snow-covered mountains inland to the estuaries on the shoreline. Much of it we had hiked together. A number of images from those hikes into secluded country flickered through my mind. "I can't tell you how pleased I was when you accepted our request to act as my guide," the senator continued. "The environmental groups offered guides, the forestry companies offered guides, the provincial government offered guides. I either had to take them all along or none." He flashed an earnestly winning smile her way. "I'd like someone along who's unbiased."

"But I am biased. Everyone knows I oppose the logging."

Starling interrupted. "But you're not really active in that opposition." His smile had a mocking crook in one corner that I found irksome.

Vhanna looked like she wanted to say something and I was pleased to see her eyes had gone kind of hard and flat as she looked Starling's way. She wasn't used to being mocked.

Turning her attention curtly from Starling to Sloan, she said, "Actually, Elias knows that country as well as I do. Would you mind greatly if he came along tomorrow?"

Sloan said that of course he didn't mind. No one thought to ask me. I minded greatly. But another round of glad handing and smiling had begun, punctuated by knowing nods of heads. I nodded and smiled in a manner I hoped imitated some of this mutual enthusiasm the rest shared for this tedious little outing into the forest.

A few seconds later, Sloan and Starling breezed off in one direction and Vhanna and I strolled off in the other, heading toward the coat rack and the exit door. As we were gathering up our coats, I found myself standing next to Samuels who was wearing an unbuttoned buckskin jacket, blue and white cowboy shirt, crisp jeans, and a wide Indian-bead necklace. "I need to talk with you," I said. He gave me a grin that was all innocence but his eyes remained cool. He joined Vhanna and I in walking outside. When we stepped clear of the bottleneck of people exiting the hall the elder appeared beside us as well as if suddenly conjured up out of thin air. In the darkness, his face was masked beneath the Stetson, so I couldn't make out any real facial characteristics.

I told Samuels about seeing the two of them arguing with Tassina on the wharf in front of the Sunshine Warriors' Flores Island cabin. "What was that all about, Joseph?" I said to Samuels.

He shrugged his big shoulders and shoved his hands into the pockets of his jeans and glanced nervously toward the elder whose hands were also tucked into jeans pockets. "I could say it's none of your business, Elias."

I waited. As an ambulance attendant he had been at enough death scenes to know my business in this matter was more than casual interest. Finally, however, it was the elder who broke the silence. "They had no right putting those things in that cabin and then not taking it all away."

My heart started pounding. "You knew about the explosives?" I said, turning to look at the older man.

Samuels stepped closer to him in an almost-protective gesture. "We don't need —" he started to say but the elder cut his hand through the air and Samuels snapped his mouth shut.

"That is our land. The cabin is part of that land now. The fishermen with their traps who built it were white, but it was long ago now and the building of it cannot be undone. Enough evil has come from that cabin. It should not be further desecrated."

"The cabin was a trap shack?" I asked.

Samuels nodded. "It was used for only a couple years because it was too far from the markets. Built around the end of the Great War."

The fish traps had been nasty affairs, constructed of rolls of heavy-gauge wire assembled like an accordion. The traps were hauled out to sea on barges and then unfurled. Each trap could haul in massive catches of salmon. I had heard that in one month in 1918, a single trap had accounted for 32,000 kilograms of salmon taken. When the fishing season ended each October, the traps were dismantled with the majority of the wire, now heavily corroded by the salt, simply abandoned to the ocean currents. This, and the terrific volume of catches each trap netted, resulted in the use of the things being banned in 1958. The cabins known as trap cabins had been used each season to construct the traps. Then, during the season it was deployed, a watchman would live in the cabin to ensure nobody vandalized or robbed the trap of its catch between emptying phases. But what had any of this to do with Tassina?

"I don't understand Tassina's link to the cabin and the explosives," I said.

Samuels sighed and stared off across the parking lot. The elder glowered from under the brim of his hat at my chest. Vhanna stood next to me, looking at the two men with a puzzled expression. I adopted her expression and chose to await some enlightenment from one or the other of them.

Finally, it was Samuels who spoke. "It was her choice to get involved with Connaught. The explosives were his and she took him up there. He was to remove all the stuff but most of it's still there. We told her that it all had to be taken away."

"But she just gave him a lift up there. Do you think she knew about the explosives before?"

Samuels face tightened, he looked to the elder beseechingly. Finally the elder spoke. "It was the people who call themselves Sunshine Warriors we came to see that day. We were going to tell them to remove the explosives." He pointed a finger at my chest. "But you were there. The woman warned us of that. So I told her to make sure it was removed."

Understanding, I said, "And she said it had nothing to do with her. So you argued, but stopped when you saw me coming down the stairs." The elder nodded. So this was possibly what Tassina had thought to tell me just before she was killed. "Are you certain the explosives were connected to the Sunshine Warriors, to Rafferty?"

Samuels shrugged again. "Ira was one of them. We knew he was involved with the explosives and had warned him to remove them from the cabin. Then he was dead, so it seemed Rafferty and the rest should be responsible for it."

"Why didn't you just call the police?"

The elder answered this in his flat, emotionless voice. "We understood the explosives were to be used for a good purpose and that purpose was still there despite the young man's death."

"What purpose?"

The elder answered my question with a dismissive gesture of both hands.

"Ira told me nobody would be harmed and that it would help bring the logging to an end. That was all I thought we needed to know." He paused. "Ira could be trusted," he added softly.

"Did you talk to Rafferty?"

Samuels said they had been unable to see the Sunshine Warrior leader. I told him that the police in Gold River knew about the explosives now and would be attending to it. But I warned him the stuff was completely unstable and might have to be blown in place rather then moved. Neither Samuels nor the elder liked that much, but there was little they or anybody else could do about it.

The two men left, obviously in less happy spirits than they had displayed during the banquet. Vhanna and I climbed into the Rover and drove off toward my cabin. "Do you think Rafferty and the others did know about the explosives?" Vhanna asked.

It was my turn to shrug. "Who can tell? If we had known this earlier, we could have confronted Rafferty. But now there isn't time. Whatever is going to happen, it must be timed to the senator's visit. If Rafferty's behind this, we'll never catch up to him now." I banged my fist on the steering wheel. "Our chance was at the banquet. He was there briefly. But he bugged out when the speeches ended. There's no time to go out to Flores and grill him."

"Perhaps we should tell Danchuk what we know," Vhanna said softly.

"And what do we know? Danchuk would just nail me for not stopping the investigation. He wouldn't act. He wouldn't get out to Flores and bring Rafferty in for questioning. Not now. Not with the senator and media here."

Vhanna gave my knee a light squeeze. "So what now?"

What indeed? I thought about it. "We go home, I guess. Get some sleep and get ready for the three-ring circus tomorrow." I stomped on the Rover's accelerator and we thundered into the night. Like it or not, I could see that my investigaton into the murders of Ira, Tassina, and Eleni was not going to be solved soon and that whatever was going to happen would happen. We just had to pray that the possibility of something more terrible being planned was an unfounded suspicion and that the senator's visit would pass without incident.

Chapter Eighteen

"It'll be like something out of a bad Vietnam war movie," I complained. "Helicopters racing into landing zones. We'll be lucky if there aren't collisions. It's going to require a major airlift to get all the security, media, and aides from one place to another. I can see your wanting to go. But why me?"

Vhanna laughed and leaned back on the couch. In her hand was a glass of Glenlivet. A small fire burned in the fireplace. Fergus snored gently at the other end of the couch. I was sitting in the big chair next to the hearth, sipping my own glass of scotch. "You'll have fun," she said. "And I wanted you along." She paused and her expression grew sort of sad. "I didn't want to go alone. Do you really mind?"

Yes, I thought. "No. Not really," I said. "It was just unexpected. And there's this other thing."

"But you've been told to stay away from it, Elias." Vhanna sipped Glenlivet, set her glass down. "I think maybe you should, too. I don't see how we can prove it's Dauphin who was behind the murders. When the senator's gone, you can give what we've learned to Danchuk and maybe then he'll do something. What more can we do?"

I thought about it. Vhanna was, of course, right. There was nothing more to be done. And, while she continued to suspect that Dauphin was responsible, there was no compelling evidence to prove this. Neither could I prove or even believe that Rafferty was guilty of the deaths of Ira, his friend, or of a woman and her daughter who he had also known. The list of suspects was short and incredibly weak. Even the other suspect that suggested himself was more dubious than the rest. Still I decided to pursue this possibility to see how far it traveled. So I said to Vhanna, "The senator said that Starling was here several times over the course of the winter."

Vhanna nodded.

"Did he call you?"

Her mouth tightened a little and the softness in her eyes slipped away. I thought myself a fool for this, but my reason for asking was more than jealousy. "No, he never called. Maybe I was overseas."

"Still it's odd he wouldn't have left word, don't you think? A message on your answering machine? A note? Something."

"I'm not lying, Elias. If that's your point."

I stood and needlessly pushed the burning wood around with a poker. "That's not what I'm wondering. It just seems bloody odd. You were friends. You are friends. Starling comes to town to smooth the way for Sloan's arrival. He talks to Sloan about you on several occasions. He even puts the idea in Sloan's head for you to be their tour guide. Yet he never contacts you. Why wouldn't he?"

"Elias, Starling isn't involved in these murders. He's on our side. Ira and Starling knew each other.

They fought the same fight from the same side. Suspecting Starling is silly."

I slumped back in my chair. "You're right," I muttered. "But everywhere we look there are always these odd deceptions or unanswered questions. That damned dynamite is still out there, Vhanna. And someone has plans for it. Plans worth killing to protect."

"But not Starling. He's part of the system now." Vhanna crossed the room, wrapped her arms around my neck and settled on my lap. "It was creepy, you know, seeing him like that. I almost didn't recognize him. It was as impossible to imagine as would be your putting on a three-piece suit and becoming a stock broker."

"I own stock."

"Yeah, in the Crab Pot Café and Artemis Adventures. And you wouldn't do that except that it's for friends. All that money would just pile up in a bank somewhere and be virtually forgotten." She kissed my eyes. "I love that about you."

"What do you love?"

"Don't fish for compliments."

I slipped my hand through a couple of buttons of her shirt I had just undone. "Okay." My fingers brushed a firm nipple, cupped the small breast. I kissed her throat.

"This is fishing of a different kind," Vhanna said.

The last button of her shirt came undone. I ran my lips down her throat, across her breast, lightly suckled a nipple. Her fingers tightened in my hair and she moaned softly. "Let's dance first," she whispered. "I've been thinking of that all evening." I took her face in my hands and kissed her mouth softly, dancing my tongue against hers. When we surfaced she got off my lap and went over to the CD player.

Accordion and rhythm guitar music came out of the speakers, folk music spiced with salsa, Tish Hinojosa's sweet voice spoke of Mexican farm-workers in California fields and nights spent crossing the Rio Grande in search of dreams. Vhanna left her shirt undone and I passed my arms inside, ran fingers gently up her spine. We moved together in a slow waltz, mouths brushing, lingering. Fergus watched wearily through one eye that often drooped shut. I pushed the shirt back and kissed her shoulder, cupped the small knob of it in my hand. Vhanna burrowed in tight against my chest.

Someone banged on the outside door with a loud fist.

When I opened the door someone standing in the shadows said, "I know it's late Eli, and I'm interrupting." I recognized the shadow as that of Vlassis Mavrikos who waved away my assurances that his being at my door in the early morning hours posed no inconvenience. "I wouldn't have come but I was down at the wharf and my truck, it won't start." His voice wavered, started to crumble and then strengthened. "I had to get away from there. I shouldn't have gone. I can call a taxi. The phone at the wharf is out of order. Nothing works." He sounded immensely weary.

"I'll drive you," I said. "Just let me get my coat."

Vlassis grabbed my arm. "No," he pleaded. "I call a taxi. I want to make no fuss. I wait outside."

Vhanna came up beside me. Her shirt was done up and hair smoothed. "Hello, Vlassis. Would you like some tea or a drink?"

"No, Miss Chan, I want only to call a taxi. I was at the wharf," he added. Vlassis's eyes were wild, his face drawn. He looked gaunt and old.

I insisted again that I drive him and he reiterated his refusal. The impasse was broken by Vhanna taking her small black leather purse from the kitchen counter and digging out the Miata keys. "Vlassis, take my car and go home. You should be with family now."

"I have no family now," he said softly.

"That's not true, Vlassis. The others are probably worried about you. Please go to them. Take my car." She held out the keys to him. He started to protest again. "Elias can bring me to get the car in the morning. It's no trouble, Vlassis." Vhanna's voice was gently commanding.

Vlassis took the keys. "I'll drive carefully. Thank you, Miss Chan." He bowed his head in a surprisingly courtly manner.

"You're welcome, Vlassis."

He turned and walked toward the Miata. I looked down at Vhanna, unable to hide my surprise. "You've hardly let me drive it," I said.

"Well, we have a dance to finish," she said and pulled me back into the house. We crossed back into the living room and Vhanna pushed the restart button on the CD. I put my arms around her. "Vlassis always calls me Miss Chan because he doesn't approve of me. He likes neither my opinions nor that I am with you." I started undoing her shirt. What Vlassis Mavrikos liked or didn't was of little importance to me at this moment. "I thought we were dancing."

"It was better the way we were dancing before the interruption, don't you think?"

"Proper girls don't answer questions like that." She sighed as my fingers grazed her nipples. "Yes. Much better. Much."

The windows in the kitchen shattered and an enormous bang crashed outside the house. Instinctively I twisted Vhanna down to the floor and threw myself on top of her. Shards of glass sprayed through the room, something stung the back of my hand. Fergus yelped. The lights went out and the CD stopped playing.

Ears ringing, I rolled off Vhanna and stumbled through the dark toward the orange glow outside. The door was open, dangling on one hinge. I went out on the porch. Across the yard the Miata burned. Both doors had blown off. Vlassis hung out of the driver's side, his body on the ground and his legs still in the car. He was burning as wildly as the car. As I ran across the yard I pulled off my shirt, wrapping my hands inside the material. I fought my way in against the flames to grab Vlassis and drag him out of the burning car. Desperately I tumbled his body across the dirt trying to smother the flames. Vhanna came running up with a blanket snatched from the back of the couch. We used it to smother the rest of the fire on him.

Vhanna was yelling something but my ears were ringing and I couldn't hear the words. I turned Vlassis over on his back. His flesh was charred away, his eyes gone. Vlassis Mavrikos was dead.

Three hours later, the last of the police cars and fire trucks left. The wreckage of the Miata remained, surrounded with yellow police scene tape. Sergeant Danchuk had been the last to leave, like a bulldog he had sought some reason to take one or the other or both of us in for questioning, but there was no cause. The car had been wired with a bomb. Jabronski, acting as fire chief, had found the remains of it attached to the starter. Obviously the bomb had been set to kill Vhanna or the two of us. He should have been offering protection rather than launching an interrogation, but Danchuk had the look of a man with a pack of pitbulls baying at his heels.

"What the hell is going on, McCann?" he had demanded at one point.

But I had no answers. There were none to be had. Finally, Danchuk went off into the night. Vhanna and I returned to the house and I swept up the shards of glass from the exploded windows. Vhanna stood outside on the deck staring at the soft light of the false dawn. When most of the glass was cleaned up, I joined her.

"Someone thinks we know more than we do," I said.

"But why my car?"

"I guess they took a chance. They must have done it when we were at the banquet. Hoped we'd both go in the Miata in the morning. At the very least they would have got one of us."

Vhanna shivered. "Poor Vlassis."

Better he then you, I thought. It was a terrible thought, but it was how I felt. I put my arms around her and pulled her back against my chest. She clung to me. "We have to find out who's doing this, don't we?"

"Once they do whatever it is they're planning, it won't matter."

Vhanna shook her head. "No, they'll still want us quiet. They think we know enough to figure out who they are. Do we? Are we just not seeing it?"

"I don't know."

"Dauphin was at the banquet."

"No alibi. He came late. And he could also have sent the Greers to do this."

"Would they know how to do that?"

I shrugged. How could I know what a Greer was capable of? Or Dauphin? Or whoever else might be the killer. I felt the terrible rage of the helpless. There was nothing I could do to protect Vhanna or myself from a killer whose identity I didn't know.

"If only we knew what the dynamite was for. It must be to kill someone, but who?" Vhanna said.

To kill someone. I had never considered that. Three people were dead. Killed by bombs made from the stolen dynamite, yet it had not occurred to me that the explosives were stolen to kill one specific individual. I had always assumed a physical target. A building. A ship. A plane. A target filled with people. A building like the community hall during the banquet. That was what I had feared. Bombs weren't used for single target killings. They were the stuff of random murder. A bomb exploding in Nicosia. A small girl sliced down by shrapnel and blast. A street full of ragged, bleeding bundles. That was the work of bombs. To kill a specific target you used a gun. A well placed bullet. I had been thinking like a soldier. And I had been terribly wrong.

"I know who," I said, and told her. Then I told her why I knew I was right. When I finished she asked what we were going to do about it. The solution seemed simple enough to me and I was pretty sure that a further killing could be averted. But there would still be a murderer to find, a killer who suspected we were closer to identifying him then we truly were.

"It won't work," Vhanna said. "Danchuk won't believe you."

"Danchuk can go to hell. The others will stop it. They won't take the risk."

Vhanna thought about this. "And whoever killed Ira and the others gets away with it." She paused, her expression grave. Vhanna didn't have to add that the killer would still be out there and might have another go at us.

"There's no other way," I said. But I new this wasn't true. And, as I feared, Vhanna had realized how a killer might be caught. She mapped out the logical path that I had seen but refused to follow.

"It's too dangerous. It could be any of the five landing zones," I argued. But, of course, we both knew it could only be one. We went inside and Vhanna lit the wick of an oil lantern. The power to the house was still severed, the pole outside charred and splintered from the explosion. I dug a topographical map of Clayoquot from a drawer and spread it on the table. Fergus tumbled off the couch and staggered up the stairs sniffing and yawning with each step. I smiled at Vhanna as the wicker bed upstairs creaked and groaned while he settled in. It had been a dreadful day for a dog, a dreadful day for us all.

Working with a protractor, I figured out the distances and the timing. "It might work," I conceded.

Vhanna took the protractor and quickly checked my calculations. She nodded agreement. "You'll have to..."

"I know," I said. The first glow of false dawn tinged the eastern skyline, filtering in through the shattered kitchen windows. Neither of us felt tired but we climbed the stairs, crawled under the covers and clung to each other with gentle desperation.

Chapter Nineteen

Morning held the promise of a fine day and only a dark band of cloud far out to sea warned that yet another storm lurked somewhere offshore. A wind, stiff with Bering Sea ice, blew in off the water. Refusing to do the sensible thing of hunkering down against the resulting morning chill I followed Vhanna through a full 108 movement Tai Chi set. Vhanna's every movement reflected coordinated agility. I trailed behind with what I hoped passed for at least an awkward grace. Vhanna was purging her spirit of doubts and fears, readying for the dangers of this day. Despite the Tai Chi's seductive rhythms, my mind was tangled with second doubts and unspoken fears. And all the while before us the wreckage of the Miata inside its corral of yellow police marker tape mocked any effort to pretend this was a morning of sanity and normality. Finishing the set, we bowed in closure toward the shattered vehicle and steadfastly avoided each other's gaze. I went inside leaving Vhanna alone to run through her Tai Chi combat ritual that required an athleticism and deadly coordination far beyond either my skill or nature. Although once a soldier, I am far too much a pacifist to study rigorously a martial art that could be used to kill a person. Or at least that's how I've fended off Vhanna's half-hearted occasional attempts to lure me into letting her tutor me in this potentially lethal discipline.

After showering, I dressed with the kind of methodical care I had been trained as a soldier to invest in preparation for combat. Sturdy canvas pants, a frayed denim shirt, scarred leather Chukka boots, Filson coat and hat at the ready. I unlocked the gun case and removed the Parker. Although it was meticulously clean I dismantled the shotgun and subjected it to another thorough servicing. Years ago I replaced the original antique barrels with hard-brazed ones that had been laser sighted. Now, although the barrels had the blued and hand-fitted look of the originals, the side-by-side barrels could handle steel shot. It was meant to reduce the likelihood of lead poisoning in game birds. They contract the poisoning by ingesting the pellets that inadvertently fall into the marshes, ponds, and streams of hunting areas. Today, if the worst happened, it would serve another less humanitarian purpose. Finished with the gun, I slipped it into a leather gun case and pulled the zipper shut.

Digging into the gun case's locked drawer I pulled out three boxes of shells — two of double-ought buckshot and one of deer slugs. I broke open the shell boxes and, being careful to keep the two types of shot separate, stowed the cartridges in the Filson's inside pockets. On the coat's left inner side were sewn loops for individual shells. These I filled with an even mixture of deer and regular slugs. Again, I made sure that I kept the two types apart and knew which I placed where. Preparations finished, I put the gun and coat into the Rover, tucking them behind the seats so they were out of sight of any prying eyes — especially those of Sergeant Danchuk.

Next, I went to work on the Rover. Checking oil and radiator anti-freeze levels, battery and brake fluid reservoirs, tire pressure. Everything seemed fine, but the Rover was a less agreeable and ready partner in the proceedings than the Parker. I would just have to hope for the best.

As I dropped the heavy hood back in place, Vhanna came out of the house, wearing black jeans and a white bush shirt. Her leather hiking boots were as scarred as my aged Chukkas. Her long hair was pulled back in a tight ponytail and she wore a rather wicked and barely-legal length Gerber hunting knife on her belt. Over her shoulder, Vhanna carried a battered bush jacket. It struck me that normally on a day when she was to play the well-photographed guide to a senator she would have been dressed to the nines in the latest synthetics that dominated the outdoor weekender recreation market. The functional utility of her clothing made me even more anxious.

Quelling my fear, I pointed at the knife. "Danchuk and the security types will have a fit."

Vhanna shrugged. I knew there was little likelihood that any of the grey suits or men in serge were going to wrestle the knife away from her. "You're wrong about who's behind this," she said in a taut voice. "It's Dauphin."

It was my turn to shrug. "We'll know soon enough." We stood awkwardly, two soldiers preparing to go into the breach and fearful of surrendering to words or gestures that might bring ill luck. I started to speak but Vhanna's fingers brushed my lips, pressing the words back.

"I know," she whispered. We hugged each other hard. Then I started the Rover and pointed its stubby front end toward the airport.

Danchuk scowled at me. "They've been all over it and found nothing. A waste of time. Tomorrow, McCann, you've got some answering to do. And I'm sure as shit going to see you're through as coroner. Understand?" He was wearing his regular Mountie uniform with the jacket done up to his throat. I wasn't sure whether it was the emotional outburst or the way the collar constricted his sagging flesh that coloured his face like an overripe tomato.

A black limo pulled up alongside the helicopter. Sloan, Starling and two security men climbed out. The two guards who had just finished searching the chopper huddled with the new arrivals. One of them glanced in my direction. His mouth was a tense line and his eyes unreadable behind the black lenses of his aviator's sunglasses. All of the guards were wearing Gore-tex foul weather jackets that did little to conceal the bulges of their guns. Each of them took a turn looking my way and each exuded an aura of hostility. I was making their job difficult, adding stress and worry to what should have been a pleasant country outing. Their grim expressions told me they were in a mood to shoot the messenger.

I ignored them and tried again with Danchuk. "Cancel the flight, Gary. After last night it's an unnecessary risk."

Danchuk snorted. I supposed it was intended to be a sound of contempt but it sounded more like he was sucking down the contents of his sinuses.

Turning my back on him I walked over to where Starling and Sloan were talking with Vhanna.

Earlier, Vhanna had agreed to this last effort to get the tour aborted — but she didn't believe it was the right thing to do. Despite my attempts to get the flight canceled, I hadn't expected to be successful. And perhaps it was for the best. Vhanna was probably right in believing if we were going to flush the killer, the flight had to proceed. She had only gone along with my trying to scrub this mission because she knew I was very afraid of the danger facing her if she boarded that helicopter. But Vhanna knew the risk and wanted to go. I wasn't sure what my own feelings were. I knew, too, that if the flight were canceled a killer would be free to strike again. But the thought of letting Vhanna get on that helicopter caused an icy fist to clutch my heart.

Sloan and Starling both greeted me with friendly nods. Each wore obviously new and well-pressed jeans and denim shirts, along with expensive-looking Gore-Tex squall jackets. They looked as if they would be more at home in the pages of an LL Bean catalogue than mucking about in the Tofino bush on a day in early spring.

"Good morning, Mr. McCann," Sloan said with a politician's professional bonhomie. "Great day for a helicopter ride." His smile flicked away and was replaced by the stern, serious countenance of the statesman. "I've been advised of the tragic events of last night and wanted to express my sympathy. I'm also aware of your concerns and would like to assure you that every step is being taken to ensure things are safe and secure."

As he talked, I watched Starling out of the corner of my eye. He looked perfectly relaxed and at ease. His cobalt blue eyes were focused on two approaching vans and several cars with the kind of keen concentration a spaniel gives a grouse trapped in a thicket. The media were arriving in a convoy. When the vehicles stopped, Starling advised Sloan that they should spare a few minutes for the media. No real prodding was required as Sloan set off immediately with Starling in his trail. Sloan moved with the well-rehearsed confident stride of a born leader. Reporters clutching notepads, television crews waving microphones and camcorders disgorged from the vehicles to circle around the senator like so many seagulls over a beached porpoise. Sloan's thoughtfully intoned murmurings drifted on the wind but were thankfully indistinguishable. Vhanna and I stood in companionable silence, waiting for the show to end. When I took her hand in mine she didn't draw it away. Her skin was cool and I wrapped her hand tightly inside my fist to warm it.

Minutes later, the senator and Starling were back and preparations to lift off were started. "I'm afraid, Mr. Senator, that I won't be able to accompany you today," I said in what sounded rather like the formal, stilted intonements the senator himself had just been uttering. At the senator's required show of protest I pleaded work commitments. Seeing as Starling had given me the rank of a businessman the night before I decided to invoke the hazy, but always urgent, duties of that calling.

Starling's eyes locked with mine. "I'm really sorry you can't come along," he said with an expression that seemed sincerely regretful and at the same time contained a threatening quality. "Perhaps you'll be able to join us all for dinner tonight before the senator flies out to Vancouver?" I promised I would, and turned to leave.

Before I could make good my escape, a finger prodded me sharply in the shoulder. I turned to find Danchuk glowering up at me. He stood barely inches away, his head tipped back and his eyes beady and mean-looking. "You can count on us to take good care of Ms. Chan, McCann." His grin was foul. "First you tell us there might be a bomb on board and then you beg off coming along for the ride. But you send her. A real piece of work, McCann, that's what you are. A real piece of work."

For a second, I considered punching him in the face but pushed the temptation aside. We scowled at each other across the uncrossable boundary of our mutual disdain. When it became obvious that Danchuk considered this a test of wills I turned my back on him and walked toward the Rover. Before climbing into the vehicle, however, I looked back at the helicopter. Vhanna was crouched in the doorway and the big rotors were starting to turn in slow motion. Vhanna raised one hand and blew a flicker of a kiss my direction. I raised an open hand in a gesture I hoped wouldn't appear to be a farewell.

In my chest I felt that hollow ache, accompanied by an all-too-familiar disorientation that grips me whenever Vhanna and I part. Whether it be for a day or a month this gloomy aura settles upon me. It is this dissonance of the soul which reminds that the love I feel for Vhanna is extraordinary, ultimately imbued with the power to award either intense joy or deepest despair. There is an old saying that for every man there is one woman and that luckily most men never meet the one meant for them. I am one of the unlucky, who, of course, don't count themselves as such at all.

Once I had loved Merriam, but it was the comfortable, secure love that most resembles the feeling one has when donning a well and oft-worn old coat. A love that is familiar, gentle, and tame. This love for Vhanna was altogether different. It was a raw thing, wild as wolves running a ridgeline, tumultuous as a flooding river, ever cutting new pathways deep into my heart. It was always exhilarating, always transmuting into something deeper and stronger, yet always a love that seemed fragile and imperiled.

I knew, too, that if anything happened this day to Vhanna I would be doomed, forever lost within a tormented nightmare of bleak personal responsibility for my having failed her. I simply must not fail. The consequences were unthinkable.

So, despite the temptation to stand there and watch the chopper fly away, to catch as long a glimpse of Vhanna as possible, I started getting on my way. The clock was running. If Vhanna and I were right, it was going to be a very tight race. A race I had to win. Were I to fail, it was all too probable that memories of Vhanna were all I would have left.

The Rover's heavily treaded tires skidded through a skim of mud slick as oiled asphalt and spun down into a chuckhole filled with mucky water. As the tires struck bottom, sloppy water sprayed up over the hood and windscreen. With a shudder the front tires clawed their way out of the hole. I cranked on the wiper and tried to smear the blots of dirty water away so that I could better see the snaking road. We fishtailed around a bend and I mashed the accelerator to the floor as the road uncoiled ahead of me. One glance at my watch told me I was late, terribly late. I cursed, but the words of anger sounded more like a prayer from the lost. The road writhed and jumped beneath the Rover's tires. I clung grimly to the wheel and ignored the howling protests of the little vehicle's sorely overworked engine. "Please," I whispered. "Please don't fail me."

This was not the way to travel rugged roads. This was the stuff of make-believe cowboys and scraggly roughnecks, of beer commercials and four-wheel truck television ads. Driving like a maniac on these kind of roads led to broken axles, to skidding over cliffs, to getting hopelessly stuck in a quagmire. It was madness to drive like this; a madness worsened by the fact that the Rover's tough little machining was intended for a pace of unrelenting determination rather than a mad rush.

I had been driven to this crazed pace because of a forty-foot Winnebago motorhome. I had fallen into its wake just past Cox Point. Like some kind of lumbering monolith, it had trundled down the highway. A small satellite television dish on the roof hunkered off to port, like a mesh steel sail topping a highway version of a modern Spanish galleon. Following every turn I swerved out to pass but with each straight-away the driver would speed up and the Rover's small engine couldn't overtake him. Then, with the onset of the merest of corners, the Winnebago would slow and list ponderously around the slight bend in a series of jagged banking manoeuvres. With the next straight piece of road the motorhome would lurch off at a rapid, weaving gait.

Finally, as we headed down the length of Wickaninnish Bay and through a series of gentle S-bends, I downshifted the Rover to third and gunned it. Shivering and shaking wildly, we rocketed out into the northbound lane toward possible destruction. The engine shrieked in defiance or fear. My hands gripping the wheel started to perspire and my eyes were transfixed toward the rapidly closing corner. Just as we came out the other end and found ourselves facing the approaching grille of a fire-balling freight truck I powered into fourth and cut the wheel over hard. With a screech of tires the Rover nicked into the space in front of the Winnebago, swerved back to the left to steady, and we were free to run. Air horns blared at us from both sides and the semi's slipstream buffeted us. In my rearview mirror I caught a glimpse of a grey looking old man in a pink baseball cap yarding on the Winnebago's horn and chomping what looked like a pepperoni stick.

A few kilometres later I turned off the highway and raced toward the northern corner of Kennedy Lake and soon shot across the logging company's bridge over the narrows located between the lake's main body and Clayoquot Arm. It was an uneventful part of the trip, but the road was so crooked and broken I gained back none of the time lost to the Winnebago. At times, during the run down the paved sections of road, I cursed myself as a fool for not taking Vhanna's big eight-cylinder Ford Bronco instead of the much less powerful Rover. With the Bronco, the Winnebago would have been dusted aside in seconds.

But as the roads narrowed and turned to gravel, then to barely-graded dirt, then to mud, muck and washouts by the twenty-five days of near-continuous rain, I was grateful for the Rover's sureness and low-ranged power. The road I followed led into the heart of Clayoquot Sound and it was a road that could have been designed by Satan. At times, the track clung to the edge of cliffs, in other moments it scaled

cliffs, or rappelled down them. In places, the road
had been gouged away by the storms. Here and there
fallen trees and boulders had been carried on flood-
waters down gorges and flung across the road, which
had also been washed away by the same waters.
Whenever I encountered these log jams, I was forced
to gear down into bull low and lurch down into the
pits cutting across the road. The Rover tottered on
the edge of wallowing into sticking mud or of high-
ending on rocks or logs. Yet, each time it clawed its
way out the other side and kept going.

There was no choice but to press on, although
I tasted the bile of fear in my mouth when the road
along cliff edges began to crumble and give way. It
was insane, I knew, to keep pushing forward at
these speeds without reconnoitering the road
ahead. But I had no choice. For always there
before me were the heavily cleated tire tracks of
another vehicle, a monstrous vehicle. They were
fresh tracks, barely hours old. They were tracks
that told me Vhanna and I were right. It was a
confirmation that chilled my heart with dread.
These were the tracks made by a killer. No other
reason existed for someone coming down this road
at this time of year.

Whoever it was had set a more cautious pace. At
the washouts he had taken the time to run a winch
line across and secure it to one of the cedars or hemlocks bordering the road. I could see the scars the
chain had cut into the thick bark of the ancient trees.
In some places a chainsaw had been used to clear
away logs fallen across the road. A couple times I
saw where the killer had used a shovel to fill in the
worst chuckholes so the truck could pass over. The
road improvements were all very methodical and

carried out with workmanlike precision. Enough to do, but not more than was required.

And slowly because of that workmanship the Rover and I started to win our race. The vehicle the killer drove was bigger, wider, possessed of a powertrain that liked to spin when it should grip. This meant more road improvements were necessary. Improvements the Rover didn't require for mere passage. Rather, the enhanced road conditions allowed the Rover to sail over parts of the road that would shatter the axles of lesser vehicles, bog down the drivetrains of a vehicle with less traction ability.

Furtive glances at the topographical map, spread out on the seat beside me, showed we were nearing our goal. But the clock was still unwinding and I knew with a sickening reality that unless Vhanna worked miracles the helicopter would arrive before we did. It all depended on Vhanna, and I had to rely on her ingenuity to stall the tour group's arrival at this last helicopter landing site.

It was a hellish place to which we raced. There is a popular misconception that before this most recent controversy Clayoquot had been untouched, was entirely a pristine old growth forest from end to end. But in the past the loggers had crept into small corners and done their work. It was to such a place that I now raced. Deep in the woods past the northwestern shore of Kennedy Lake there is a ridge where trees that were eight hundred years old once grew. Massive trees with trunks as big around as some houses, tall spires that rose higher into the skies than most European cathedral towers. Beneath the canopies of these trees it was always a gentle dusk.

But the loggers came. Now the same ridge is barren of trees. Saplings of poplar and alder are slowly reclaiming the land. Salal and Oregon-grape snake out from under the stumps and carnage of fallen trees deemed too small for market use but cut anyway and left to rot. Stumps, blackened by half-hearted attempts to burn the piles of slash from the branches of the fallen timbers, rise up out of the new growth of brush and offer silent witness to the glory that used to live here. To the locals it's known simply as The Ridge and everyone knows the place to which you refer when you mention its name.

The senator might have wished Vhanna as his guide so he could maintain a semblance of neutrality on the to-log-or-not-to-log Clayoquot issue, but that didn't mean Vhanna had planned a trip that would allow him to avoid taking a stand easily. The landings had been carefully scripted with the same fusing of education, adventure, and dramatic impact that all Artemis Tours were packaged. First the helicopter would visit the old growth meccas, places where the world was hushed by soaring giants. Places from which, beneath the shelter of dense wooded canopies, the ocean surf could be observed far below rolling into sheltered inlets. Then, when the senator had been lulled and soothed by the beauty of Clayoquot, The Ridge would jar him rudely to wakefulness — an awakening that would demonstrate vividly the fate promised Clayoquot by governments and logging companies. She would bring him to The Ridge and let The Ridge relate its own story — the tale of a land's old growth forests being gutted by greed. It was about as subtle as a chainsaw's roar, but it was quintessential Vhanna at work. How could it fail to slice Sloan right to the heart?

And so, of course, it was to The Ridge the helicopter was coming as the sun started drifting downward in the late afternoon sky. It was on The Ridge also that a killer waited. And it was to The Ridge that I hurried as fast as a Rover meant for slower paces could take me.

Chapter Twenty

There's an axiom in military lore that he who dares wins. All the planning and careful assembly of forces and timetables are, in the end, mere chaff if you don't know when to set them aside and exploit an opportunity — to risk failure by seizing a moment which, if successfully grasped, may guarantee success. I seized such a moment now. The Rover was nakedly exposed on the edge of the clearcut known as The Ridge. At the very heart of the open ground stood a high summit that gave the logged area its name. Any watcher waiting up there could not help but see the small green and white body of the Rover chugging persistently up the torn roadbed. My original strategy had called for leaving the vehicle in the woods and creeping up on The Ridge by foot. Such a strategy promised the chance that I could arrive at the bridge unseen by the enemy I suspected was emplaced there.

But time was also my enemy and I had arrived at The Ridge late. If the tour was on schedule, and I could only assume this to be the case, then I had thiry-five minutes to get to the ridge and undo whatever ambush the killer had set. There was just no bloody time for skulking about. I had to dare. To risk everything on the conclusion that a murderer wouldn't be able to, or feel the need, to place an observer on the skeletal spine of the ridge.

For two kilometres the road switchbacked up the steep incline and every roll of the tire carried me across an open moonscape. Enormous blackened stumps dotted the ground like craters. Surrounding the stumps was a dense growth of salal, salmonberry, tall Oregon-grape, and alder saplings. In many places the thickets created by this growth appeared impenetrable and I knew it would have been a hellish task to move across this landscape on foot.

Going boldly forward in the Rover was a brutal test of nerves. The closer I came to the ridgeline, the tighter was pulled the wire of tension circling my chest. I cringed ever more deeply into the driver's seat, literally pulling back from the dashboard and windshield. In my overheated imaginings, I could sense a high-calibre bullet leaving the rifle of a sniper watching me from that ridgeline. I could almost hear the slug smash through the small windshield to rip at my flesh and organs.

The fear made me want to shove the accelerator to the floor and roar across the open ground, to close with the enemy before he could squeeze off that killing shot. My sense of time hastening away also called for speed. I quelled both these urgings to hurry and with concentrated effort drove the Rover with a steadiness that avoided engine revs and the growl of powershifts.

The wind blew through the side window and brushed my face. It was a high gusting wind that flowed out of the northwest and funneled over the ridgeline to rush down the slope toward me. This was the kind of wind that plucked at clothes and brushed eardrums with sounds swept before it. It was a wind that worked for me, a wind that would carry the sounds of a smoothly working engine far away from anyone waiting on the ridge's other flank. Were it not for the wind, I could not have taken this risk of driving up to The Ridge.

I pushed the risk further when I crested the ridgeback by driving across the flat top to the northern edge. Twenty-five minutes remained. Off to my right I saw a skidder track cut away from the road and curve in behind a screen of salal. The Rover bucked and shuddered along this rough path. When I could no longer see the road behind me, I cut the engine and quietly stepped out. I pulled on my Filson coat, unlimbered the shotgun from its bag. After breaking the breech open I pushed two cartridges into the gun barrels. The left barrel took a deer slug, the right double-ought. As I started walking, I snapped the breech closed. In seconds I was back on the road trotting along the edge with the gun held at port arms.

How many times had I moved down narrow Nicosian streets like this? Then, I had worn the blue helmet of a peacekeeper. Despite the helmet of peace, I had carried an automatic rifle and feared the bullet of a hidden sniper. It was the same fear I had now.

At each turning in the road I paused, and with the shotgun at the ready, carefully exposed my head to see if the road was clear. My palms slipped sweatily on the gun's well burnished stock, my breath came in ragged gulps, and the thudding of my heart threatened to drown out all other sounds. Scanning the road ahead, I repeatedly encountered only shoulders choked with brush and an empty stretch of naked brown soil uncoiling like a dusty ribbon between the green hedges. Birds sang their reassurance that all was clear, but I knew better than to trust them. Only in movies is nature so aware of the movements of men that it hushes at the approach of soldiers. A grouse flushed from cover, wings thrumming wildly as it fled before me. Not knowing who had been more startled by our encounter I lowered the shotgun from my shoulder and was grateful my finger had not reflexively squeezed the trigger.

The road was descending now, gently wending down into the valley. I was off the ridgeline and headed toward the bridge. The slope was long and the grade gradual, so I couldn't see the valley bottom where the bridge stood. I glanced at my watch. Fifteen minutes remained. It was going to be tight. Too bloody tight.

Three minutes later I found the truck. It was backed into a sapling thicket. The blue Chevy with monster tires was well hidden and yet ready for a hasty escape back up the road. I wasted two minutes carefully circling through the brush to come up on the truck from behind only to find it empty. In the truck box lay a tangle of log chains and on top of a few rusting links was perched, as if carelessly dropped, a solitary red stick of dynamite. It was clean and new-looking, showing no sign of the damage evident on the damp explosives in the old shack. Both doors to the truck cab were unlocked. The passenger side contained an open toolkit jumbled full of grease-covered wrenches and screwdrivers. An orange and white Thermos waterjug lay on its side in the footwell. Next to it were a couple of dirt scummed empty Labatt Blue bottles. The keys were in the ignition. I gently eased the door open, removed the keys and tossed them far off into the brush. Then I unfolded my clasp knife and slashed all four tires and the spare. Like some behemoth inflatable water toy the truck slowly settled down in fits and lurches onto its wheel drums. Its crown of halogen spotlights rocked back and forth, like eyes, and the deflating image of the truck would have been foolish-looking were it not for the deadly intent that its presence here presaged.

I moved more slowly now, for it was clear the enemy was close. This was a killer who wouldn't walk far. Eight minutes remained. Perhaps I had longer. Hopefully Vhanna had managed to delay the schedule or it had been disrupted naturally. Maybe the chopper wouldn't come at all. The wind was stronger, clouds were piling high on the northwestern horizon. They were ashy grey, cored with black. A storm approached. Prudence would suggest the helicopter should have returned to the airport. But the storm was just as obviously still hours away and the senator would want to finish his tour, to gather his facts, and be able to say he had come and seen all there was to see.

The road turned another tight corner. I slipped across to the inside edge and crept into the turn. And froze. Four hundred metres ahead, down a small incline, the bridge straddled a stream choked with boulders and logging debris. Slowly I withdrew a couple of steps and stepped off the road into the brush. Dropping to my stomach I crawled through salal toward a large charred stump. The stump topped a small rise next to the roadway. My movements were slow, measured, contained of a soldierly professionalism I had thought long lost. No sound betrayed me. Vines were carefully lifted and set aside so they wouldn't rustle. Loose rocks were cleared to avoid elbows, knees, or toes setting them rolling. There is no fast way of doing this. Minutes slid by, sweat flowed out from under my hat to sting my eyes.

I removed the hat when I reached the stump and set it aside. Then I inched my head around the corner and looked down on the bridge and the ground surrounding it. I had chosen my position well, but it was still a surprise to see him there below me. I had, of course, expected it and known from the time I found the Greers' truck who it would be. Vhanna had been right after all and my own suspicions unfounded. I was struck by how truly simple most mysteries are to solve, how a killer is usually obvious and only the proving of complicity in murder is difficult. But now the evidence was plain to see.

He sat with his back against a boulder. His legs were splayed out before him, beige boot-cut cowboy jeans stuffed dude-style into a shiny pair of black cowboy boots with white hand-tooled scrollwork on them. A long-billed sports cap with the logo of a logging truck manufacturer cast his face into shadow. His head was down on his chest so that he appeared to be asleep. Between his legs was a small box-like object that had a twist knob built into its top. Wires were hooked to its side and trailed away into the brush. The wires ran in the direction of the bridge. Propped against the boulder next to Phil Dauphin was a high-powered clip-fed rifle. The stump behind which I was positioned was a mere thirty metres or so from where Dauphin had set up his observation point. From the boulder's shelter, he could easily see the bridge. I examined the bridge's footing carefully and thought perhaps I saw the wires, only lightly covered with dirt, running down beneath it to where undoubtedly a dynamite charge was placed. When the helicopter landed Dauphin would need only to twist the crank on the plunger and an electric current would snap down that line to spark the detonator and blow the charge. The helicopter would be torn to pieces in seconds and there was scant possibility anyone would survive.

From my vantage point above him, I pondered what to do next. Given time, I could circle down on the boulder, work up on him from behind and take him by surprise. That was the obvious approach.

When I had first seen the Greers' truck I had been afraid that the brothers might be the killers or that they might have accompanied Dauphin to this killing zone. But the toolkit on the passenger seat, the rubble in the passenger footwell, all suggested Dauphin did this day's work alone. No doubt one or both of them had helped string Ira Connaught from a tree, perhaps they had assisted him in placing explosive charges on Tassina's boat and inside Vhanna's car. I suspected their complicity in Dauphin's plot, but saw no trace of them here today.

Dauphin, it seemed, was alone and unaware of my presence. He obviously sensed no danger. Why should he? We were all supposed to be on the helicopter. And when it touched down on the bridge the big man would twist the little knob on the top of the plunger and we would die in a fiery explosion. An explosion that would be linked to the death of a Sunshine Warrior, the subsequent dynamiting death of a woman who had manned a protest line against the logging companies, the further attempted murder of the investigating coroner and his lover. Somehow in Dauphin's twisted mind he must have thought that road ultimately would lead to the suspicion that this bombing had been the work of the Sunshine Warriors or some other eco-terrorist group. I couldn't follow the logic of this train of thought, but his actions allowed for no other explanation.

There was also no time to think about it further. No time, either, for crawling up on a killer and taking him by surprise. There was only time to act. For out of the northwest came the whop-whop sound of an approaching helicopter and a small dark image materialized on the darkening horizon and began quickly to take on recognizable form.

I put my hat back on, cocked the shotgun and left the stump's cover to walk up on Dauphin. I didn't call out because I wanted to close the distance as much as possible. Dauphin had a rifle. The advantage of my shotgun would be heightened if I was closer to him. The man's casual calm amazed me. He hadn't stirred at the sound of the chopper and he obviously didn't hear my approach. His hands remained loosely gripped around the plunger, his head stayed rested on his chin. The ground between me and Dauphin was mostly bedrock and so lightly overgrown. I walked quietly, the gun at the ready and aimed at him. If he moved for the rifle I had every intention of discharging the left barrel and putting a solid-core deershot slug through his chest.

In my short military career I never fired a gun at anyone. I had killed or wounded nobody. But I was certain that should I need to I could kill this man. Dauphin had tried to kill Vhanna, had murdered Tassina Mavrikos and her daughter, had choked the life from Ira Connaught. Dauphin even now planned the deaths of several more people and again Vhanna was among the potential victims.

I stepped off the slope and onto the level shelf that was dominated by Dauphin's boulder. The chopper's thumping blades rumbled loudly overhead. Dauphin still lazed against the boulder. I came right up to him, stood with my boots nearly touching his own. He must be asleep, I thought. It was madness but he must have drowsed off and still slept even now despite the helicopter's roar. I placed the barrel of the shotgun between Dauphin and his rifle, so if he reached for it I could push it beyond arm's length. Then I leaned over and with my free left hand grabbed the plunger and wrenched it from his grasp. At the same time I swept the rifle away with the barrel of the shotgun and stepped back in a smooth movement that left Dauphin disarmed of both gun and plunger.

My shotgun was trained at his chest and at this range even holding the gun with one hand I knew if I pulled the trigger the shot would find its target. I expected Dauphin to lunge upright and was prepared to let him find his feet. I wouldn't shoot him then. If he moved toward me I would shoot, but only if he threatened me.

Dauphin didn't jump up in startlement. Instead he listed slowly over on his side. The hat fell away and I stared down into the wide-eyed vacant gaze of a dead man. His mouth was open and, from the gap, a twist of blood snaked. The boulder against which he had been leaning was smeared with blood and grey or white bits of brain. Where the back of Phil Dauphin's head had been there was now only gore.

I knew then. I saw it all clearly and in the moment of that flash of revelation I also moved, desperately diving into a shoulder roll. The roar of the helicopter was in my ears and the air around me was being thrashed by the suction of the blades. Within the racket of the chopper's engines and propwash, however, I heard a sharper cracking noise. Stone splinters flaked away in shards from the boulder. Still rolling, I looked up to the stump where I had earlier hidden and saw the silhouette of a man. The man was lean, his hair long and blowing back in the wind. At his shoulder was a rifle and he was tracking me with it.

In my left hand I still held the plunger, my right hand clung to the shotgun. My finger was on the trigger. I stopped rolling, flattened on my stomach, raised the shotgun, pointed it at the silhouette and squeezed the trigger. Firing a shotgun one-handed was an act of desperation for which I knew I would pay dearly. The Parker crashed loudly and its recoil jerked the gun from my hand so that it flew over my shoulder into the brush. My hand felt like it was broken and blood spurted from where the metal of the trigger guard had flayed my index finger to the bone. The pain was hellish, a great burning and throbbing agony that blurred my vision with tears.

Through these tears, I saw that the skyline above me was empty. I realized the sound of the chopper was fading, the engine and props winding down. It had landed. And it was still in great danger. Lawrence Rafferty could still kill me and finish his job. But I could stop him. So, instead of trying to roll to cover, I focused through the pain of my injured hand, gripped the wires connected to the plunger and ripped them free. Then I threw the box as far into the bush as I could.

Still no bullet had found me. Scrambling to my feet, I retrieved the shotgun. My right hand was useless, so I gripped the trigger with my left hand, pressed the butt against my hip, and balanced the barrel across the top of my right forearm. Then I walked up the slope toward where Rafferty had been. As I crested the small hill I glanced over my shoulder and saw the chopper disgorging people. Vhanna pointed up the hill at me and I saw the two security men draw their pistols. I turned my back on them, trusting Vhanna to prevent their shooting me.

I heard Rafferty before I saw him. He was making a low mewling sound like that which might come from an abandoned and hungry baby. He lay curled in a fetal ball, hands clasped over his stomach. Blood trickled through the fingers. There was a much larger hole in his back that he seemed unaware of and through which the bulk of his life's blood was flowing. The rifle lay forgotten among some rocks. Rafferty's face was the colour of chalk and the pool of blood in which he lay was rapidly growing into a lake. I dropped the Parker, clumsily tugged a hiker's first-aid kit from a jacket pocket, and went down to him.

"It's over," Vhanna said as she finished sewing the last tidy little stitch necessary to close the wound in my finger. "Fourteen stitches. I don't think there will be any scarring." She knelt before me on the hard planks of the bridge. For the past few minutes I had been sitting on one of the ties running along the outer edges of the bridge and studiously looking off, over the ruined landscape while Vhanna did her emergency nurse routine on my injury. Behind me, the helicopter's rotor was slowly starting to turn in preparation for lift off. Rafferty lay just inside the open side door. One of the security agents hovered over him, continuing to check vital signs while feeding this information through the commandeered co-pilot's radio headset to the emergency room people at the Tofino hospital. Fortunately for Rafferty the agents had carried with them more than guns and little earplug radios on this outing. They had brought a full medical kit containing a cornucopia of bandages, blood plasma, and morphine all put to good use in saving the man's life by one of the agents who had paramedic training. Lying next to Rafferty was the larger bulk of Dauphin. The body had been covered with a simple blue plastic tarp, the only thing available. Several other agents, senatorial aides, and an ashen-faced senator were grouped just outside the chopper.

Danchuk stood off to the edge of this group like an unpopular child eternally hopeful but always overlooked when a pickup basketball team was cobbled together on the schoolyard. My antique Parker was tucked under one arm. From under the brim of his cap he continued to glare malevolently in my direction as he had for the entire time it took the agent doing first aid to stabilize Rafferty's condition sufficiently to permit his evacuation on the helicopter. Left to his own devices, Danchuk would have had me in irons rather than just having confiscated my firearm. But the senator had praised my heroism and it's a hard thing to arrest a hero in front of a grateful American senator. Such things play very badly in the media, some of whom circled overhead in their own helicopters, dipping and turning like violet green swallows chasing mosquitoes.

Having wrapped my finger in gauze and tape to hold it in place Vhanna closed up the smaller first-aid kit from which she worked, crouched forward to kiss my cheek delicately, and stood up dusting off the knees of her pants. "When you get to town, I want you to see Tully and have him check my work okay?" I nodded distractedly, eyes drifting up to the spot where my deer slug had struck Rafferty down and come within a hair of ending his life. An inch or two one side or another of where the shot had hit and some vital organ would have been irreparably rent. Not good marksmanship on my part, just plain good luck. A wave of relief washed over me that I would not have to bear the responsibility of killing the man.

I tugged my attention back to Vhanna and slowly pulled myself up to stand before her. With my good hand I lightly stroked her cheek. "I still can't believe it," Vhanna said. Her eyes shifted from my face to where the helicopter stood. "What was Rafferty thinking? How could he have done all this?" Having no simple answer, I shrugged, took her hand and walked with her toward the helicopter. The senator, his aides, and security men were piling in, understandably anxious to escape this place. Danchuk followed and then hung out of the doorway like a bad parody of a crew chief, waving impatiently at us to hurry. The chopper blades started to thump and whump, causing us instinctively to bend forward despite their being well clear of our heads. I followed Vhanna right to the door and held her hand as she stepped inside. "There's room," she yelled. "We could send Jabronski for the Rover."

I shook my head. "It's okay. I'll meet you at Tully's office," I shouted and then retreated beyond the chopper's prop wash, which plucked at my coat and pant legs and tousled my hair roughly. It rose slowly, dipped its nose so that the machine looked ready to topple into the gully over which the bridge stood, and then turned sharply to the north gaining elevation as it roared away. I watched until it and the pursuing media helicopters all disappeared into the distance like a flock of migrating geese with the senator's helicopter leading the rest forward in a ragged V-formation. Then I trudged up the hill to where my hat had fallen during the battle with Rafferty, scooped it up, and made my way wearily back to the Rover. Although I knew I should be hurrying, because this long danger-fraught day was not yet over, I could not.

Firing up the Rover, I backed this way and that to face it toward Tofino and started retracing my path down the narrow, rough track. After a few minutes, I began to think and perhaps understand why I remained uneasy — why my instincts told me the mystery surrounding the killings of the past few days was not yet fully solved by the foiling of Rafferty's plot. And with that knowledge came the realization that a killer was still loose. Not only a killer, but also the mastermind behind all the killings.

Even as I thought this, the devil's advocate inside my brain argued that I was wrong or — even worse — motivated by no more than petty jealousy to imagine the worst of Barry Starling. I pondered that possibility. Yes, I was jealous of the place he had held in Vhanna's life. When it comes to Vhanna, I am unable to avoid the temptation toward jealousy of anyone who captures her affection in the way that Starling had managed. There had been a happy contentment in her expression in the photograph where she was settled back inside the envelope of his arms. That expression I knew well, having brought it to life at times myself. It was a look reserved for when she was feeling in love. Vhanna had loved Starling.

Loved him at a time when my own life was shattered by Merriam's suicide. I resented him for that. Both for winning Vhanna's love for a while and for doing so at that particular time. But I rejected that my emerging belief that he was a murderer had anything to do with jealousy. The thread might be thin and hard to trace, but following it carefully led me inevitably to Starling.

Ira Connaught had been a professional soldier who had served as an adviser to the Contras in Nicaragua at one time in his career. I had never realized what that meant before until now, but I should have. No regular infantryman would have played at that role. If Ira was advising Contras then he had been Special Forces, probably a Green Beret or Ranger. Starling had served with him, ditto same training. Both men were trained killers. Ira, of course, other than for the tree spiking and his wild plans for Native resistance, had largely forsaken this path. He had been working in the woods around Tofino for several years without resorting to explosives.

And Rafferty? Tassina had described him as a man who planned and sent forth the Sunshine Warriors without ever putting himself in harm's way. Physically, he lacked the sheer power necessary to throttle someone as large and undoubtedly well-trained in combat as Ira Connaught. Starling, however, could easily have been his match or better — especially as they were friends, indeed co-conspirators in a wild plot intended to forever discredit the loggers and turn popular opinion decisively in favour of the ecotagers and their struggle to save the old growth forests of Clayoquot. It would not have been too difficult for Starling to get close to Ira and, using his skills, disable the man long enough to throttle him to death. A brutal way to kill and one to which I suspected only someone who had once been at home with such deadly violence would resort.

I believed Starling, rather than Rafferty or Ira, was the mastermind of the entire plot. I believed he had approached Ira almost immediately after coming into the good fortune, which he had probably orchestrated, of being hired by the good senator. It was within weeks or days even of Starling being hired by Senator Sloan that Ira started following the senator's pronouncements in American and Canadian newspapers. Sloan was not the only politician babbling platitudes about Clayoquot from various pulpits. But only Sloan was monitored by Ira, a man with little money but who still went out of his way to buy copies of *The New York Times* and other papers that were hard to find and expensive to buy in Tofino.

Then Ira approached the devil himself to buy explosives. Would Ira have done this on his own? Or even if Rafferty had asked him to? I thought of Tassina's disdain for Rafferty and could not imagine Ira coming under his spell to the degree that would countenance murder. Rather, I imagined Starling approaching Rafferty, Starling outlining a decisive strategy that would bring victory and the salvation of the forest without any risk of detection. A plan that would also provide Rafferty a pulpit to stand upon that would enable him to emerge from marginalized ecotager to legitimacy. He and Starling would be two voices crying out in the wake of the senator's death and they would be heard as one and they would profit from it in the same way. I imagined Starling stepping easily into the senator's political shoes back home in whereverville Kansas. And to attain this all Starling had to do was provide the senator and ensure he was in the right place at the right time. Dauphin would be lured there to recover the stolen explosives that could indict him. Ira would kill him and prop him up before the detonator and then blow the helicopter and escape overland to a nearby road where Rafferty would be waiting with a truck.

I was sure that had been the original plan. But what if Ira had tried to back out, threatening to scupper the entire thing? So Starling had come to town ostensibly to plan for the senator's visit, but in reality to stop Ira betraying the plan. He and Rafferty had done so by killing him. I could easily imagine Starling lifting Ira's body into the tree while Rafferty tied the knot around his throat. I saw how his complicity in this crime would give Starling complete control over Rafferty, ensuring that he would assume Ira's role in the plot despite the man's aversion to the risk inherent in direct involvement. They could trust none of the Sunshine Warriors with such a task. They were mostly idealists who carried their hearts on the tattered sleeves of their wool sweaters and tie-dyed shirts. I could imagine none of them turning into killers. It was only this complicity in Ira's death that had actually forced Rafferty to become a soldier following Starling's direction. A complicity that also meant that Rafferty would take the fall if the attempt on the senator should fail and the dynamiter be captured.

And Tassina? Eleni? Incidental. Had Tassina not taken Ira in her boat to the cabin to retrieve the explosives both she and her daughter would still be alive. I would never know for sure if Starling would have killed them had I not been snooping about and beginning to blunder ever closer to uncovering what he was planning. It seemed likely that Starling acted from fear of exposure and also a professional's tidy mind that wanted no loose ends left lying around that could be unravelled in subsequent investigations. So he had set explosives and two people had died.

But I kept probing and I kept getting closer. Vhanna was not only helping me, but also knew far too much about Starling that might, if examined in the right light, cast him into suspicion. So even though he had wanted her as the senator's guide, had ensured her role as that guide, he had decided to kill us both. Guides presumably were easily found and his affection for Vhanna aside — which I grudgingly accepted must have been real at the time — he was willing to kill her to safeguard himself. This didn't really surprise me. He had obviously known Ira well, had served shoulder to shoulder with him in dangerous places. A man who would kill a comrade in arms would also be capable of killing a casual lover. So he wired a bomb to Vhanna's car and Vlassis Mavrikos became its innocent victim. Four deaths and each at the hands of Barry Starling and not a thread of evidence to prove any of it in a court of law. As I turned the Rover off the logging tracks onto pavement and rolled more quickly toward Tofino, under a darkening late afternoon sky with a storm front building out to sea, I realized Starling was likely to escape. Danchuk would never listen. In a couple of hours, Starling would join the senator at the airport and together they would wing off to the land of the free and if ever some evidence were forthcoming Starling would simply disappear. Looking at my watch, I realized I had but one chance and very little time. I stepped hard on the accelerator and pushed my beleaguered Rover to drive at speeds for which it was not constructed.

As I roared into the parking lot and jumped from the Rover I saw the senator and Starling waiting on the tarmac as the ground crew finished refueling the two-engine executive-style plane. Vhanna was standing with Sloan and Starling. The senator was leaning close to Vhanna, smiling widely and talking in an animated fashion at the same time. He looked a happy man; a man who had come for answers and found those he sought from the outset. Vhanna had helped him find those answers. But Starling had written the script, manoeuvred events in a bloody way to make sure that even in failure he would win. The senator might still be alive, but he was a senator who would be seeking the blood of all loggers from this day forward.

Walking briskly toward them, I saw that Danchuk was there, too, as were a small pack of security men and police. Seeing me approach, Danchuk raced to intercept, but I brushed his restraining hand aside and walked up to Starling. The man wore the same foul-weather jacket and jeans he had that morning when he was to have gone on the helicopter tour. He looked at me now with calm blue eyes that betrayed no trace of apprehension.

"Feeling better, Mr. Starling?" I asked.

He nodded. "It was just a passing bit of indigestion, I guess."

"Shame you missed the tour, then." I paused and let the moment drag. "And the danger." It was when we were loading the wounded Rafferty into the helicopter that I realized Starling wasn't there and learned he had been taken ill just after the chopper lifted off at the airport. So they had flown back and left Starling behind and continued the tour without him. Had I stayed to watch the helicopter disappear over the horizon, I would have witnessed this and probably realized that Dauphin wasn't the killer. This was the final shred of information that had confirmed in my mind that my intricately woven version of Starling's murder plot was correct. Starling ensured the senator was on the helicopter and that it would go to the bridge where a bomb waited. But being no suicide, he also ensured he was not on that helicopter. Even then he had been willing to trade Vhanna's life for the senator's death and the benefits he believed would accrue.

"You almost got away with it didn't you?" I added.

Behind me I heard Vhanna say, "Elias." Her voice was reproachful and embarrassed sounding. Vhanna knew nothing about Starling's guilt. She sounded like a woman might who is trying to constrain an embarrassing outburst by a well-seasoned drunk.

The mocking twist of Starling's mouth turned up ever so gently — in that look of arrogant self-assurance that I had come to detest in the few short hours I had known the man. "What do you mean, Mr. McCann?" he asked in a voice redolent of innocence and a humouring tolerance of my intemperate behaviour.

The senator stepped between us. The sky was grey overhead now and the clouds heavy with rain. The wind had picked up and it tugged at Sloan's well-groomed hair but couldn't seem to disrupt whatever spray combination held the locks in place.

"You're surely not suggesting that Barry had anything to do with this are you, Mr. McCann?"

"I'm suggesting nothing. I know he was responsible." I put a hand out and gently pushed the senator out of the way. It was like pushing aside a tall, spindly twig. Sloan's security men started to close on me, but I saw the senator inexplicably wave them off. Perhaps he still hoped to avert a scene that the media might notice. "You were smart, Starling, I'll give you that. If it had all gone the way you planned then Dauphin would have taken the blame. It would have been the perfect murder-suicide wouldn't it? And even when that failed you were in the clear. Because there wasn't any link between you and Rafferty. And Rafferty's a true believer, so you didn't have to fear that he'd shop you to save himself."

Starling was smiling openly now. It was the kind of smile a passerby gives the crazed souls that stand on city streets blathering incoherent foolishness. He caught Vhanna's eye and gave her a little shrug. I couldn't bear to look Vhanna's way for fear of the dismay I knew would be on her face.

And, indeed, I shared her dismay. For I had no proof. All I had was my own certainty and the determination to brazen through to somehow force a confession from this smug and capable killer. I had hoped to shock Starling into this, to play on the fear of discovery that I expected he must feel. But, meeting his relaxed gaze, I saw not the slightest trace of fear. There was only confidence in his eyes and I sensed it was I who was doomed. Doomed to look a fool. Doomed to let a murderer walk free. A murderer to whom Vhanna might once again be drawn, perhaps even by a desire to negate my unproved and cruel accusations.

"You made some mistakes," I said hastily improvising.

"Did I?" Starling asked with mocking curiosity.

And in that second I knew I was right. For a moment the man's eyes had ceased glowing with amusement and the mocking twitch at his lip had disappeared. It had been replaced by a hard tightness and in his eyes I had seen nothing but the flat watchful cruelty of a large hunting cat. I saw this for only a second and then the expression flitted away and was again masked behind one of mocking attentiveness.

"Really, Mr. McCann, I must insist," the senator was saying. His hand closed on my arm in a friendly restraining grip, as if he feared I might strike out at his apparently falsely accused aide.

I shook his hand free and took a step toward Starling. It was a threatening step but Starling held his ground. The action, however, had the desired effect. This time the tightness that might be fear or murderous intent returned to his face and remained there. The blue eyes burned out at me and I saw that his big hands were forming fists, then unclenching, only to curl again into fists. This was a man quick to violence. I was certain of this.

It was time to gamble all. In Tai Chi there's a movement called "Move Hands Like Clouds." The move entails sweeping both arms from full extension at one side of the body to a duplicate extension on the other. It involves an intricate simultaneous movement of the hands in a delicate choreography. The movement unfolds quickly and gracefully. When it's completed, only the hand motions are remembered by the watcher. But the moving of the hands like clouds is purely illusion, it gives the sense that somehow all the movement that takes the Tai Chi adept across about fifteen metres of space is powered by arms and hands. Mesmerized by the hand motions, the observer doesn't recognize that the real power and motion emanates from the legs and feet.

"Hands, Starling, that was your mistake. You shouldn't have strangled Ira. Of course the suicide ploy nearly worked, didn't it? But nearly isn't good enough, as they must have taught you and Ira in the Rangers or whatever it was you served in during your army days."

"For godsake, McCann. Are you drunk?" This was from Danchuk and I sensed him coming up to grab my elbow. To buy a few more precious seconds before the RCMP sergeant could drag me off, I stepped closer to Starling so our chests almost touched.

"We can't wait for the final results, Sergeant," I said. "We have to arrest him now. If he gets on that plane he'll disappear and we'll never hunt him down."

As I had hoped he would, Danchuk abruptly halted, wondering, no doubt, if he had forgotten something about the tests. It would take a few more seconds before he realized he hadn't. They were seconds I exploited to the full. I hurried on, waving my hands now in the way lawyers and politicians do to intensify the authority of their words, turning them into pointers of guilt. "We found your fingerprints on the skin below the surface of Ira's throat, Starling. It took time and there's still some confirming tests required, but the preliminary tests showed enough traces for us to run a check.

"You didn't think of that did you? Didn't think of how your fingers would leave marks on the layers of skin below the surface. You figured the rope marks on his throat would cover up any evidence like that because the bruises the rope left would be larger than those of your fingers." I was motioning at Starling with a bandaged hand, ramming each point home with a flash of white gauze. And Starling was starting to yield ground. His eyes were widening and I could see the thoughts spinning inside his head. "But your science was out of date. And because of that we've got you, you murdering thug." It was all a preposterous lie, of course, but there was enough logical possibility in it, I hoped, to unnerve even the steeliest of killers. And it worked.

"No," Starling said to my accusations in an icy voice, but the word was more a confirmation than a denial. I felt the relief of a runner successfully reaching the finish line after a long marathon. I had him, now all I had to do was squeeze harder to make him act.

But I had no time to say anything further for a large fist flashed out from Starling's side and chopped me in the throat. I sagged to my knees and my hands jumped up to grasp a throat that didn't work properly anymore. I panted but no air passed down my windpipe. I was distantly aware of Starling standing behind Senator Sloan. One of the man's big arms was around the senator's neck. Sloan's face was very red and his mouth was gasping like a fish cast up on a dock, which was probably much how my own mouth was working. The security men and Danchuk all had guns out and leveled, but Sloan was between them and Starling. Using the senator as his shield, Starling retreated deliberately toward the plane.

I tried to rise but my body refused to respond. Instead, my legs crumpled and I flopped down on my side to the tarmac. My rasping for air was the only sound I could hear. Out of tear-blurred eyes I saw Danchuk and the security men lowering their guns and crouching to abandon them on the ground. The senator was drooling and gasping.

Then suddenly Starling and the senator convulsed together, arching inward as if a pile driver had struck Starling in the back. I heard a bellowing sound of agony that cut through my own gasping sounds. Starling lost his grip on the senator, who slithered down to the ground and lay on his side retching for breath. Starling staggered as he twisted around and now I saw Vhanna facing him and coming up out of a wind-up crouch. Starling swung a haymaker but Vhanna's left forearm snapped up like a spring released by a button to deflect his blow upwards and harmlessly off to her left. As she did this, Vhanna sprang forward, rear leg unleashing her body like a piston so that her shoulder slammed into Starling's sternum. Her hand closed on Starling's extended right arm and as her still rising shoulder thrust him up off his feet she twisted his helpless arm. Starling landed on his back with a flat slapping sound that cut through even my desperate gasps for air. Even as Starling recovered and tried with a vicious sweep of his leg to tear her feet from under her, Vhanna rotated clear of him with an easy skip.

With Vhanna safely outside Starling's counter-attack it was all over, for the security men and Danchuk had recovered their guns and now crowded in warily on the big man. Starling stared at the gun barrels with a look of violent, caged rage. But then he obviously saw that further resistance was futile. Slowly, he responded to the orders to turn on his stomach and knot his hands behind his back.

I was winning my own battle and could feel some air trickling down my throat to reinflate my burning lungs. With a lurch, I managed to sit up. I blinked and the fuzzing that had been crowding the edges of my vision cleared. I looked up as the next breath came sweetly into my lungs and saw Vhanna kneeling in front of me. She touched my cheek and said something, but I couldn't hear the words. She was smiling and there seemed a dampness at the corner of her eyes, but when I reached out with a shaking hand to brush the moisture away Vhanna closed her hand on mine and squeezed tightly. Then she pressed my cheek against her breast and I let her hold me.

Chapter Twenty-one

Fergus and I wandered along the beach in front of Vhanna's house until we found her finishing her Tai Chi routine. The sun had set and the last remnants of clouds from the night's passing storm were a rusty red. I settled on a tide-smoothed boulder. Fergus sat beside me and pushed his back against my leg. In the companionable silence old friends can share, we watched Vhanna complete the set.

When Vhanna came over she scratched Fergus behind the ears and then joined me on the rock. I took her hand in my undamaged left one and held it. The three of us sat without talking until the light faded from the sky and the stars came out to shine through the big gaps between clouds. It was a good moment, one that could last forever as far as I was concerned.

But eventually, as it always does, time started moving again. And Vhanna, ever restless of spirit, turned to me with a question. "How did you know?"

"It was mostly just suspicion. But he did make a small mistake that gave me some certainty besides the suspicions. When we met the senator at the banquet he introduced me as the coroner."

Vhanna shrugged, not seeing it. "How did he know?" I asked. "It's not something that's in a phonebook. I didn't become coroner until after he left this area. He could only have known I was the coroner if either Dauphin or Rafferty told him so. They were setting Dauphin up for the stooge so that the loggers would take all the blame. I suppose they thought the adverse publicity would lead to the government reversing its decision to log."

"That's crazy, though. They hurt everything we've done so far to stop the logging. We'll be lucky if this violence doesn't tar all the environmental movements."

A freshening breeze had come up and was trying to pluck my hat away, so I pushed it more firmly down on my head. It was growing colder and nearly time to seek the shelter of indoors. I wondered passingly where Fergus and I would sleep this night. There had been no invitation as yet, but we were ever optimistic. I concentrated on Starling's plot again, although in truth I was tired of the issue. "Imagine, though," I said, "if they had got away with it. A mass of deaths, a dead senator, a deranged logger who committed suicide with his rifle after blowing up the helicopter, Starling alive and well to become the public voice of condemnation. He would have had a pulpit and a probable shot at stepping into the departed senator's shoes. Rafferty could have been the voice shouting back here at home. It was bloody close, too." They had set Dauphin up perfectly, dropping him a hint of where the last of the explosives were hidden so he would come looking, desperate to recover the stuff and try to prevent his being linked to further deaths. Rafferty had then killed the man and set him in place to look like he was operating the detonator. Had I not come along, everything would have gone smoothly. Rafferty would have set off the charge, and hiked back through the hills to the road, where he had parked his truck, and then carried the explosives in to set the trap. There would have been no sign of his having ever been there; nothing but Dauphin's body, the plunger, and his truck where Rafferty had left an errant stick of dynamite in the back to make the connection all the neater.

Vhanna shivered, but I didn't know whether this was from the closing evening chill or the thought of Starling's criminality and willingness to have killed her to achieve his goals. We left the rock and walked over the sand toward the stairs leading up to her house. Fergus trotted ahead of us, running along the shoreline with an innocent joy. "I'm leaving in a week," Vhanna said.

"I know."

Her hand tightened on mine. "It'll be longer than just the tour. There's something I need to do."

I thought of a woman going alone into Cambodia. A woman who, as a child, had been sent to the Khmer Rouge death camps and had escaped across the Chuor Phnum Dangrek escarpment to Thailand. I thought of that woman now returning to a still tortured land to seek family and her heritage. What dangers would she face? How would the things she discover there, the cruelties she must bear witness to, indelibly mark and change her? I was afraid for her and for myself.

"I could come," I said.

"No. It's something I need to do alone." She didn't have to add that a remittance man would stand out and attract attention in a country hovering on the brink of chaos and violence. Although Pol Pot was reportedly dead, Khmer Rouge remnants were still afoot in Cambodia and their pathological violence still walked its ancient roadways if only in the form of millions of uncharted landmines. On those same roads, a small Eurasian woman might blend and pass without notice. But with me blundering along at her side there would be no anonymity. Vhanna sought to blend into Cambodia's landscape and travel down its pathways in search of some trace of surviving family members or knowledge of the fate that befell them all.

"You will take good care of yourself?" She nodded, her face shadowed by the approaching darkness. "How long do you think?"

"A month. Maybe longer. Counting the Nepal mountain expedition, probably two months."

I said nothing. My thoughts were of two months without Vhanna. Months filled with worry about her safety. It seemed an eternity but I told myself that the weeks would go by quickly enough. They would pass as they always passed. Fergus and I would walk the woods and, if we were lucky, flush some game. There were books to read, music to listen to. Father Welch and I could play chess. I could try to convince Mayor Tully that a more suitable coroner should be found, even though he was now convinced I was an investigator of great talent. Time would pass and Vhanna would come back from the darkness. Then we would start again trying to harmonize our lives until she had to leave again on some other quest. While she was gone, both this time and in the future times that must inevitably follow, I would live well enough. I always did.

At the bottom of the stairs leading up to her house, Vhanna climbed onto the first step and turned so that she was looking almost evenly into my eyes. The starlight dusted her pupils to create bright motes that sparked within the darkness. Despite the dancing of these starlight reflections her eyes held a certain sadness that I thought must flow deeply all the way down to her soul. It was a sadness I wished to exorcise from her but which I knew was beyond my power to alleviate.

For the first time, however, I saw within the sadness touching her eyes the slightest flicker of uncertainty and a hesitation to speak. "What is it?" I prompted.

Her eyes broke from mine and she looked down. Fergus was already far up the stairs and I heard him huff sharply with impatience at this delay that kept him from a warm hearth. Vhanna was speaking and her words were so softly released that I had to bend forward slightly to make them out. "When I get back you'll still —" she was saying. Before she could finish I touched her lips with my fingers to ensure the last words remained unspoken.

"Yes," I said.